A PENNY URNED

A Den of Antiquity Mystery

TAMAR MYERS

AVON BOOKS
An Imprint of HarperCollins*Publishers*

For Susan and Jack Timberlake

AVON BOOKS
An Imprint of HarperCollins*Publishers*
10 East 53rd Street
New York, New York 10022-5299

ISBN: 0-7394-1276-0

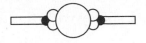

1

Lula Mae Wiggins drowned in a bathtub filled with champagne. She was fully clothed. It happened on New Year's Eve.

Though someone had sent me a letter, I wasn't informed of her death until a full three months had passed, thanks to my ex-husband, who returns all my mail unopened. Fortunately the delay was no cause for added grief. Lula Mae was my daddy's second cousin, or something like that, and had never been a part of my life. Frankly, her name didn't even ring a bell.

"It was cheap champagne," Mama said that day we got the fateful call from Savannah. "The kind you kind buy from Food Lion for $3.75 a bottle."

"How do you know?" I asked. We were playing Hearts with Wynnell and C.J., two of my closest friends and coworkers. I had just been passed the queen of spades and was trying to maintain my cool.

Mama grinned. It was she who had passed me the queen.

"The coroner said so. He said the taste was sweet enough to set your teeth on edge."

"Did he taste it?" C.J. asked.

"Yuck," Wynnell said. "*Did* he?"

"I don't rightly know," Mama said, and passed me the ace and king of hearts. "I didn't speak to the

1

coroner himself. I spoke with the executor of Lula Mae's will."

"Did this executor say how it was this Lula Mae person happened to drown in a bathtub of champagne?"

"Apparently she had a heart attack while bathing. And get this, Abby. She was dressed to the nines."

"She was bathing in her *clothes*?"

Mama nodded. "You know, dear, your daddy's family has always been a little on the strange side."

C.J., Wynnell, and I all rolled our eyes. For Mama to call anyone strange was like the pot calling the kettle black—in every language on earth. My mama, Mozella Gaye Wiggins, dresses like June Cleaver. Her sister Marilyn not only dresses like Marilyn Monroe, but also claims the blond bombshell stole both her name and her style from my platinum-coiffed relative.

"What the heck am I going to do now?" I asked. I was referring to my lousy hand, having stupidly forgotten this was still Mama's conversation.

"You drive down and get her, that's what," Mama said. Her tone left no room for argument.

"*Excuse me?*" I set my cards down, fortunately face up.

"Don't show us your cards, Abby!" the trio chorused.

It was my turn to grin now that a redeal was in order. "What's this about me driving down to Savannah to bring back a dead aunt?"

"Cousin," Mama corrected me. "And she's been cremated. We could have them ship the ashes, but the executor said he'd been instructed to tell the mortician to place the cremains in an urn that was part of her estate. But get this." Mama paused to take a deep breath."The mortician, who claims to be something of an expert on antiques, thinks the urn is worth a pretty penny. Said it might be something called a truck-san. Is that Japanese, dear?"

"He probably said Etruscan, Mama. That refers to the Tusci people who were contemporaries of the ancient Romans and lived in what is now Tuscany. So, shall we deal again? I mean, it isn't fair now that you've all seen my cards."

"Whose fault is that, dear?"

"Yours. You distracted me with this gruesome story of a dead cousin I've never even seen."

"Actually, dear, you did see her once. I think you were about three years old. Lula Mae came up here to visit. You called her a witch."

"I did not!"

"You most certainly did, and to her face."

"Well, if I did—like you said, I was only three."

"Still, I can't imagine why she'd leave you every- thing."

"Say what?"

"You heard me right, Abby. Your daddy's cousin left you all her worldly possessions. The executor—a Mr. Kimbro—said your brother Toy wasn't even mentioned."

"Mama, was that call intended for me?"

"Well, they called *here*," Mama said, pretending to study her cards, "and it *is* my house."

It did not surprise me that my mother had been able to intercept a call, even one of this nature, in- tended for someone else. Mama could charm a fly out of its wings, and barring success at that, could lay on such a guilt trip, the poor fly would leave behind his antennae and a leg or two to boot.

I glared at Mama, who of course didn't notice.

"Maybe you should go down to Savannah to pick up Lula Mae's cremains. After all, you were married to her cousin. And I'll bet you anything you pretended to be me on the phone when Mr. Kimbro called, didn't you?"

Silence.

"Didn't you?"

Mama sighed. "I can't believe your attitude, dear. I should think you'd jump at the chance to do this. That urn could be worth a lot of money."

"The Etruscan urn is most probably a fake," I said, speaking from experience. "And besides, what do you propose that I do? Buy a cheap vase at Kmart and dump Lula Mae's ashes into that?"

Mama squirmed. "Well, I don't see that we have a choice, dear. I already told the man you'd be there day after tomorrow."

"*You what?*"

Mama cringed. "Well, it was either that or tell him to mail the urn and sell off your cousin's estate. But seeing as how you're an antique dealer, I thought you might like to look over Lula Mae's things first. There might be some items you'd like to keep and maybe others you could get more for up here in Charlotte than you could get in Savannah."

"Or maybe you could have told him the truth, that your name isn't Abigail Timberlake, and maybe you should have given him my phone number and told him to speak to me directly."

"What's done is done, dear. There's no use in beating a dead horse, is there?"

"I'd wager the old gray mare has enough life left in her to go down to Savannah by herself with a U-Haul and bring back Lula Mae's estate," I mumbled half to myself.

Wynnell gasped. Her hedgerow eyebrows had fused into one long, black bush.

"Abby, is that any way to talk to your mama? Besides, she couldn't possibly bring back your cousin's entire estate."

"You stay out of this," I said gently. One of the disadvantages of having a friend twelve years older than I was that she tended to act like *she* was my mama.

C.J., on the other hand, is young enough to be my daughter, and every bit as impertinent as my real daughter, Susan. C.J. giggled.

"Abby, don't be ridiculous. Your mama can't bring a house back in a U-Haul."

"House? Who said anything about a house?"

"Oops," C.J. said, and clamped a big hand over her big mouth.

I looked at Mama, whose cards suddenly hid her face. "Mama! Out with it! What have you told Wynnell and C.J. that you haven't told me?"

Mama put down her cards. "Well, I guess we're not going to finish this hand, are we?"

I gestured at the queen of spades. "Not if I can help it. Now, what's this about a house?"

"It was going to be a surprise," Mama said, glaring at C.J. "But I suppose you have the right to know. Your daddy's cousin left you her row house as well."

"Get out of town! I mean, you're kidding, right?"

Mama shook her head. "I may be guilty of withholding a few facts—just temporarily, mind you—but I would never kid about such a thing."

"And what facts might you be withholding right now?"

Mama cleared her throat and patted her pearls.

The necklace was a gift from my father shortly before he died, and to my knowledge Mama hasn't once removed it in seventeen years. When Mama gets agitated, she strokes or pats her pearls. When things get truly bad, she twirls them.

"Why, nothing, dear, except that this row house is located on Gaston Street and is worth a great deal of money."

"How much?"

"He wouldn't give me an exact number, dear. But he did recommend a real estate agent. Anyway, I should think it would be worth several hundred thousand. Maybe even half a million."

Who knew that insulting a relative could be so lucrative? My brother, Toy, ever the suckup, had yet to inherit a thing. I, on the other hand, had already inherited an antique shop from an aunt and now a house.

"Well, well, well," I said, feeling both exhilarated and guilty. "I suppose I should drive down to Savannah. Do U-Hauls come with automatic transmissions?"

Mama smiled. "They do, but that wouldn't be a problem in any case. C.J. here has volunteered to come along."

"*She what?*" I turned to my young friend. "How long have you known about this?"

C.J. is a big gal, a natural dishwater blonde with an expressive face. "I just found out, Abby. Honest."

"C.J., you're lying!"

"Okay, your mama called me a couple of hours ago. Just after she got the call from Savannah. But don't blame her, Abby. She wanted to surprise you."

I turned to Mama. "Surprise me with what?"

"Well, dear, I thought it might be nice if the four

of us made the trip together. Sort of a girls' week off."

"Mama, you don't even work, but both C.J. and Wynnell do. Besides, Wynnell is married. She can't just go trotting off like that."

"Actually, I can," Wynnell said. "I have an assistant now, remember?" She lowered her voice, although there was no danger of anyone else hearing. "And Ed's decided to work at home for the next two weeks. They're remodeling an office next to his, and you know how he is about dust. Anyway, he's been home one day, and already he's driving me crazy. Besides, you'll need a car to get around in when you're down there. We can take mine. *Please*, Abby."

Wynnell never begs. Apparently she really needed a change of scenery. As for C.J., who knew what her motive was?

I looked at the woman who birthed me. Thirty-six hours of excruciating labor, to hear her tell it. And a ruined figure. No amount of daughterly servitude was ever going to make up for that. Nonetheless, it was my duty to try.

"This is a setup, isn't it?"

Mama shrugged. "But just so you know, dear, I haven't been to Savannah since your daddy was stationed there during World War II. Why, only this morning I was looking at a photo of him taken at one of those lovely squares, and then that call came." She brushed away a tear. "It's almost as if this was meant to be."

I groaned. "Okay, okay, you guys win. I'll take y'all with me to Savannah. But if anything terrible happens down there—anything at all—you three are going to pay!"

They nodded, mute but grateful.

Lest you think it was rude of me to have spoken like that to my mother and our friends, I've traveled with this trio before. These ladies make the Three Stooges seem like Emily Post. Besides, I had a gut feeling that nothing good could come out of acquiring the estate of a cousin I barely knew—not when she drowned in a bathtub full of champagne. *Cheap* champagne.

"And we're taking Dmitri," I said firmly, referring to the one male I'm used to having around on a daily basis.

They nodded again, and the die was cast.

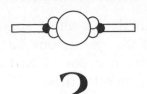

2

Dmitri is my cat, not my boyfriend. Greg Washburn is my boyfriend—well, off and on. Lately more on than off.

You already know that I'm Abigail Timberlake. You might not know that I'm forty-eight years old and not ashamed to admit it. In fact, I'm rather proud of my age, given the fact that nature has blessed me with a somewhat girlish figure and dark hair that has yet to turn. My eyes are green and, I am told, sparkle with youthful vitality. I weigh a mere ninety-three pounds—give or take a few.

The one category in which nature shortchanged me was height. I stand four foot nine in my stocking feet, and that's with wool socks! Of course I could wear high heels, but I don't have a hankering to ruin my feet, and besides, the style selection in the little girls' department is limited.

But genetics deals only half our cards; we pick the rest. I chose to marry Buford Timberlake, a timbersnake of a man, who two-timed me with a bimbo named Tweetie. This happened on my forty-fifth birthday. Tweetie, I think, was twenty then. In retrospect I'm surprised Buford didn't trade me in for two twenty-year-olds. Perhaps the cost of silicone was especially high.

At any rate, Buford is a divorce attorney and has

9

more connections than a set of TinkerToys. Before I knew it, he had the house, our bank accounts, but most importantly, our son, Charlie. Susan, thank God, was on her own by then.

I had to scramble to support myself, but I managed. Today I more than manage. Luck has been on my side more times than not—knock on wood—and my shop in Charlotte, North Carolina, is squarely in the black. In fact, the Den of Antiquity has done so well that I, too, have an assistant.

It was in the capable hands of this assistant, Irene Cheng, that I left my shop the morning I set out for Savannah.

"Don't forget that the Kefferts will be picking up their Khorassan carpet this afternoon," I said, one small foot still inside the shop. Wynnell waited for me in her car, C.J. and Mama in the U-Haul, but I felt reluctant to leave.

Irene rolled her eyes. "I won't forget."

"And tomorrow morning that woman from Hickory will be stopping by to show you pictures of the living room suite her grandmother left her. Don't even agree to look at the stuff if it's run-of-the-mill Victorian."

"Don't worry," Irene said. "I'm not a complete idiot."

I smiled. Irene's bluntness is also her charm.

"Well, then, I guess I'd better be going."

"I guess you'd better. You look pretty stupid standing there just looking at me. People might get the wrong idea."

Against my better judgment I said good-bye again and climbed into Wynnell's car.

*   *   *

From Columbia on, we took the back roads down to Savannah. I always eschew the interstate. I know, it is often the fastest route, but not always, and this time it was far from being the most direct. Besides, I like seeing something besides pine trees and mud flaps.

Route 321, on the other hand, takes me through cotton fields and charming little towns with distinctly American names like Norway, Sweden, and Denmark. Virtually free of trucks, traffic is light, and I always make as good if not better time as I do on the interstate. But then again, I have a Carolina license plate. Buford once told me of an Ohio couple who got lost on a Carolina back road, stopped at a police station to ask directions, and, to make a long story short, ended up making license plates *for* the state of South Carolina.

At any rate, I didn't plan to stop, but it was lunchtime when we reached Denmark, and Wynnell made me pull over to the Little China House. We left Dmitri in the car, window cracked, and went inside. Normally I would advise against eating Chinese food in Denmark, South Carolina, but the Korean cook there was really quite accomplished, and we enjoyed a very tasty lunch.

We also enjoyed each others' company, and I was beginning to think the trip was a good idea after all.

"Hurry up," I admonished the slow eaters. "Time's a-wasting!"

Wynnell's hedgerow eyebrows rose in tandem. "Abby, you're not finally getting excited, are you?"

"Well—okay, so maybe I am. But you can't blame me, can you? I've never been willed a house before. If it really is nice—and if the area can support another antique shop—well, maybe I'll just move down to Savannah."

"You wouldn't!" Mama wailed.

"Why not?" It's always fun to yank Mama's chain, even though in the end I invariably end up paying for my sin.

"Because of your two dear precious children, that's why."

"My two dear precious children are both away at college. And there's no telling if Susan will even be home this summer. She wants to go to Europe with Erin."

"Who's Aaron?" Mama asked in alarm. "Who are his people?"

"Call her mother and ask her that yourself." I stood, gathering my refuse. The Little China House is strictly self serve. "Have y'all read The Book?"

"I read it every morning," Mama snipped. "I may be Episcopalian, dear, but I start my days out right."

"Not that book, Mama, The book, John Berendt's *Midnight in the Garden of Good and Evil.*"

Mama shook her head. "I heard it was filth and lies. Sudie Dunbar says she knows half the people in it and they aren't anything like that man portrayed them."

Wynnell snorted. "John Berendt is a Yankee, a literary carpetbagger if you ask me."

"I liked the book," C.J. said. Mercifully, her mouth was now empty. "I especially liked the character who kept those flies glued to little strings. My Uncle Festus back in Shelby used to do the same thing."

We said nothing.

C.J. scratched her head. "Although come to think of it, it wasn't flies Uncle Festus kept on strings but pigeons. And he didn't glue the strings on the birds but made little harnesses for them and tied the strings to the harnesses and then to his belt. Must have had a hundred of them tied on there at one time, because one day a pack of dogs came running through Uncle Festus's yard and scared the flock. Next thing Uncle Festus knew he was airborne, headed west toward the mountains."

She stopped again, and again we said nothing.

"Did I tell you how far those pigeons carried him?"

Mama made the mistake of shaking her head.

"All the way to Tennessee, that's how far. Some hunters finally shot a few of the pigeons, and Uncle Festus landed in a little town called Alcatraz. And you know, he wasn't even hurt, except for a turned ankle. Anyway, it was in all the papers, and some guys from Hollywood came out and made a movie about it. Uncle Festus actually got to play himself. The film was called *Birdman of Alcatraz*."

We groaned again. C.J., as you might have guessed, is a flapjack or two short of a stack. Still, she's a remarkable businesswoman, and at age twenty-four is one of Charlotte's youngest antique dealers. She is also a loyal friend, and we have long ago come to the consensus that her friendship is worth the price of listening to her stories.

"But I thought Burt Lancaster—" I clapped a loving hand over Mama's mouth before she had a chance to spur C.J. into a long-winded defense.

"Let's hit the road," I said firmly. "Fortune, if not fame, awaits us."

We made no further stops.

I should have known better. Late March, early April is azalea season in Savannah, and the city is swamped with tourists. Getting a reasonably priced motel room was an impossibility. We finally had to settle for a so-called suite at the Heritage Hotel on River Street. It was basically just one very large room, but contained a kitchenette as well as a sitting and dining area. However, there was only one bed. A king-size bed to be sure, but you just try and sleep with three other women—especially C.J.! Triathlon competitors expend less energy during their events than C.J. does in her sleep. I bet that gal would weigh three hundred pounds easily if she ever settled down long enough to stop burning calories.

"Do you at least have a rollaway?" I asked. We were, after all, paying two hundred and fifty a night for the room.

The clerk, a young woman named Ashley Hawkins, shook her head. "I'm sorry. We normally do, but I'm afraid you've come at a bad time. It's the peak of azalea season, and the *Today* show just did a segment on Savannah gardens. We've had folks coming from as far away as Oregon."

Mama, who was standing at my elbow, sighed. "We should have known better. We're not tourists, you see—well, not in the conventional sense. We're here to pick up my daughter's dead cousin."

"Oh?"

"I guess that didn't come out right. Lula Mae's not just lying around; she's in a jar."

Ashley recoiled. "I beg your pardon?"

"Make that an urn," I said.

"A fancy Italian urn," Mama said. "One that could be worth a lot of money. Abby, what's the name for that again?"

Ashley smiled. I could tell from years of parenting

experience that she was struggling not to roll her eyes.

"Mama, please, we don't need to be boring Miss Hawkins with silly details."

"Drowning in champagne is not boring, dear."

"She's not boring me." Ashley's face was suddenly very earnest.

Mama's chin tilted in triumph. "Like I said, she drowned in champagne. You ever hear of somebody doing that?"

"Yes, ma'am. Y'all's cousin. It was in all the papers. It happened New Year's Eve, right?"

"Right! Did you know her?"

Ashley shook her head. She would have been a plain girl had it not been for the thick strawberry-blond tresses that swirled now in front of her face.

"No, ma'am, I've never met y'all's cousin. But I've heard about her from time to time."

"You see, Abby? Your cousin is famous! Maybe she's in The Book."

"Mama, she isn't—" I turned to Ashley. "*Is* she?" After all, when I read the book, Lula Mae was the furthest thing from my mind.

The golden-red curls collided and parted several times. "No, ma'am, she's not in the book. But everyone in Savannah knew her—or at least knew of her."

Mama smiled proudly. "You see?"

"Mama, that's not necessarily a good thing."

"Don't be ridiculous, dear. Your daddy's cousin was famous. Go on," she said to Ashley, "tell my daughter some of the stories."

Ashley glanced at the clock. It was three minutes to four.

"Like what?"

"Like what was Lula Mae Wiggins known for."

"Well, uh—I—uh—"

"Go on, dear."

"She drank a lot."

"I beg your pardon?"

"Every afternoon about this time she'd come into the Heritage and head straight for the bar. An hour later security would be escorting her out—well, to be truthful, they'd be carrying her out. Frankly, Miss Lula Mae's death didn't surprise anyone. But we were surprised there was any champagne left in the tub."

Mama gasped, and her pearls got a good workout.

It was time to change the subject. We needed to get down to business anyway.

"Miss Hawkins, if perchance any of your guests decided not to use their rollaways after all, can we have first dibs on them?"

Ashley nodded. She had a million freckles, many of them connected, and smiling pushed them into an interesting pattern.

"I'll make a note of that. I'll also have housekeeping round up extra blankets and pillows. Maybe someone could use the sofa."

"Thanks."

Mama poked me. "What about Dmitri?" The price of our room had yet to register with her. Trapped in the 1950s by a time warp, she no doubt thought we were *buying* the suite for two-fifty. Even then she probably thought we were paying too much.

I ignored Mama and fumbled with my credit cards. I try not to use plastic money generally, but I do carry it with me for emergencies. The trouble is I have so many of the dang things, all with different rates, that I can't remember which is which.

"Abby, ask about Dmitri."

"Shh," Wynnell said. C.J. giggled.

"Well, I wouldn't feel right about sneaking a cat into a place this nice. Would you, dear?"

The jig was up. I had indeed been planning to sneak my ten-pound bundle of joy into the hotel. But please understand, Dmitri is not just any old cat. My fluffy yellow tom has been neutered and is meticulous about using the litter box. And of course he's very quiet.

Ashley looked stricken. "I'm sorry, ladies, but we don't allow pets."

"I *know*," I said through gritted teeth. "You wouldn't happen to know a place where I can board my cat, would you?"

Ashley glanced around, as if we were all part of an Oliver Stone conspiracy. "Well, we do keep a list of kennels, but I'm afraid they're all full as well." She paused, and when she resumed speaking, her voice was barely audible. "Tell you what, I know someone who boards pets but isn't on this list. Let me give her a quick call to see if by any chance she has room."

"Oh, would you please!"

"I'd be happy to. But first, would you mind terribly if I waited on these people?"

I turned. Somehow a tourist family in Bermuda shorts, their necks bent forward under the weight of cameras, had managed to sneak up behind us.

"Not at all," I said.

We waited in the open lounge area, in the faux shade of ficus trees and dusty Kentia palms. While we waited, three more families demanded Ashley's time, and she made or received half a dozen calls. In the meantime, a bored C.J. wandered off to the bar and returned with cold sodas for all of us.

Finally Ashley Hawkins nodded to me. I left my soda with Mama and trotted over.

"Here," Ashley said, and thrust a folded slip of paper into my hand. "It's on Bonaventure Road, just about a quarter-mile past the cemetery. I know it's a ways out, but I'm sure you'll be satisfied. Look for a white sign on the left-hand side. It has a black paw mark on it. Velvet Paws is the name."

"Thanks."

Ashley had been very kind, but for some reason I felt like a goose had walked over my grave—no, make that a whole flock of geese.

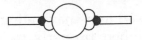

3

C.J. and Wynnell declined to accompany me to Velvet Paws. While at the bar to get a refill on her soda, C.J. had looked out the panoramic window at the Savannah River directly below and seen porpoises. This was the poor girl's first glimpse of these splendid mammals in the wild, and for a few heart-stopping seconds she thought she was seeing sharks. But sharks or porpoises, it didn't matter which. From then on, C.J. and Wynnell were glued to the window. I must admit, even I had a hard time dragging myself away to tend to my cat.

"But why do I have to come?" Mama whined.

"Because you're my mother, that's why. And because on the way we're going to stop in and see Mr. Dewayne Kimbro, the executor of Lula Mae's estate."

"Do you have an appointment?"

"Of course." And I did, too. Never mind that it was for the following morning at nine o'clock. I just wanted to touch base. Surely there was no harm in that.

Unfortunately Mr. Kimbro's office was located on Montgomery Street near the County Courthouse. It was a long way from Velvet Paws. Equally unfortunate was the fact that north of West Broughton the street becomes one way—the wrong way. Mama, who was supposed to be navigating but hadn't even got the map aligned properly by then, refused to accept responsibility for the fact that I nearly hit a van of bewildered tourists from one of the square states. She placed responsibility on poor Dmitri who had his tail in her face. At any rate, by the time I had located the building in which Mr. Kimbro had his office and found us a parking space nearby, it was nearly five.

I cracked the car window for Dmitri and dragged Mama down the sidewalk. You can bet she complained the entire way, especially when, during a brief tug-of-war, she whacked her free arm against the trunk of a palmetto, which had no business being planted in the middle of a pedestrian thoroughfare.

"Ouch! You see what you made me do?" Mama, holding her injured arm, staggered dramatically across the sidewalk and straight into the path of a man who had just exited Mr. Kimbro's building and who was very much in a hurry. The man did a deft little sidestep but just barely missed being knocked to the ground.

"Excuse me," Mama gasped. She was utterly mortified.

The man stopped and stared at us over the tops of bottle-thick glasses. He was perhaps in his midfifties, pudgy, with strands of graying hair held desperately in place over an expanding pate. To his credit, the white suit he wore was impeccable, as was the white tie. The pale blue shirt with buttondown collar accented both nicely.

"Are you all right, ma'am?"

Mama gave him the widow's once-over and much to my surprise found him attractive. I could tell by the sudden twinkle in her eyes, although pearl-patting and crinoline-fluffing were dead giveaways as well.

"I am fine," Mama said, stretching those three little words out into twelve syllables. "How about you?"

"Fine. Well, if you ladies will excuse me." Jowls shuddered as he bowed slightly.

"Just a minute," Mama said. "We're looking for somebody named Kimbro. Maybe you—"

But the portly man was off and running. I mean that literally. Perhaps he had a bus to catch or had taken one too many laxatives the night before. He disappeared around the first corner in a blue and white streak.

"Well, I never!" Mama said. "Abby, have you in all your born days ever met someone so rude?"

"As a matter of fact, I have, Mama. What I can't believe is how you just threw yourself at him."

Mama blushed. "He didn't have a ring, Abby. Not even a tan line."

"Mama, he was wearing white, and Easter is still two weeks away."

She sighed. "Well, there is that. But Abby, I've been so lonely since your daddy died."

I grabbed Mama's elbow and steered her into Mr. Kimbro's building. A group had exited the courthouse and two of them were headed our way. I wasn't about to let strangers hear what was undoubtedly going to be a very personal, if not embarrassing confession.

The exterior of Dewayne Kimbro's three-story building was red brick and perhaps two hundred years old. To reach the front door one had to go up a flight of steps flanked by black wrought-iron handrails. The thick glass pane in the front door was etched, depicting a scene of egrets perched on dead tree limbs. It had the look and feel of old glass.

The inside of the building was not at all what I expected. The walls were peach, and the hardwood floor in the hallway was covered with a runner of plush navy carpet bordered with a gold geometrical design. Greek, I think. Little lamps in gaslight style with navy and gold shades lit the corridor. To our right was a wooden staircase, it, too, protected by the plush runner, more simulated gaslights ascending its walls. Understated elegance were two words that immediately came to mind.

A black velvet sign on a gilt easel dominated the small foyer. A single gold braid tassel hung from the right corner of the sign. The only discordant note in the scene was the white plastic letters that informed us of the building's occupants.

Apparently the entire bottom floor was reserved for Miss Mimi Merriweather and her School for the Refinement of Young Ladies. The five visible doors were all closed, and there was no sign of or any sound from Miss Mimi and her girls. The second floor contained the offices of Gerald Paynter, Registered and Certified Hypnotist; the Courtney Bouchard Modeling Agency; and the International Pecan Praline Export Company. The third floor, thank heavens, was home to the law firm of Kimbro, Rathbun & Cohen.

"Is there an elevator?" Mama asked needlessly.

We hoofed it up the stairs. It was clear to me that the three-story building had once been a private home. It was fun to imagine ladies in hoop skirts and ringlets ascending and descending the very same steps, Scarlett O'Haras all of them.

On the second-floor landing Mama craned her

short neck for a peek at Gerald Paynter, the hypnotist, and I sniffed the air for pralines, but we were
both disappointed. The door to the Courtney Bouchard Modeling Agency was open, however, and we
heard the faint sound of voices. Female voices.

"Do you think she handles male models?" Mama
whispered.

"I doubt it. And if she does, they're either children
or gay."

"Stereotypes," Mama hissed. "Abby, didn't I teach
you any better?"

"You taught me well enough, Mama. I have plenty
of gay friends, you know that. But a fact is a fact.
Besides, I doubt if she handles men your age. No
offense, of course."

Mama glared at me. "There you go again, stereo-
typing. For your information, dear, I prefer younger
men."

That was, in fact, quite true. Just a year or two ago
Mama had had a brief, and I hope platonic, fling
with a male maid, Stanley Morris from Scrub A Tub-
Tub. Mercifully Mama must have forgotten the party
incident when Stan, who was her date at a society
party in Charlotte, dumped her in favor of the butler. The male butler.

I hustled Mama up the second flight of stairs. I
wasn't about to haul a male model back up to Charlotte with us. I mean, what if by some miracle the
guy was straight and she ended up marrying him,
thereby giving me a stepfather at the tender age of
forty-eight? Even worse, what if he continued to
model? What a mistake that would be! I didn't want
to contemplate a faux pas faux pa who primped.

The third floor, alas, was deserted. There was just

one door for Kimbro, Rathbun & Cohen, and I knocked until my knuckles were sore.

"What do we do now?" I wailed.

"We rest," Mama said, and sat on the top step.

I joined her. The thick navy carpet made it a comfortable seat. The peach walls were easy on the eyes.

"So, Mama, what's going on with you and men? What is it you were going to tell me outside?"

"Forget it, Abby, you wouldn't understand."

"Try me."

"You really want to know?"

"Of course I do—well, as long as it doesn't involve body parts."

"Oh, Abby, you are so old-fashioned." This from a woman who wears a full circle skirt puffed up by crinolines, patent leather heels, and always carries a matching purse. She was the last woman in Rock Hill to wear a hat and gloves to the supermarket.

"Mama, just tell me!"

"I'm lonely, Abby, that's all there is to it."

I breathed a huge sigh of relief. "I'm sorry I haven't been spending much time with you lately. I guess it's good you talked me into bringing you on this trip."

"Yes, and I'm grateful dear. But there's more to it than that."

"Of course. And we discussed before the problem of you getting a cat of your own. Like I said, a cat can live to be twenty years old. Maybe you should consider a dog. You know, one of those breeds that doesn't live past ten."

"I don't want a pet! I want a man!"

"Well, don't we all," I said with mock cheer. "Look, Mama, you have plenty of men friends. Many more than I. Why, there's Phil at church. And

Bill at Shepherd's Center. You're always talking about them, how much you enjoy their company."

"I don't want just a man's friendship. I want his body. I want to feel a man's body next to mine. I want to—"

"Mama!"

"Well, it's the truth. A woman my age still likes to be touched. To be held."

I put my arm around her. I didn't know what to say. I couldn't very well advise her to put an ad in the personal columns, now, could I?

We sat there in uncomfortable silence for several minutes. Finally Mama spoke.

"I need chocolate."

"What?"

"Something sinfully rich, jam-packed with fat and sugar. Something in which you can actually taste the calories."

"Dark chocolate or milk?"

"Dark chocolate, of course. Milk chocolate is for wimps."

I was about to argue the merits of *good* milk chocolate when we heard the sound of footsteps and heavy panting. We stood, and Mama fluffed her skirt. Seconds later a cloud of acrid cigar smoke rose from the stairwell. Arriving shortly behind the stench was a bald-headed man, and several steps behind him was a heavyset woman with a preposterous shade of silver-blond hair.

"Good afternoon, ladies," the chrome dome said. "I'm Ralph Lizard, and this lovely lady"—he gestured with the cigar at the bottle blonde—"is Miss Duvall."

"Raynatta Duvall," the plump platinum floozy puffed. "That's Raynatta with an A and a Y."

Stopping just below us, both the man and the woman held out their hands so Mama and I were obliged to shake them. Clearly the couple wanted us to tell our names as well.

"I'm her mother," Mama said cagily.

"And I'm her daughter," I said, proving I could be just as cagey.

Ralph Lizard stoked his stogie with cheeks like bellows. "Wouldn't either of you happen to be Abigail Timberlake, would you?"

I coughed and waved my hand to clear the air. "That's me, but I have to warn you, I have a black belt in karate."

"You do?" Mama asked in a tight little voice. "Oh, Abby, when did that happen? I've been begging you to take classes with me at Chop a Block Karate School on Cherry Road. Begging for ages, and you keep turning me down. So now you spring it on me, and in front of strangers yet!"

"Mama! I was just—well, trying to play it safe. Of course I don't have a black belt. I've never even been near Chop a Block."

Mama smiled, the relief painfully evident in her eyes. She wants to do an activity with me—anything—so we can bond. Fortunately I live in Charlotte, and Mama lives across the state line in Rock Hill, South Carolina. Bonding activities are possible but not practical.

"I'll buy us both lessons for Christmas," she said. "Only we won't be in the same class, dear. I decided not to wait for you and bought a book on it. *Karate for Idiots*. I'm already on Chapter Three and I can do a pretty mean karate chop, if I say so myself."

The smooth and smoky Mr. Lizard rubbed his pate with the palm of his free hand. "So, what's the verdict, ladies? Is one of you Abigail Timberlake?"

"I'm Abigail," I said, and shifted my purse so that I held it only by the straps. I'm embarrassed to admit that I'm one of those folks who still carry a pocketbook the size of a gym bag. In theory I tote with me everything I might need to facilitate my outings—if only I could find the items when needed. At any rate, a good hard swing with it and Mr. Lizard, who was still a couple of steps below the landing, would do a back flip from which there would be no quick recovery.

"Good to meet you," Mr. Lizard said, and pumped my hand again. "I had a hunch it was you. Dewayne said you would be coming, but he didn't say when. Miss Duvall and I were just passing by and figured we might give it a try. Dewayne not in?"

"Mr. Kimbro is not in," I said, "if that's who you mean."

He nodded, while blowing another puff of noxious smoke into my space. "Well, it doesn't matter now, because you're here."

"Oh?" The grip I had on my purse straps tightened.

"It's all strictly on the up and up, ma'am. Dewayne keeps his fingers in a lot of different pies, but real estate isn't one of them."

"Please, Mr. Lizard, get to your point."

Mama gasped but said nothing. No doubt I'd hear later—ad nauseam—just how rude I'd been.

Ralph Lizard laughed. "I like a woman with spunk. Yes, ma'am, I do. And you," he said, waving the disgusting cigar, "have spunk."

"Hey!" Raynatta with an A and a Y was not amused.

"But I like you most, sugar doll."

Raynatta beamed and waggled a finger sporting a rock so large and clear, it could only have been cubic zirconia. If not, well, I had no objection to changing my name to Abigail Lizard. Or course, the cigars would have to go.

"Please," I begged, "I have a pussy waiting for me in my car."

Ralph laughed again. "Here." He thrust a business card at me, which I reluctantly took. "My home phone number is on there as well. You can reach me night or day."

"This is all very nice, but why would I want to?"

"Because I can get you top dollar for it."

"For what?"

"Why, for your aunt's house."

I shoved the card in my purse. "She was my cousin, not my aunt, and I haven't even seen the place. Who knows, I may just want to keep it."

His frown was barely perceptible. On a man with hair it might have gone unnoticed.

"Well, in case you do decide to sell, remember Ralph Lizard. Just like the reptile."

"I'm sure," I said pleasantly. He was free to interpret that as he pleased.

After rejoining Dmitri, we backtracked to City Market, where we found a little shop that sold melt-in-your mouth, to-die-for pecan fudge. We had a couple of pieces each, and of course Mama had to find a chocolate shake with which to wash her share down. I, I'll have you know, settled for a diet cola.

At any rate, it was already dusk by the time we drove past the famed Bonaventure Cemetery. The live oaks hung low over the road, forming a veritable tunnel. Spanish moss hung from their limbs like fragments of a tattered shroud.

We drove the specified quarter-mile but didn't see a white sign with a black paw on it. About a mile down the road I turned around, and we searched again. Still no sign. Desperate, I turned around in the drive leading into Bonaventure Cemetery.

In fact, I was so agitated at having missed the Velvet Paws sign I almost ran down a woman standing just outside the wrought-iron gates. Mama and I both gasped, and Mama even threw her arms protectively in front of her face. For one heart-stopping moment the woman stood there, just inches from my car, my headlights full on her, and the next second she was gone. I mean that literally. The woman had totally and utterly disappeared.

My only thought was that she had fallen. I hadn't felt a thud, but perhaps I'd hit her just hard enough to knock her off balance.

I jammed the gear into Park and jumped out of the car. "Mama!" I screamed. "Come help me!"

But there was no one there. No one at all. Just the hard pavement of the drive and a fallen clump of Spanish moss. I got on my hands and knees and looked under the car. No one.

"This is too spooky for me," Mama said.

"So you saw her too?"

"Did I ever!"

"Straw hat? Bright orange top? Long purple skirt?"

"And the beads," Mama said. "She had on about eight strings of beads."

"A black woman?"

"Yes. Abby, I'm getting back in the car."

Call me a chicken, but I got in before her. The

second her door slammed shut, I locked all the doors. It was only then that I thought to check the back seat.

I've never screamed so hard in my entire life.

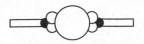

4

"Well, it's about time," the woman said. "W-w-what are y-y-you d-doing in my c-c-car?"

"Help!" Mama shrieked. "Help! We're being car-jacked!"

The interloper laughed. She had deep voice that resonated of cigarettes and age.

"I ain't no car-jacker. And if I was, I sure wouldn't get me a bitty little car like this. No, ma'am, a Lincoln Town Car is more my style."

"Who are you?" I was trying to feel under my seat with my foot. I sometimes keep an umbrella there. It wouldn't be of much use against a real weapon, but deployed at the right time, it might allow Mama and me to escape.

"My name is Diamond," the woman said. "And who might you be?"

"That's none of your business," Mama snapped. "Abby"—her voice was now a whisper—"step on the gas and ram the gates. She's probably not wearing a seat belt."

Instead, I flipped on the interior lights. "Diamond who? And what are you doing in my car?"

"Just Diamond. And girl, I've been waiting. What took you so long?"

"Excuse me?"

"Miss Amy say you'd be here at five on the nose. I reckon it's a good deal after that."

"Who, pray tell, is Miss Amy?"

"Little white girl over there in the north corner. Drowned in the Savannah River when she just nine. Miss Amy see everything. Know everything, too. And if you follow all the steps right, she tell all, too."

"Mama," I muttered. "We've got another C.J. on our hands." That was meant to be code, but when it comes to things like this, Mama is as subtle as Tammy Faye's makeup.

"Do you mean this woman's crazy?"

Diamond's laugh was like gravel rattling in a galvanized bucket. "Yes, ma'am, I be crazy. But we all be crazy."

"I'm not!" Mama said, and puffed her crinolines.

"Yes, ma'am, you is. But I ain't gonna argue." Diamond tapped me on the shoulder. "Whatcha waiting on, girl?"

"I beg your pardon?"

"Let's ride. Let's get us a move on. Y'all can't be sitting here after dark—not without taking all the steps."

"What on earth are you talking about?"

"You really don't know?"

"I haven't a clue. Now if you'll you be so kind as to get out of my car."

The back driver's side door opened. "Miss Amy's gonna get herself a good talking to."

"Give Amy our best, dear," Mama said. No doubt she rolled her eyes.

"Yes, ma'am. But you be talking to her soon—real soon."

"Somehow I don't think that's going to happen," Mama said primly.

"Yes, ma'am, it is."

The second the back door closed, I jumped out. Diamond was nowhere to be seen. I even made Mama get out, which was almost as hard as giving Dmitri a bath.

"N-n-no," Mama said, her teeth chattering. "I don't see her either."

"Do you think we just imagined her?"

"Of course not, dear. No one looks good in orange, but if you have to wear it, for heaven's sakes forget the purple."

"Maybe we hallucinated. Maybe there was something in the fudge."

"Been there, done that,' Mama said dryly. "What happened here was not a hallucination."

"What?"

"She was too clear. Distinct, I guess you'd say. And the colors didn't vibrate."

"Mama! What do *you* know about hallucinations?"

My petite progenitress patted her pearls, which gleamed in the light of the rising moon. "It only happened once, Abby, and it wasn't even my idea."

I leaned against the cool metal trunk of my car. "*What* happened?"

"*It.* Our one experience. And it wasn't my idea, mind you, but Thelma Lou's."

She paused, and her pearls got a good workout. Thank heavens for the moon, because if the string had broken, we'd have had a devil of a time finding them in the sand.

"Go on, Mama."

"I think it was 1971. Thelma Lou and—I'm not going to tell you all their names, Abby—anyway, a few of us gals who were mothers of college kids got together and decided we should do a little experimenting of our own. Just a little, mind you. Just enough so that we could know what it was y'all were trying. You know, so we could see the pitfalls for you and maybe be of some actual use instead of just wringing our hands."

"Mama, you didn't!"

"Like I said, just the once, dear."

"I can't believe this! My mama smoked marijuana."

"Oh, no, dear. It wasn't marijuana. Just some little pills Thelma Lou bought up in Charlotte."

"Oh, no!" I wailed. "I'm the daughter of a psychedelic drug user. My mama's a freak!"

Mama let go of her pearls and put her hands on her hips. "Why, Abigail Louise! What a thing to say to your mama. It was only that one time. And don't tell me you never took drugs in college."

"I only smoked pot! That was it. And I never inhaled!"

"Don't be silly, dear. You can level with me."

"But it's true! You know I hate smoke. Lord knows I tried to inhale, but it just made me choke."

Mama's eyes widened. "Oh, my."

I shook my head miserably. "I can't believe this. I've got to be the only woman alive who came out of the seventies with less drug experience than her mother."

"Oh, no, Abby! There's Thelma Lou's daughter Angie, and Lauren's daughter Christie, and Connie Sue's daughter—" Mama clapped a hand over mouth. "Now see what you've done!"

"Me?"

"Well, I've never claimed to be a saint," Mama wailed. "And it *was* the seventies—drugs, sex, even something called swinging. I remember once—"

I hustled Mama back into the car before I had opportunity to learn other tidbits that a daughter has a right *not* to hear. Of course, I didn't believe, not even for a second, that Mama and Daddy had swung. Well, maybe if the swing had consisted of a sturdy wooden seat suspended from a stout oak limb by ropes or chains. But even that image was going too far.

"Look for the paw sign," I barked.

"Aye, aye," Mama said smugly. She was, I knew, immensely satisfied that she had gotten my goat.

We found the Velvet Paws sign, but it was a quarter of a mile *before* the cemetery, not after. The little white house was set well back from the road at the end of a sandy drive. The front door was almost hidden by a pair of enormous camellia bushes.

I held Dmitri while Mama found and rang the bell. My yellow bundle of joy was decidedly unhappy. He was growling the way he always does when he smells another cat.

The door opened a crack. "May I help you?"

"Yes, ma'am. The clerk over at the Heritage sent us. I need to board my cat."

"What's the clerk's name?"

I drew a blank. "Mama, what's her name?" I whispered.

"Lord, Abby, don't expect me to remember. Besides being so much older than you, I'm a freak."

"Mama!"

The door started to close.

"She's a strawberry blonde with more freckles than Opie!"

There was the scrabble of chain, and the door swung open to reveal a strikingly beautiful woman.

Skin like that seldom, if ever, saw the sun, and either she owed parts of her body to the hands of a skillful surgeon, or she'd been blessed with exceptional genes. Of course, no one is perfect, and this woman was wearing a white T-shirt *and* white slacks. I'm sure Mama was fit to be tied.

"Sorry, about that. But ever since The Book, I've had to be real careful. Especially at night. Tourists do some pretty strange things."

"I bet."

"Lougee Hawkins," she said, and extended her hand. She had large brown eyes that were warm and welcoming. Never mind that her hair resembled a haystack that had been through a wind tunnel.

Mama shook her hand, but I couldn't, because Dmitri was struggling. Lougee leaned over to pet him, but when her hand came within six inches of him, he hissed.

"This ferocious beast," I said, after Mama and I had introduced ourselves, "is Dmitri Timberlake. He's eight years old. Aren't you, boy?"

Dmitri produced a moan that sounded like it had escaped from the gates of hell. "Stop that, boy!" I smiled at Lougee. "I don't know what's gotten into him. He's not usually this antisocial."

Lougee had the grace to return my smile. "Strange place, long car ride, it's not so unusual. Maybe he smells other cats. Maybe dogs. You board him a lot?"

"No, ma'am. This is only the third or fourth time."

"That explains it, then. He's just insecure. But he'll adjust. Won't you, big guy?"

She reached out again, and this time Dmitri swiped at her with a paw. Fortunately he missed, or it would have been a spontaneous game of connect the dot with Lougee's freckles.

"For shame, Dmitri! Now, what do you say?"

My baby's meow was a pitiful, high-pitched squeak that made me want to fold my body over his protectively and run him back to the car. But unless I planned sleeping there with him, that was not an option.

I sighed. "Well, this has to be done, I guess. So, where does he go? Where's his room, so to speak?"

"Follow me."

We followed Lougee through a house that made her hairdo seem neat. I mean, who am I to judge, but one can at least put away dirty dishes when expecting clients, can't one? And what were panties doing on the living room floor?

The cat kennel appeared to have been made by converting a screened back porch. It consisted of six compartments, three on either side of the door. Each compartment was approximately three feet wide, three feet deep, and four feet high. The main floor was concrete slab, but halfway up the back wall of each cubicle was a carpet-covered sleeping shelf. The doors were metal with wide mesh screen. There was a full water dish and what appeared to be fresh cat food. Above all, and much to my great relief, the cattery was clean.

Five of the six cages were occupied, and their inhabitants regarded us with baleful muteness. Dmitri was still on a roll, so he hissed dutifully at each in turn.

"The house sits so that each cage gets a little morning sun," Lougee said, reading my mind.

I kissed Dmitri. "You see, dear, it isn't so bad."

"And each cat gets an hour turn-out in the common walkway here, if they want. Most prefer to stay in their quarters."

Quarters? Now that was a generous use of the word! Still, I had seen worse, and beggars can't be choosers.

I lowered my precious to the floor. "Mama will be back soon, dear. Just two night-nights and my snuggle bunny will be back in his own widdle bed."

Lord only knows why it is that folks like me talk human baby talk to a feline with a walnut-size brain. But there you have it.

Now, I'm not claiming that Dmitri understood my words of comfort, but he did feel confident enough to wiggle free from my grip and gingerly inspect the cage. This he did by sniffing. I waited patiently while his nose led him on the grand tour, confident that he would at least return to say good-bye. But when my youngest and hairiest child reached the far side of the box, he leaped up to the sleeping shelf, flopped over on his side, and proceeded to glare at me.

And that's how I left him, burning holes in my back with his yellow-green peepers.

Mama and I stopped for a bite of fast food, McDonald's I think, but then went straight to the hotel. We were both exhausted, and besides, we wanted first claim on the bed. Neither of us was surprised to find that C.J. and Wynnell were still somewhere out on the town. I won the coin toss and the privilege of sleeping at the edge of the bed.

At exactly ten minutes after midnight—I looked at the bedside clock—the door opened, and our friends tiptoed in. One or both of the ladies smelled like a brewery. No doubt they'd switched from cola early in the evening. At any rate, they made very little sound getting into bed but once there immediately began snoring like the drunks they were.

I put up with the double assault of auditory and olfactory abuse for about a minute, and then quite wisely sought the couch. Ashley, bless her golden-red tresses, had been unable to come up with a roll-away but had made sure we were amply supplied with sheets, pillows, and extra blankets. There may not be many perks to being my size, but being able to stretch out, with room to spare, on a hotel couch is one of them. No doubt I had the best sleep of all of us. Lord knows, I was going to need it.

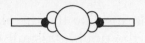

5

My plan was to grab a toasted bagel in the City Market and walk to Dewayne Kimbro's office. Mama was still in bed, snoring it up with C.J. and Wynnell, and early morning, if I'm awake, is my favorite time to be alone.

But when I got to City Market, I stumbled into a wonderful place called Seasons and had an Eggs Benedict breakfast served with champagne. The bubbly seemed particularly appropriate, given the means of my cousin's demise, but rest assured, I did not drink to the point of inebriation. In fact, given my rather compact frame, I never drink more than a glass of anything.

Nonetheless, it was a warm spring day, the sun was shining and the air filled with the sounds of sparrows, mocking birds, and several thousand tourists. Every azalea bush in town was blazing with color, and every deciduous tree and shrub shimmered in a haze of bright, fresh green. In short, it felt good to be alive. After breakfast I practically bounced my way over to the Kimbro building. One more sip of champagne and I would have skipped, that's for sure. The only thing standing between reality and perfection was the absence of Greg Washburn, my gentleman friend.

My appointment was for nine, and that's when I

arrived. In fact, I got there a little early, so on Mama's behalf checked out the Courtney Bouchard Modeling Agency. I was told by a receptionist with a thick German accent, who was built like a panzer, that they did indeed handle male models—under the age of twelve. I had better luck at the International Pecan Praline Export Company, where a receptionist with a soft southern accent, built like the *Hindenburg*, foisted several fistfuls of free pralines on me. Fortunately I'd forgotten to tuck my hairbrush in my purse that morning and had extra room.

I knocked on the door of Kimbro, Rathbun & Cohen. No answer. I knocked again, louder. I was about to try the knob when the door opened and I found myself face to chest with the pudgy man in the white suit and tie Mama had tried to pick up the day before. He was still wearing the same suit, by the way. I could tell by a fleck of orange on his left lapel. He may have been wearing the same blue shirt, but I can't swear to it. His sparse hair was still plastered to his pate, and he was still wearing bottle-thick glasses. Yup, it was definitely the same man.

"Miss Timberlake?" he asked almost casually. His breath smelled of curry.

"Yes, sir. I'm here to see Mr. Kimbro. A Mr. Dewayne Kimbro."

"That would be me."

We shook hands.

"We sort of met yesterday," I said.

He said nothing. Perhaps his eyes were asking for more, and I just couldn't see it through the thick lenses.

"My mama almost ran into you on the sidewalk yesterday afternoon. Not in a car, of course, but on foot."

Again nothing.

"You seemed to be in a hurry to get someplace."

He shrugged. "Miss Timberlake, won't you please come in?"

I followed him into a reception area that had been obviously abandoned. The desk was clear save for a bulbless lamp and an upside-down wastebasket. There was no chair. On the wall behind the desk was last year's calendar.

To either side of the desk was a door, and I followed him to the left into a room only slightly better furnished. He gestured at a vintage wooden chair with sweat-stained armrests. I took the seat. His chair behind the desk was black leather, but a short strip of electrical tape placed diagonally across the back was the sure sign of a tear.

"It isn't as bad as it looks," he said.

I nodded, surprisingly at a loss for words.

"I've been thinking of retiring anyway. Got a nice little fishing boat down by Tybee Island. Creek side. Ever since Cohen quit to join his brother-in-law's firm in Atlanta—well, it just doesn't make sense to break in a new partner at my age."

"And Rathbun?"

"Never was a Rathbun. That was Mama's maiden name. Did it for her."

"I see."

"She was a Yankee from Ohio," he added, almost as a confession.

"Your secret is safe with me."

"Well, Miss Timberlake, shall we get down to business?"

"By all means."

He flipped open a manila folder. "As you know,

your aunt, Miss Lula Mae Wiggins, left her entire estate to you. It—"

"Excuse me, sir. I hate to be picky, but Lula Mae was not my aunt. She was some sort of a cousin. Second or third, I think. Throw in a couple of 're-moveds.' "

He shook his head carefully and slowly, so as not to disturb his coiffure. "No, ma'am. It says right here Miss Lula Mae Wiggins was your father's sister."

"Where? May I see that?"

Dewayne Kimbro passed me photocopies of several handwritten pages. "These are yours to keep."

I read the first paragraph. Not trusting my eyes, nor the effects of one glass of champagne, I reread it. It read the same.

I, Lula Mae Wiggins, being of sound body and mind, do hereby leave my entire estate, and all my worldly belongings, to my niece Abigail Louise Wiggins Timberlake, daughter of my late brother, Clarence Rufus Wiggins III, originally of Atlanta.

"But this can't be! Daddy didn't have a sister. He was an only child!"

Dewayne Kimbro pushed the heavy glasses up and massaged his eyes with sausage fingers. "Ma'am, your father was Clarence Rufus Wiggins III, originally of Atlanta, was he not?"

"Well, actually Daddy was born in Madison, Georgia, but he grew up in Atlanta. After the war and after college, he moved to Rock Hill, South Carolina."

"And you are Abigail Louise Wiggins Timberlake, are you not?"

"Yes, sir. Timberlake is my married name. I only kept it because of the kids."

"Well, ma'am, then I believe we have established that it is you mentioned in this will. Shall we continue?"

He read the entire document aloud, and I followed along. Well, to be honest, I touched base every couple of paragraphs. The rest of the time my mind bounced all over the place, wanting to think about anything other than the fact that Daddy, and Mama too, had lied to me my entire life. *Unless*—I mean, maybe even they didn't know! Stranger things have happened, believe you me. Just watch the Jerry Springer show.

When he was through reading, Dewayne Kimbro folded his massive hands. "Are there any questions?"

"No, sir—well, maybe just one. Is this document legal?"

The glasses fell back into place. "Ma'am?"

"Well, it's that part about her being my aunt. Let's say I'm the right Abigail Timberlake but she really isn't my father's sister, do I still inherit everything mentioned in there?"

"Ma'am, let me get this straight. Is it your intent to prove that you are *not* the party mentioned in this document?"

"No, sir. But what if I get all this stuff, and then someone proves later that they are the niece to whom Lula Mae is referring. What then?"

For the first time he smiled. "It is my professional opinion that were this to be the case, your ownership would still stand. In many instances, and I believe this to be one of them, possession is indeed nine-tenths of the law."

"Are you sure?"

The smile receded. "Ma'am, your aunt appointed me executor of her will, and that is what I intend to do. You are, however, are free to seek counsel elsewhere."

"No, no, I believe you! It's just that I'm still having a difficult time believing Daddy had a sister."

He nodded, eager to get on. Perhaps he had a date with the dust bunnies under his desk.

"Ma'am," he said, opening a side drawer in his desk, "your aunt wanted you to have this."

He handed me a cheap plastic bust about four inches tall. It was bubble-gum pink with a rose felt base. I took it to be the bust of a composer, perhaps Franz Schubert. Maybe Beethoven. All those men look alike to me with their long hair and grim expressions. At any rate, it was hideously ugly, and I promptly dropped it in the cavernous maw of my purse. With any luck I would never see it again.

"And here are keys to your aunt's house. This is the key to her safety deposit box. And this"—he handed me a slip of paper—"is the mortuary that handled her cremation and where her cremains currently reside. You have to go there in person and sign a release. You can, of course, make arrangements with the mortuary to inter the cremains there or do with them what you wish. They are yours to keep."

I grimaced.

He appeared to grimace back, although perhaps it was just a distortion of his lenses. "Ma'am, when your aunt made out her will, she left a vase—an urn, I guess you would call it—with me. She made a verbal request that you deliver the urn in person to the mortuary." He rubbed his eyes again. "Since you could not be immediately located, I took the liberty of delivering the urn myself. I trust that will not have been a problem."

"No problem at all."

"Good. Any questions?"

Yes, I thought. How does a hard-working, clean-living, law-abiding citizen suddenly find herself in possession of the ashes of an aunt she never knew existed? What guarantee did I have that tomorrow something even more bizarre wouldn't turn up in my life? Perhaps Mama would reveal she was really an alien from outer space or that I was the love child of Clark Gable. Now, the latter I would have been willing to believe.

"No, I think you've covered everything," I said.

"Well, if you think of anything, feel free to give me a call." He started shuffling papers as if I wasn't even there.

I practically ran all the way back to the Heritage, and I wasn't wearing running shoes, either, but sandals—seasonally correct sandals that were *off*-white. The only chance I had to catch my breath was in the elevator up to our floor. Wouldn't you know it, I'd forgotten my key card and had to knock. At any rate, I was still panting when Mama opened the door.

She was wearing a lavender silk robe that trailed behind her like a royal train. It obviously belonged to C.J. or Wynnell.

"Oh, it's only you."

I stepped inside. "Who were you expecting? Prince Charles?"

"Well, I was hoping for someone named Bjorn. Or Sven. I've heard the Swedes give the best massages."

I staggered over to the couch and collapsed. "Massages?" I gasped. Not from surprise but from exertion. Nothing Mama could do would shock me.

"Well, I must have gotten whiplash from that horrible fright I got last night in front of the cemetery. So I called the concierge and asked her to send up a masseur."

"And they have one on staff?"

"No. But you know I don't take no for an answer, don't you, dear? Beverly finally said she'd see what she could do."

"I see. Where are C.J. and Wynnell?"

"They both have hangovers, but they're out doing the tourist thing. Can you believe that? Wynnell wanted to take the *Midnight in the Garden of Good and Evil* Tour, and C.J. wanted to visit the Juliette Gordon Low Birthplace. She wanted to protest."

"Protest?"

Mama nodded. "C.J. claims her great-great-granny Ledbetter back in Shelby started an organization of farm girls in the eighteen hundreds and called it the Girl Sprouts of America. She says Miss Low stole that name when she started the Girl Scouts. According to C.J., her granny's group fell apart then, and so did her granny. The Ledbetters have never been the same since."

"C.J.'s four-wheel drive is definitely missing a tire," I said kindly. "So, Mama, until blond and buff gets here, why don't I give you a massage?"

Mama grimaced. *"You?"*

"Sure, Mama. Greg says I have magic fingers. Why don't you come over and sit beside me, and I'll give you my special neck rub. In no time at all you'll feel like a different person."

"That's very nice of you, dear, but I couldn't take advantage of my own flesh and blood."

"Mama, I insist!"

"Oh, all right." She sounded as enthusiastic as my ex-husband Buford used to sound when I would suggest we turn off the television and go to bed early. Of course, unbeknownst to me, by then he was already tuning in to Tweetie.

"Now, sit right here beside me," I said, "but turn so your back is toward me."

Mama reluctantly did as she was bid, and I put my hands around her neck. "I'm afraid you're going have to remove the necklace, Mama."

"I could never do that!"

"Okay, I'll try and be real careful. But you can be glad I'm not Sven. Those big Swedish hands of his might have—well, you could be on your hands and knees right now looking for pearls."

"Oh, my! I hadn't thought of that."

I smiled to myself. "Now, Mama, while I rub your neck, you and I are going to have us a little chat."

"That's nice, dear. Have you been attending the church of your choice?"

"What?"

"It doesn't have to be the Episcopal church, dear. Catholic, Methodist, even Baptist. Why I always said—"

"Mama! We are *not* going to be talking about my spiritual life. We are going to be talking about the aunt I never knew I had."

"Don't be silly, dear. Your Aunt Marilyn held you in her arms the day you were born. And you just saw her Christmas."

"Not her, Mama. My *other* aunt."

"Why, I don't have the slightest idea what you're talking about." I felt Mama's neck stiffen under my fingertips.

"My Aunt Lulu Mae," I said through gritted teeth.

"Oh, *that* aunt," Mama said, just as innocently as you please.

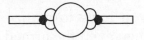

6

I dug my nails into the base of Mama's neck.

"That feels good," Mama crooned.

"It isn't supposed to. Now, spill it, Mama. Why did you lie about Lula Mae? Why did you say she was Daddy's cousin, and not his sister?"

"Well, dear, there some things one just doesn't talk about."

"Like what? She was my aunt!" I dug so deep, I swear I could feel her pelvic bones.

Mama's sigh was one of pleasure. "Abby, you don't think I'm prejudiced, do you?"

I did and I didn't. I have gay friends, Rob and Bob—the Rob-Bobs, I call them—and Mama is very fond of them. Rob happens to be Jewish, and Mama has no problems with that either. Nor do I think she has a problem with race. My shop assistant, Irene Cheng, is Chinese-American, and Mama adores her. We both have peripheral friends who are African-American. We even have tall friends.

On the other hand, Mama hates to see women over thirty in shorts, and gum-chewers drive her right up the wall. No need to say more about people who wear white out of season.

"You don't appear to have any major prejudices," I conceded. "What does this have to do with Aunt Lula Mae?"

"Well, dear, you have to realize this was a long time ago. Back then even the armed forces were segregated. Why, even in Rock Hill we had separate public facilities for whites and coloreds—that's what we called black people in those days."

"I can remember, Mama. Well, not the armed forces, but the separate drinking fountains and bathrooms. And going to an all-white school."

"Then you can imagine that for a white woman to fall in love with a black man—well, that was just unthinkable."

My blood raced. "You mean Aunt Lula Mae—"

Mama nodded.

I turned Mama around to face me. "Wow! Tell me everything!"

"I don't know a whole lot!" Mama wailed. "It was all so hush-hush. Your Daddy didn't like to talk about it."

"You mean *he* was prejudiced?"

"No, I don't think so. I really believe he wasn't. But his parents were. So were mine, come to think of it. Anyway, this thing with your aunt—well, your grandparents forbade anyone in the family to ever have anything to do with her again. They gave him an ultimatum; either he turned his back on Lula Mae, or they would turn their backs on him. Your grandmother Flora—forgive me, Abby, but she was a very bitter woman. She didn't even approve of me at first, because I was a Presbyterian and my people dirt farmers from upstate. It wasn't until I became an Episcopalian—well, anyway, out of respect for his parents, Daddy went along."

"That kind of ultimatum doesn't deserve respect," I said. "Aunt Lula Mae was Daddy's sister. It should have been up to him to decide whether or not to see her."

"Don't judge your daddy too harshly, Abby. He was very close to his mama."

I swallowed my anger. Believe me, it didn't sit too well on the Eggs Benedict and champagne.

"Grandma Wiggins died just a year or two after Daddy, didn't she? And Grandpa Wiggins was already dead by then. Why didn't you—"

"Abby, I already know what you're going to ask, and I don't have an answer. Maybe because I thought your Aunt Lula Mae would hate me for having ignored her all those years. Or maybe it was because I didn't know how to explain to you what happened. You see, dear, it was easier just to let sleeping dogs lie."

"This sleeping dog was my aunt!" I said with surprising vehemence. "And she isn't sleeping now—she's dead!"

Mama shook her head. "You see how strongly you're reacting? Do you honestly think you'd have taken the news well if she were still alive? I mean, what if she told you to go to hell?" Mama gasped and dutifully slapped her own mouth for swearing. Gently, of course.

"Yes, Mama, I do think I would have taken the news well. But even if I hadn't—even if I'd been mad as blazes at you for keeping the secret from me, and even if Aunt Lula Mae had spit in my face—I had a right to know. She was my flesh and blood!"

It pleased me to see tears in Mama's eyes. "Okay, Abby, so maybe I made a mistake. A big mistake. Can you forgive me?"

I longed to give Mama a long, easy hug. Not one of those quick, backslapping things I'd slid into as an adolescent and never quite grown out of. Not with my own mama at least. I am capable of giving my children slow, tender hugs, and my lovers too— not that I've had that many, mind you—but the second I put my arms around Mama, my hands start flapping like the flippers of a seal.

"Of course I will forgive you, Mama. In due time."

Mama's right hand flew to her pearls. "What does that mean?"

I smiled. "I want to experience the joy of being mad at you. At least until lunch."

Mama let go of her necklace long enough to wipe away the tears. "I can live with that."

"But you need to tell me everything you know about Aunt Lula Mae."

"I'm afraid I don't have much to tell, dear. I only met her once, when I was dating your daddy."

"But you said I insulted her when I was three."

Mama turned the color of a Yankee sunburn. "I lied," she said in a voice that matched her physique. "But that was before Mr. Kimbro hung our dirty laundry out to air."

"He did no such thing, Mama. He merely told me the truth. Besides, yesterday you came right out and asked Ashley, the desk clerk, if she knew Lula Mae Wiggins. Weren't you afraid she'd spill the beans?"

Mama paled to the color of a ripe peach. "I was testing the waters, so to speak. I was hoping the scandal had blown over. And Abby, it has!"

"What an awful thing to say."

"Not that I was scandalized, mind you. But Abby, it really was a big deal back then—especially in our social set. You can't imagine how big a deal."

"Yes, I can," I said reluctantly. "My elementary

school was segregated, remember? And our church might as well have been."

Mama nodded, her normal pasty complexion completely restored. "Even though I only met Lula Mae that one time, I wasn't surprised when I heard the news."

"How so?"

"Well, your aunt was very much a free spirit. A bohemian, we called folks like that in those days."

"Was she tall, thin, short, fat? What color was her hair?"

"As I remember, she was a big girl, like your daddy. Dark brown hair. Very pretty. But she dressed different." Mama began rotating the pearls around her neck as if they were worry beads. It amazes me the nacre hasn't worn off after all these years of abuse.

"Different how?"

"Well, she wore pants, for one thing. Women just didn't wear pants back then—not in the South. I'll never forget that your Aunt Lula Mae had on this pajamalike outfit the day I met her. And the biggest gold hoop earrings I'd ever seen, and a barrette in her hair that looked just like a grasshopper! A green enamel grasshopper. Can you imagine that, Abby? Oh, and not only did she smoke, but she had this ivory cigarette holder about a mile long. She could blow perfect smoke rings."

"What was her personality like?"

"That's hard to say from just one meeting, but I thought she was very friendly. And smart. She had gray eyes, I think. Anyway, you could just look into those eyes and tell she was smart." Mama sighed. "That's really all I can remember."

"You did good, Mama. But can you remember

anything—anything at all—about the man she became involved with? Besides his race? Something somebody, maybe Grandma, said about him?"

The pearls stopped in mid-rotation, the clasp at the front of her neck. "I think maybe he was a teacher."

"Oh? What level?"

Mama shrugged. "I think it was something your grandmother Flora said *before* your Aunt Lula Mae broke the news her new beau was black. Something about dating a teacher, which was at least a step up from the sailor she'd been dating the month before. Like I said, Abby, your aunt was a free spirit."

"I'm surprised you two weren't related by blood," I mumbled.

Fortunately Mama didn't hear me. "So, dear, is the interrogation over?"

"Yes, Mama. Have you had breakfast yet?"

Mama looked like the cat who has stolen the cream. "After C.J. and Wynnell left to go touring, I ordered room service."

"I don't see any dirty dishes."

Mama looked like the cat who has stolen the creamer as well. "I washed the dishes."

"Yes, I know we have a kitchenette, but where are the dishes? In the cupboards?" I hoisted myself off the couch and headed toward that corner of the room. "Mama, it's not your job to wash them, you know. And if you put them away in the cup—"

Mama leaped off the sofa and intercepted me. "Don't look in the cupboards, Abby."

"Why not?"

"Well, because they're really filthy. The Heritage should be ashamed. Don't worry, dear, I'll put the dishes out in the hall like everyone else does."

I may be short, but I'm not stupid. Not *that* stupid. My antennae were up, just as sure as if Mama were one of my children. I didn't have time to play the onion-peeling games I did with my own children to get to the truth. Instead, I started to walk back to the couch, which put her off her guard. Then I turned abruptly and dashed past her.

The cupboards were bare. Just bare as Mrs. Hubbard's.

"Mama! You didn't!"

Mama hung her head.

"You did! You packed them in your suitcase already, didn't you?"

"It's only one place setting, dear. It's not like they don't have plenty more. And they're charging you so much for this room. It's only fair."

"It's stealing."

"I would have sent them a nice thank-you note. Anonymous, of course."

No doubt she would have, at that. I could just see and smell her flowered, perfumed paper, across which she'd have written something like *Thanks so much for the lovely china. It goes so well with my grandmother's lace tablecloth.*

"Mama, I have half a mind to call security."

"You wouldn't dare!"

"Try me. Now you go put it back on the tray and out in the hall—no, better yet, take it down to the kitchen yourself. But put some clothes on first. In the meantime I'll call to cancel the masseur. Then I'm going to freshen up a little. Then you and I are going to do something that's long since been overdue."

"Oh, Abby, not the birds and the bees talk. I tried telling you when you were in the seventh grade, but you refused to listen."

"Not that, Mama. We're going to go pick up Aunt Lula Mae. It's time for a family reunion."

Moss Brothers Mortuary & Memorial Gardens was out near the Bamboo Farm and Coastal Gardens, southeast of town. The wide, sweeping oaks on the grounds were hung so heavily with moss that I suspected the establishment owed its name to the epiphyte rather than some siblings.

Calvin Bleeks, the owner and director, confirmed my suspicion. "Yes, ma'am, my granddaddy was an only child. But he loved that moss." He looked around the plain walls of his windowless office as if someone had hidden a listening device in the crumbling plaster and then whispered, "Granddaddy was a Yankee."

Mama and I both gasped. I, for one, was just pulling his leg.

He nodded somberly. With each forward movement I thought he was going to lose his head. I mean that literally. It may have been just an average-size noggin, but it was set on the skinniest neck I'd ever seen on a full-grown man and set off-center at that. He was wearing a black-and-white-check bow tie, and I had the impression that if I pulled on one end of the tie and loosened it, Calvin Bleek's head would either come crashing down on his desk or float up like a helium balloon. Surely it was not connected to his rather normal torso.

"Yes, ma'am, my granddaddy was a full-blooded Yankee. Came all the way down here from Boston, Massachusetts, in a goat cart."

"A goat cart?" Mama and I exclaimed simultaneously.

He nodded again, despite my prayers to the contrary. "It was the Depression, you see, and Granddaddy couldn't afford a car, and the Boston Bleeks never took public transportation. Anyway, that cart was the prettiest little thing, all painted up red and gold like a gypsy wagon. Of course, granddaddy had to take the back roads, and it took him over a year to get down here. By then he'd gone through eight or nine goats. Granddaddy got awfully good at cooking them, though. Became a regular goat gourmand. Even wrote a cookbook titled *Getting Your Goat and Grilling It Too*."

Mindful of my manners, I rolled my eyes discreetly. "You don't say."

He checked the cracks in the walls again, and I can't say that I blame him. They're making microphones awfully small these days.

"My grandma on my mama's side was a Yankee, too. I reckon that makes me one-quarter Yankee."

Mama gasped again. By her reckoning there is no such thing as a part-Yankee. If your ancestors were Yankees, then you are a Yankee. When the memory of their tainted blood dies, and *if* you have married into an upstanding local family, well, then just maybe you qualify for a dinner invitation. But you can forget about Junior League and Cotillion.

"Mr. Bleeks," I said pleasantly, "that would make you half Yankee, not a fourth. Now, as I said when we met, I'm here to pick up my Aunt Lula's remains."

"Yes, ma'am." He stood and bowed slightly before leaving the room. It may have been an involuntary movement.

"Abby," Mama said, clutching my arm like it was a rail on the sinking *Titanic*, "did you notice?"

"That his head is off balance? In more ways than one?"

"No, silly. That he isn't wearing a ring."

"Give it up, Mama. You're not having a fling with a mortician."

"Oh, I wasn't thinking of me, dear. I was thinking of C.J."

"Well, maybe you have a point—"

Calvin Bleeks returned, carrying a blue and white ginger jar. He set the vessel reverently on his desk.

"These are the cremains of Miss Wiggins."

I stared at the jar. It wasn't at all special. I'd seen hundreds like it at Pottery Barn, Kmart, you name it. True, this one had a nicer glaze than some I'd seen, and the painting was competently done. But I had bras that were older than it and no doubt more expensive.

"I don't mean to be crude at a time like this, Mr. Bleeks, but Mr. Kimbro said you thought it might be a very valuable urn." My voice rose, forming a question.

He smiled, and that merest of movements caused his head to bobble. "I didn't know if I could trust him," he said, his voice barely above a whisper.

"I don't get it."

He opened his desk drawer and withdrew a small plastic bag, the kind you store a sandwich in. It was folded several times.

"That was taped to the inside of the jar lid," Calvin said. "I reckon *it's* worth a fortune."

7

I took the bag and spread it on the desk. In the space following the word CONTENTS, someone had written with a black felt-tip pen: *Ashes to ashes, dust to dust, there's plenty more, if this you trust.*

"Hmm, wonder what that means."

Calvin shrugged, thereby putting his cerebellum in danger. "I assumed you would know. As I understand it, you were supposed to be the one to deliver the urn to me. Instead, Mr. Kimbro brought it."

I nodded. "Ex-husband problems." There was a coin in the bag, and I fingered it through the plastic. "What's this? Some kind of foreign coin?"

"No, ma'am. That's an American one-cent piece. It was minted in 1793."

I started to open the bag. "This I've got to see!"

Calvin Bleeks was quicker than Mama when I try to sneak a bite of her dessert. He did not, however, poke me with a fork.

"You shouldn't touch it with your bare hands."

"Says who?"

He bobbled apologetically. "It's very valuable, ma'am. I took the liberty of speaking to my brother-in-law, who is a numismatist."

"That's very nice," Mama said politely, "but your family's religion is really none of our business."

"A numismatist is a coin collector," I mumbled.

"What was that, dear?"

"Nothing, Mama." I smiled warmly at Calvin Bleeks. "How valuable is it?"

The mortician looked pointedly at Mama and then at me.

"If I can hear it, so can she," I said.

"Yes, ma'am. Well, then, the penny—or, as I should say, one-cent piece—is worth hundreds."

I raised an eyebrow.

He cleared his throat. "Perhaps thousands."

"Perhaps? What exactly did your brother-in-law say?"

"Please, Miss Timberlake, I would much rather you take that up with him." Calvin Bleeks was looking at Mama again.

I tried my best to sound patient. "Okay, I'll see your brother-in-law. He does live in Savannah, doesn't he?"

"Yes, ma'am. His name is Albert Quarles. You can find him on West Perry, which is right off Chippewa Square. That's the square where Forrest Gump sat waiting for the bus."

"How interesting," Mama said with genuine enthusiasm. *Forrest Gump* is her favorite movie. Mama is convinced that Sally Field based her interpretation of Forrest's mother on the one and only Mozella Wiggins.

Calvin Bleeks jotted down the address, his head jiggling, while I signed Aunt Lula Mae's release forms. I know that sounds like an odd way to put it, but I felt a need to liberate her from Moss Brothers Mortuary & Memorial Gardens. To say nothing of the bobbling Mr. Bleeks and his black-and-white-checked bow tie.

I placed the urn, which was surprisingly heavy,

on the back seat of my car and buckled it safely in place. As we drove off, Mama burst into her own rendition of "Moon River." The woman couldn't sing for a snack, much less her supper, but she means well. The choir director at the Episcopal Church of Our Savior in Rock Hill fondly refers to Mama as her mercy member. As in *Lord have mercy* every time Mama opens her mouth.

"Three drifters, off to see the world," Mama sang.

I'm sure Aunt Lula Mae, looking down from above, was happy to at last be included in a family event.

The address Calvin Bleeks had given us was not a business but a private home. West Perry is lined by restored stately houses. Wrought-iron railings, oak trees, palm trees, cherry laurels, azaleas—if there is a more beautiful residential street in this country, write me in care of the Den of Antiquity, Charlotte, North Carolina.

The house we sought was fronted by a cherry laurel and an unusual shade of azalea, almost salmon-colored. Next to one of the flowering shrubs was a downspout in the shape of a dolphin. I coveted the spout in my heart as I rang the doorbell.

Albert Quarles opened the door immediately. He was a small, swarthy man whose black hair betrayed its bottle origins. He had a clipped black mustache, rather like Hitler's, incongruous silver eyebrows, and tiny, wrinkled ears that reminded me of dried apricots. His cream suit, white silk shirt, and yellow paisley tie only served to accentuate his sallow complexion. The monocle, however, was a nice touch.

"Come in," he said, without even asking our names.

I meant to introduce myself, but he immediately led us through a foyer with a gleaming parquet floor and into a sumptuous drawing room. The peach, silk-covered walls soared ten or twelve feet—height has always been a difficult thing for me to judge. The heavy damask drapes were also silk, as was the Chinese rug.

"A million silkworms gave their lives for this room," I whispered to Mama.

"Oh, Abby, look at that chandelier," she said aloud.

It was definitely worth spraining my neck for a look at the Baccarat crystal chandelier. The fixture measured at least eight feet across, and what's more, I couldn't spot a single spiderweb.

"And that mantel!" Mama gushed.

Even I drooled on the silk carpet when I saw the snow-white chunk of Carrara marble that surrounded the fireplace. The artist who carved the classical frieze into Albert Quarles's stone was a worthy successor to Michelangelo.

"Please, ladies, have a seat." Our host possessed a deep Georgia accent. Any Yankees lurking in his woodpile had long since been burned up in that beautiful fireplace.

I chose a powder blue love seat—silk, of course—which had been gilded by the addition of an eight-inch gold fringe. Mama, ever the queen, selected a veritable throne of a chair upholstered in faux leopard skin. It was on the far side of the room, so I didn't get a close look, but my hunch is plenty of worms died for that as well.

Albert Quarles waited until we were seated before slipping into a well-worn leather armchair close to the fireplace. A cow or two and maybe a tree had died for his seat, but no worms.

"May I offer y'all something to drink?" he asked politely. "Maybe some coffee? Or tea?"

"No, thank you," I said, before Mama had a chance to answer.

He nodded, head safely attached. The monocle, however, slipped, so he readjusted it.

"I understand this has to do with the coin my brother-in-law Calvin found taped to the lid of an urn."

"Yes, sir. I'm dying to know—" I stopped and stared at a massive oil painting above the fireplace.

Albert Quarles smiled, but not a hair of his mustache moved. "That's my wife, Miranda. She's at a Junior League meeting this morning."

"Calvin Bleek's sister," I said. It was not a question. The woman in the picture had a normal enough head, but her neck was no bigger around than my wrist. Were it not for the five-strand pearl choker, Miranda Quarles would have been wearing her head in her lap.

"Yes. Calvin is Miranda's younger brother."

Mama gasped. "A Yankee in Savannah's Junior League?" I'm sure it was an involuntary outburst on her part, because she immediately clamped a hand over her mouth. If only she used Super Glue for lipstick.

Albert's smiled broadened, and the mustache finally twitched. "They made an exception in her case, because my family tree more than compensates for hers. My ancestors arrived February 12, 1733, along with General James Oglethorpe in the first landing party. In fact, it is believed by some in the family that our ancestor, Cornelius Quarles, arrived a good five minutes earlier, thanks to a bit of bad jerky he'd eaten the day before and his subsequent need to find some privacy. Besides, as part of our premarital agreement, Miranda agreed not to pass any Yankee genes on to our children. Ah, but I digress. What is it you were dying to know, Miss—uh—I'm afraid I didn't get your name."

"Timberlake. Abigail Timberlake." I waved at Mama on her gilded mahogany throne. "And this is my mother, Mozella Wiggins."

"I'm pleased to meet you both," he said with a courtly bob of his head. "I can't remember when two ladies as lovely as yourselves have graced this room."

Mama's purple face clashed with the peach walls and Albert's sallow skin. "Oh, go on," she said. I'm sure she meant it literally.

I decided I liked the swarthy Hitler look-alike with the silver eyebrows and bottle-black hair. "Mr. Quarles—"

He held up a well-manicured hand. "Please, Albert."

"Then please call me Abby."

"You may call me Mama," Mama said shamelessly. No doubt she was already planning for the day when Albert would come to his senses and divorce Miranda. Because Albert's tastes were not limited to the 1950s, a union between Mama and him was obviously out. But there was always second best. Mama would happily settle for being mother-in-law to a scion of one of Georgia's oldest families. Back in Rock Hill, South Carolina, this liaison would automatically bump Mama up a notch or two on the social scale. Who knows, some day she might even be admitted to the Perihelion Book Club.

"Albert"—I dug into my purse and pulled out the sandwich bag—"your bother-in-law said this penny was worth hundreds. Maybe much more. How much more?"

He sat forward in the leather chair. "As I recall, that is a 1793 Flowing Hair type, with a Chain Reverse. Or is it the Wreath Reverse?"

"I beg your pardon?"

"On one side of the coin there is a portrait of a woman—Liberty—with flowing hair. On the reverse side there should be a chain. Either that or a wreath."

I turned the coin over, still in the bag. "It looks more like a wreath."

"Ah, yes, I remember now. Wreath Reverse. Still, if it's in extra fine condition—which I believe it is—it could bring well over a thousand dollars."

I hopped off the blue silk love seat and skipped across the room. "Is this extra fine?" I demanded, practically shoving the coin in his face.

He took the plastic bag from me, a look of horror on his face. "It isn't sealed!"

"Yes, it is. That's a Ziplock bag."

"Who put it in this—this—bag?"

"Your brother-in-law. Calvin Bleeks."

"Idiot," he muttered.

"What did you say?"

He was holding the bag at arm's length, as if it contained the remains of a dead rodent. "The coin hasn't been sonically sealed."

"Excuse me?" I must admit, I knew next to nothing about collecting coins.

Albert sighed. "Amateurs think that because coins are metal, they're indestructible. Nothing could be further from the truth from a collector's point of view."

"I don't understand."

"A person's hands contain natural oils that can do irreparable damage to the surface of a coin. It may not seem that way to the ignorant, but a single fingerprint can take thousand of dollars off a coin's value. Especially a mint state coin."

"You don't say!"

"Always hold a coin by its edges, and never, ever let it come into contact with abrasive materials. Never polish a coin. In fact, it is best not to clean coins at all. They should be professionally graded as to condition and sonically sealed in hard plastic. Only then should they be handled by amateurs."

I felt like saluting, but at the same time my heart was sinking. "Is this coin ruined?"

Albert sniffed and wiggled his mustache. "Ruined is perhaps too strong a word. This is of course an old coin and has seen a good deal of wear. It wouldn't have been mint in any case. You are fortunate, Abby, in that it is still probably worth a thousand dollars or more."

It was my heart's turn to skip. "And how much would it be worth if it was in mint condition?"

"Many times more than that. I tracked one in very fine condition that sold in an Internet auction for fifteen grand."

"You don't say!" I scampered joyfully back to my fringed perch.

Mama shook her head and patted her pearls at the same time. "Imagine all that money for a penny. What is the world coming to? Most pennies aren't worth a dime these days. People don't even stoop to pick them off the pavement anymore. Well, in my day a penny was worth something. Not that kind of money, mind you, but *something*."

"Like what?"

"Like candy. You could always get some kind of candy for a penny. And five pennies bought you a Coke."

"You can still buy a Coke for pennies," I said smugly. "It's just that it'll take eighty-nine of them. But on the plus side, it will be a twenty-ounce bottle now and not one of those little two-sip glass bottles it used to come in."

Mama frowned. "Still, I can't see paying fifteen thousand dollars for a penny."

"A very rare penny, Mama." I turned to Albert. "I very much appreciate your time. You've been very kind allowing us to barge in this way. If you don't mind, though, I have one more favor to ask."

"Ask away," he said, suddenly pleasant.

"Well, you see, I deal mostly in period furniture and home furnishings. I have a small case of good quality costume jewelry and a few unimportant pieces of the real thing. But the cost of insurance is prohibitive for me to carry easily portable high-ticket items."

"Abby, tell him what happened to that ruby ring."

I sighed. "Well, you see, I did a brief stint in estate jewelry. It started when I found a Burmese ruby ring in a box of paste and plastic junk I bought at auction. Awful rings, not even fit to come out of a gum machine, but they were part and parcel of a lot I bid on and won."

The white eyebrows lifted with interest. "Was it a genuine Burmese ruby?"

"From the fabled Mogok mines—well, that's what one appraiser said. I had it appraised three times. Anyway, I started paying more attention to jewelry and had a nice little collection going up there by the register. My shop's in an upscale neighborhood, you see, and stuff like that moves pretty fast. But like I said, I wasn't geared to selling easy-to-steal things."

"And then," Mama said, squirming impatiently on her throne.

"And *then*," I said as I glared, "this well-dressed couple came, looked at a few rings, and then suddenly started showing a lot of interest in a rice plantation bed that was taking up too much room in my shop and for which I'd paid far too much. So of course I trotted on over, hoping to unload it, but they ended up not buying it. In the meantime a confederate of theirs had replaced all my estate rings with the same kind of junk rings I found the ruby in. As fake-looking as those things are, they do take up space, and from a distance—well, I didn't notice the switch until after the well-dressed couple had left the shop."

The white eyebrows knit with concern. "And you weren't insured for the full amount?"

I could feel myself blush. "Not quite."

"Not at all," Mama said. "Abby here had no extra insurance on that ruby ring."

"*Thanks, Mama.*" I turned to Albert. "So you see, I don't want to carry merchandise that easy to lift. What I was wondering is, could you possibly broker the coin for me? I'd be happy to pay the going fee."

Albert cleared his throat. "It would be my pleasure, but on one condition."

"What is that?"

"That you let me broker the rest of the collection when it comes up for sale."

"What collection?"

Hitler's mustache twitched in delight. "The famous Lula Mae Wiggins American coin collection."

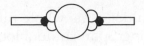

8

"*E*xcuse me?"

He set the monocle on a rosewood side table. "Your aunt was well known in numismatic circles—no, let me take that back. Lula Mae Wiggins was legendary."

"Get out of town!"

"I am told that's how she supported herself. Every now and then Miss Lula would put something extraordinary on the market that had collectors salivating. I would wager this coin is just the tip of the iceberg."

I wanted to hang my head in shame. Here was a relative whose livelihood was essentially the same as mine, but I hadn't had a clue. It hadn't even occurred to me to think about her means of employment. But I should have. One doesn't get paid for being a bohemian, after all.

"How big a collection?" I asked, ignoring my shame. "How much do you think it is worth?"

Albert shrugged. "Who knows? But like I said, we all feel it's just the tip of the iceberg. She dropped little hints, you see."

"What kind of hints?"

" 'There's plenty more where that came from.' That kind of thing. Once she attended a coin show dressed like a pirate. She had a real live parrot sitting on her shoulder—the whole nine yards."

"Was she selling Spanish doubloons?"

"Something better. She had an Indian Head gold dollar. 1861D, mint condition. It sold for over thirty grand."

"Wow! So you actually knew my aunt."

"Let's just say I knew of her. In fact, *everyone* in Savannah knew of her. Although I met her on numerous occasions—well, she was a very private person. If you know what I mean. Didn't do the social scene."

Mama and I exchanged glances. I wanted to ask Albert if he'd ever met Aunt Lula Mae's African-American lover but didn't know how to word it. I wanted to ask him if he knew the man's name, but how would that look? What kind of niece doesn't know the name of the man responsible for her aunt throwing away her social position? Believe me, Queen Elizabeth II knows about Wallace Simpson.

"Albert, I've seen my aunt's will. There is no mention of a coin collection."

"Oh?' He looked like Mama did the day I told her I had broken off my engagement with Greg "Studmuffin" Washburn of the Charlotte Police Force.

"But that doesn't rule out a collection, does it? I mean, maybe she didn't want me to have to pay inheritances taxes on it. Something like that."

Albert chuckled. "That sounds like Miss Lula, all right. Taping this coin to the inside of her funerary urn may have been another one of her clues."

"Exactly! That collection could be hidden somewhere in her house. I'm going right over there to look for it."

"Good luck. The old gal was really clever—no disrespect intended."

"None taken, I'm sure. And you're right, she was very good at keeping secrets." I rubbed my hands together in lustful anticipation. "This is going to be fun. Now, where to begin?"

Mama raised her hand like a schoolgirl. "I know! I know!"

I smiled patiently. "Yes, Mama, I'll look under the bed." That's where Mama hides everything. Christmas presents, birthday presents, her silver (when she travels)—even a copy of *Muscle Magazine*.

Mama lowered her hand to pat her pearls. "Well, dear, you can look under her bed if you like. But I was going to suggest you start by going to the bank and taking a peek in her safety deposit box."

You could have made an omelette with the egg on my face. "That might be a good idea."

Mama beamed and turned to Albert. "She means well. But she's very tidy and not a bad cook, if I must say so myself. And she really does have her own business."

I thanked Albert Quarles and hustled Mama out of there before she had me officially inscribed in his list of replacements for the Yankee-tainted Miranda. Another twenty minutes and she would have had us choosing our china pattern. Hmm, let's see. Noritake Hemingway or the Wedgwood India? The silver was a no-brainer. I'd just ask for the box under Mama's bed.

We didn't make it much farther than Albert Quarles's front door before our quest was thwarted. On the public sidewalk in front of us a small band of tourists was being mesmerized by a woman with a high-pitched voice. I don't think it was the information being disseminated that held the group's attention but the guide herself.

She was wearing a straw hat piled high with every conceivable variety and color of silk flower. Her pink, pearl-studded glasses swept away from her nose like bats' wings. Her pearl necklace was obviously newer than Mama's, but her dress was almost identical to the one Mama had on. Nipped at the waist, the frock fanned out into a full skirt buoyed by layers of starched crinolines. She had on gloves—something even Mama gave up wearing years ago—but since it was not yet Easter, these gloves were a tasteful ivory shade. The stiletto heels were a bit much, if you ask me, but at least they were black and a good quality patent leather.

"Behold your look-alike," I whispered to Mama.

"Abby, don't be rude!" Of course Mama couldn't take her eyes off the woman.

The tour guide ignored us. "And notice the dolphin downspout," she chirped. "Because Savannah is a major seaport—"

"Excuse me, ladies." A tourist had broken free of the ranks and was coming up the walk toward us.

"Run," I growled, but there was no place for us to go.

"Do you ladies live here?" I couldn't pinpoint the man's accent, but it was American and the vowels only one syllable in length. Chalk-white legs sprouted out of baggy shorts, like mushroom stems. A wrist no bigger around than mine sported a genuine gold Rolex worth twice as much as my car.

"No, we—"

"Of course we live here." Mama flounced her petticoats and smiled. She had seen the watch.

"Hi. My name is Bob Crane. I'm what they call an

advance scout for Reels and Runs Productions."

"I don't know anything about fishing, dear, but my daughter Abigail here is quite the expert. Fishes all the time."

"Mama, I do not!"

"Yes, you *do*." Mama keeps her nails short, but they're miniature bolt cutters.

"All right," I wailed. "I go fishing every week."

"Tell the nice man what you catch."

I twisted my torso out of Mama's grasp. "I catch Mrs. Paul's at Harris Teeter and Gorton's at the Bi-Lo."

Bob laughed. "Reels and Runs Productions is a movie company. I'm scouting for locations. We're going to be filming a movie about a murdered food critic who comes back as a ghost and gets her revenge on the chef who did her in."

"What's the movie called?" I asked. "More importantly, who is going to be in it?"

"It's called *Midnight in the Garden of Food and Evil*, but I'm afraid I'm not at liberty to divulge the cast just yet. We don't want the town going crazy just yet, like it did when Clint was here."

"What does that have to do with us?" Mama asked shrewdly.

"Well, this is basically a ghost story, and we thought it would add an aura of authenticity if we filmed at a real live"—he chuckled—"haunted locale."

"I still don't get it," Mama said. Her eyes didn't leave the watch.

"Then I apologize for not making myself clear. You see, my sources"—he paused to consult a pocket notebook—"state that one of the houses on this street has a reputation for being particularly haunted."

"That would be our house," Mama said.

I gasped.

Bob grinned. "Fantastic! Would it be possible to tour your house?"

"Absolutely," Mama said, and patted her pearls.

"Mama, that's not possible!" I hissed.

"Shh." The bolt cutters found the merest suggestion of a love handle and closed.

I yelped. The tour guide with the squeaky voice stopped her recitation midsentence and glared at me from beneath her bouquet-laden bonnet. I in turn glared at Mama.

"I'm afraid our house is a mess at the moment," Mama said smoothly. "Yesterday was the maid's day off, and she isn't expected in until"—she leered at the Rolex—"until eleven. Could you come back this afternoon?"

Bob glanced at the troop of tourists, who were being led down the street by the glaring guide. He seemed torn.

"What time this afternoon?"

"How about three, dear? I could serve you tea. No, wait, I've got a better idea. Why don't we meet you for lunch someplace at noon. We can fill you in on the ghost then."

"But I will get to see your house, right? Maybe even meet the ghost?"

I cleared my throat. "Actually, they prefer to be called Apparition-Americans."

"I beg your pardon?"

"Ghost is a pejorative term, and I'm afraid that Hollywood has added insult to this injury. *Casper*,

Ghostbusters, that kind of movie—Apparition-Americans find those very offensive."

"Oh?"

"Ignore her," Mama said.

I braved the pinchers. "Bedsheets and chains, that used to be the stereotype. Now it's ectoplasm and goo. Can you blame them for being upset?"

Mama stamped her right pump. "Enough, Abby! Besides, Patrick Swayze played a ghost, and he was far from gooey."

"True. I believe you referred to him as yummy. You said you wanted to eat him with a spoon. But that movie was an exception, Mama. No, I think Maynard is going to want editorial control over this project."

"M-maynard?" Mama stammered.

"Yes, Mama, our resident Apparition-American. And I'm sure that Esmerelda—she's Maynard's wife—will want to get involved with costuming. She used to be a set designer in real life—oops, I shouldn't have used the R word. Esmerelda is very sensitive about that. And whatever you do, don't use the word 'haunt.' 'Inhabit' is the word of choice. Apparition-Americans *inhabit* a house, they don't haunt it."

"I see." Bob Crane was backing away from me like plague from penicillin.

"And be careful of sound-alike words, too. They can be just as painful. Mama here got in big trouble for using the word 'ghastly' in front of Maynard. He wouldn't speak to her for a week. Made her apologize big time."

"That's all nonsense," Mama said, but it was too late. Bob Crane's mushroom legs had already melded with those of the rest of his group. Mama whirled. "Abigail Louise! Why on earth did you do that?"

"Exactly, Mama. What were you going to do? Tie up Albert Quarles while you served a stranger tea in his house? And what about his wife? She's not going to stay at Junior League all day."

"I would have thought of something," Mama wailed. "That's why I suggested lunch first. You might have been able to hook him over a good steak. Or better yet, something French."

"*Hook* him?"

"Snag him. You know, get him really interested."

"And what do you mean *I* might have been able to hook him? Why me?"

"Well, you must admit, he's not exactly my type, dear. But he's rich and works for a movie company. Need I say more?"

"Absolutely not, Mama."

I, on the other hand, had plenty that needed saying. I grabbed Mama's hand and literally dragged her down the walk and over the square to the nearest Bank America. Along the way I gave her Lecture Number 384. I tried to make it clear that my love life is none of her business, and even if it were, Greg Washburn and I are doing just fine. We both just have trouble committing. If you think about it, this is better to figure out *before* wedding vows are exchanged. Mama had no choice but to listen, although I doubt if she heard a word.

Suddenly she gasped and tugged on my hand like a child headed for the candy counter. "Abby, look over there! It's Tom Hanks."

I glanced at the park bench she indicated. The man sitting on it looked nothing like Tom Hanks. This guy was drop-dead gorgeous. I'm ashamed to admit that, like an acquiescing parent, I allowed Mama to pull me over to the candy.

"You're Tom Hanks, aren't you?" Mama gushed. "I've seen all your movies, but *Forrest Gump* was my favorite."

Gorgeous grinned but said nothing.

Mama was undeterred. "I just know Sally Field's part was based on me, wasn't it? Go on, tell my daughter it's so."

"Mama, please!" I hissed. Like I said, the man did not look like Tom Hanks, but he did look familiar. Perhaps he resembled some young star I'd seen in the movies lately.

Mama let go of my hand and patted her pearls. "Not that I mind you basing the part on me, you understand. But you should at least give me credit."

I tried not to roll my eyes, but they may have slipped a little. "Mama, even if he was Tom Hanks, what would you expect him to do? Have the credits changed on rental videos?"

"Well?" she demanded of the bench-warming man.

He had the nerve to nod.

Mama beamed and turned to me. "I told you so, didn't I? Maybe next time you'll take my word for it, Abby."

"Mama, this is *not* Tom Hanks. This man has a full head of hair, and besides, he's a lot younger."

"Abby, don't be rude!" Mama turned to the impostor. "Say something from the movie."

Boy Gorgeous blinked. "Ma'am?" he said in three syllables.

"Aha!" I said triumphantly. "This is a southern boy!"

Mama was undeterred. "Say something from the movie!" she commanded.

Her victim swallowed hard. "Life is a box of chocolates."

"Wrong!" I practically shouted. "Forrest Gump didn't say that. Forrest said, 'Life is *like* a box of chocolates.' "

Mama's pearls began to rotate slowly around her neck. "Well, one word isn't such a big deal. The poor man had a lot of lines in that movie." She turned to her hapless prey. "Tell my daughter who you really are."

He blinked again. "My name is Joe, ma'am."

Mama's hand froze in midtwirl. Then, much to my surprise, she giggled.

"Of course it is. We wouldn't want our little secret to get out, would we? Heavens, no! You'd be swamped with pushy tourists."

I snatched Mama's free hand and hauled her, feet dragging, from the park.

Harriete with only one T led us back to the vault. Against my better judgment I allowed Mama to tag along.

"What's in that box is going to make my daughter very rich," Mama bragged.

"Mama," I whispered, "enough."

"But it's true. Her Aunt Lula Mae died, you see, and left her a coin collection worth millions."

"We don't know that," I said through gritted teeth.

"Albert Quarles thinks it's so, and he's an expert pneumatic."

"Numismatist!" I hissed.

"That's what I said. Anyway, we didn't even have

a clue about the collection until the mortician showed us a penny that had been taped inside the lid of Lula Mae's urn. Fortunately for us the mortician was the numismatist's brother-in-law. I guess it's also fortunate that Lula Mae left her safety deposit box key with her lawyer. Abby, you still have the key, don't you?"

I stopped and rummaged through my purse. The key was in a small white paper envelope, but alas, my pocketbook is the final resting place of good intentions. In it you will find the button that fell off my blue cardigan winter before last, and which I still mean to reattach—provided I can find the sweater; antique store brochures, collected from my rivals, that I intend to file; a ragged envelope of grocery coupons so old they might be even more valuable now than when they were valid; price tags from a blouse I never quite got around to taking back to Sears; a half roll of petrified, lint-covered breath mints I've been meaning to throw out; ditto for four spent alcohol swabs and a wad of tissues; two combs (one was borrowed from my daughter, Susan); a church bulletin from the last time Mama forced me to go, which lists an address to which I can send parcels to needy folks in Honduras; a book of stamps which now need auxiliary helpers; and two wallets, one old, one new—I've been meaning to switch my cards and license ever since Mama gave me the Lady Buxton for Christmas—and several fistfuls of pralines.

"Well, dear, do you have the key or not?" I'd memorized the box number off the envelope, and Harriete with only one T had led us there, but we needed both keys to open the box.

"It's in here someplace," I growled, my fingers

sifting through a mound of small change, most of it pennies, and none of them valuable. At least not to my knowledge.

Harriete with only one T sighed impatiently. "Ma'am, if you don't have business here, I'm afraid I'm going to have to ask you to leave."

"But I do have business here. I have—well—in here someplace I have—uh—here!" The little envelope containing the key had been hiding inside the larger envelope with the coupons.

"You see!" Mama said triumphantly. "Now just wait until she opens the box!"

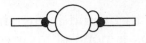

9

Mama and I stared at the empty box. Harriete with only one T stared too. She, of course, had no business being there.

I found my voice. "Well, if stale air is selling at a premium, then we're rich."

"But it has to be in there!" Mama wailed.

"Obviously it isn't. And anyway, we have no proof there even is such a collection."

"Mr. Quarles is an expert, and he said—"

"He said he suspected there might be a collection *somewhere*. It could be hidden somewhere in her house."

"Ha!" Harriete with only one T snorted. She was hovering over me like the Goodyear Blimp at a football game.

I turned, and since I am a southern lady, spoke without rancor. "This really is none of your business, dear."

"Well, ma'am, maybe it is."

"I don't see how," Mama said icily. She is, of course, southern as well, but her age permits her more latitude.

"Maybe it is," Harriete with only one T said defensively. "If you ask me, it's kind of strange, y'all coming in here and not finding the key right away, and the box being empty."

I stood as tall as I could in my size fours. "What I keep in this box is none of your concern. I'm free to deposit hot air in here if I want to. Heck, I could even store Mama's old dentures in here, and you'd have nothing to say about it."

"I don't wear dentures!" Mama hissed.

Harriete with only one T had hands like catchers' mitts, and she propped them on her ample hips. "Maybe I should report you to the manager. In fact, I will. This isn't your box, I just know it."

"I knew the number, didn't I?"

"That doesn't mean anything."

"Go ahead and report me to the manager. Call security if you want"—I took a minute to eye her hovering hulk—"although that would be overkill. Just as long as my key is the one that opens the box, it's none of your damn business."

"You go, girl!" Mama may be my biggest critic, so to speak, but she's also my biggest fan.

"Harrumph!" Harriete with only one T was the first person I'd ever met to actually pronounce that word as it's written.

Emboldened, I waved her back. "Just run along, dear. We'll call you if we need you."

Harriete with only one T took a second to give me the once-over. "I've memorized what you look like. Both of you. If I need to, I can give the police artist a photographic description."

I started blowing air into the long metal box just to irritate her. Too bad Mama didn't really wear dentures.

"Think you're funny, don't you?" Harriete with only one T stomped off, presumably to fetch a security guard.

"I smell something," Mama said quietly.

"The box smelled that way before I blew in it!" I wailed.

Mama's nose twitched like a rabbit in a carrot patch. "Not that. I smell trouble."

I knew then what she meant. You might find this hard to believe, but my mama, Mozella Gaye Wiggins, can literally smell trouble. She has proved this claim so many times that I now take it seriously.

"What kind of trouble?"

"I don't know, but it's big trouble."

"How big?"

Mama's nose twitched so fast her entire body shuddered. "B-b-big trouble. L-like s-s-somebody's going to die."

My heart did the rumba. "It's not you or me, is it?"

"No."

"Wynnell and C.J.!"

"Not them either. At least, I don't think so. Oh, Abby, let's get out of here. This vault gives me the creeps."

I slid the drawer back into place and turned the key. "Okay," I said, just as Harriete with only one T returned, a burly young man at her side.

Mama and I skedaddled without further ado.

Stepping into the lobby was like coming up for air from a long dive. Stepping outside into the bright spring sunshine was utter bliss. While Mama's olfactory track record is amazingly accurate, adjustments must be made for latitude and longitude. Perhaps her amazing shnoz had sniffed the odor of Aunt Lula Mae's death, albeit rather tardily. Surely folks didn't die on days like this.

"Mama," I said, and then gasped as talons dug deep

into my elbow. I whirled. "What the hell!"

"Shh!" The old woman who called herself Diamond held a crooked black finger to her lips. "It only me."

"I know who you are," I snapped, my heart now racing to a jitterbug beat. "What the hell is it you want?"

"Abby," Mama clucked. "You shouldn't swear so much."

"But she—"

"And you," Mama said to Diamond, "a woman your age! Don't you know any better than to wear white this time of the year?"

I glanced at Diamond's ensemble. Same straw hat, but she was wearing a white cotton dress studded with eyelets and elasticized at the waist. Above the band hung two breasts (completely covered, of course), and between them a black felt pouch on a dirty string and what looked to be a chicken's foot. Below the band, the gathered skirt fell almost to the wearer's feet, which were clad, alas, in white plastic sandals.

"You have broken the eleventh commandment," I informed her somberly. "Thou shalt not wear white between Labor Day and Easter."

Diamond cackled. "And folks think I'm strange!"

I did my best to smile. "Perhaps it's that chicken foot. What are you, some kind of voodoo practitioner?"

Diamond cackled again. "I don't do that devil stuff. No, ma'am, I stay away from curses and such. I'm what they call a herb doctor."

"You fix sick plants?" Mama asked, suddenly willing to abandon her position as chief of the fashion police for a little free horticultural advice. "My rose-mary bush has been dropping its little leaves, and it's not supposed to, is it? I thought it was an ever-green."

When Diamond shook her head, her entire upper body moved. Breasts and chicken foot swayed.

"I don' doctor no plants. I fix people. Folks like you and me. I give them herbs—potions some-times—to cure what ails them."

Mama sniffed the air dramatically. "Abby, I think she's telling the truth. At least she's not dangerous. Not to us."

"I ain't dangerous," Diamond agreed emphati-cally. "But somebody is. I needs to talk to you la-dies."

I glanced around. We were still standing in front of the bank, and people were coming and going with regularity. Some of these people were giving us mighty strange looks.

"Okay, let's talk. But how about over there in the square. Chippewa Square, isn't it?"

"Where they filmed *Forrest Gump*," Mama purred. She tugged at Diamond's forbidden white sleeve. "I shouldn't be telling you this, but he's there right now."

Diamond scowled and took a step back. "Who there?"

"She thought it was Tom Hanks," I said quickly. "But it was some other guy. Just a kid really."

Mama shook her head vehemently. "It's *him*. Just look for yourself—" She gasped. "Abby, he's gone!"

The bench was indeed empty. In fact, the park was devoid of people altogether unless you count the statue of James Edward Oglethorpe. It was such a handsome likeness, it should count for at least half a person. Nine feet tall without his pedestal, the bronze founder of Savannah is splendidly arrayed in the uniform of a British general of the period, a sword in his hand, a palmetto leaf under his foot. His creators, I am told, also did the seated Lincoln Monument in Washington, D.C.

"See what you did?" Mama wailed. "You chased him away!"

"I did no such thing!"

Diamond cackled. "This ain't no time for fighting."

"She's right," I said, and dashed across the street. Fate must have been looking the other way, because I nearly got creamed by a car. The driver—a woman on a cell phone—made no attempt to swerve. Her front bumper came within a radio wave's width of my rear bumper, which, Buford's aspersions aside, is not all that big.

Mama and Diamond followed suit, but instead of dashing dangerously across among an onslaught of cars, they took their sweet time, walking just as sedately as you please. Horns honked, and brakes squealed, but they made it to my side safely.

I headed toward the nearest park bench. My legs felt as if they'd been carved from warm butter, and I desperately needed to sit.

"Not there, Abby!" Mama called. "I want to sit over here."

"What's the difference?"

"Do what your mama say," Diamond growled softly and headed off with Mama.

By then I was irritated with both women, but nonetheless I trotted obediently after them. As we plopped ourselves down on a single bench, with yours truly in the middle, Mama let out a long but satisfied sigh.

"I wanted to sit where Tom Hanks sat," she said almost shyly. "I wanted to put my buns where he put his."

That sent Diamond into a spasm of giggles.

"Mama!" I was genuinely shocked. "I thought you wanted Forrest for your son."

"Don't be silly, dear, I already have a son. Your brother, Toy, remember?"

"How could I forget? Toy the Perfect, now that he's decided to become an Episcopal priest."

Mama smiled. "Just think, Abby, three years from now hundreds of people will be calling your little brother Father Wiggins."

"Maybe hundreds of bamboozled people," I muttered.

"Abby, you're jealous!"

"I am not."

"Of course you are, dear, but there's no reason to be. You could become a priest too."

"If I do, will you call me *Mother* Timberlake?"

"Well, I—I don't know what folks call a woman priest. We've never had one at the Church of Our Savior."

"But *if* they call her Mother, could you handle that?"

"Well—"

"Maybe I should become a nun," I said wickedly. "Surely you could handle Sister Abigail Louise."

Mama flushed. It was only last year that she ran off to the Episcopal convent in Dayton, Ohio, to become a nun. Fortunately for everyone involved, Mozella Wiggins was not an asset to the abbey. Not only did Mama whistle on the stairs and wear curlers under her wimple, but she organized a slumber party at which she served S'mores. According to

Mother Superior, she even started a pillow fight.

"Abby, there's no need to bring up the past in front of perfect strangers."

"I ain't no stranger," Diamond said. "We met last night, remember?"

"How could we forget," I growled. "I didn't have a single gray hair until then."

"You still don't," Mama said. She leaned over me to speak to Diamond. "I'm the one with all the gray, and you can imagine why. Do you have any children, dear?"

Diamond blinked. "I got me a granddaughter."

Mama leaned back. "Well, then you know about kids. So, what is it you had to say, Miss Diamond?"

"That just Diamond. Don' go by no other name."

"Right. Like Cher."

"Yeah, like Cher." Diamond spread her legs so the white eyelet skirt formed a shallow bowl. She removed the chicken foot from her neck and placed it gently—almost reverently—in the center of her lap. Then she slipped the black felt bag over her head and carefully removed its contents. Around the shriveled bird's claw she arranged three brittle leaves of different sizes, a cluster of tiny dried leaves, a clump of bleached grass, an unfamiliar nut, and a desiccated mushroom.

Mama nodded. "Ah! Witchcraft!"

"Watch yo' mouth!" Diamond said with sudden vehemence. "I ain't no witch!"

I could tell Mama was taken aback. "Perhaps you could explain them to us," I said gently.

Diamond glared at Mama and then cleared her throat. "They herbs. I ain't got nothing to do with that witchy stuff, nor voodoo neither."

I patted Mama's knee to calm her. "We understand," I said to Diamond. "Please continue."

"All right then. This here"—she pointed to the small-leafed cluster—"is mistletoe."

"The kind you kiss under at Christmas?"

Diamond rolled her eyes, and I clamped a cluster of tiny fingers over a much too active mouth.

"Go on, please," Mama said, happy to be out of the hot seat.

"You wear mistletoe around your neck, ain't no voodoo lady going to curse you."

"Hmm, maybe I should try that. And what's this one for?"

"That be tansy. Make a tea and it clean out your system good. Sometimes too good. It clean out the worms, clean out everything. Girl get in the family way—well, I don't approve of using it for that. Folks can die, they drink too much."

"Then why do you carry it around on your neck?"

"Because it keep the bug away."

"What kind of bug?"

"Flu bug, that kind of thing."

"I see. But what I don't understand is why you are showing us these things."

" 'Cause I wanted to show you I ain't got no black magic in here. Just herbs and things. My ju-ju, they only the good kind."

"*Ju-ju?*" I asked. That was a new word for me.

"What you white folks call spells."

"Aha!" Mama cried, switching sides again. "So you do cast spells!"

Diamond spread her wrinkled hands over the contents of her lap as if to protect the items displayed from Mama's assertion. She growled before finding a speaking voice

"I casts only good spells!"

This fascinated me. Good spells or bad, I have sometimes fantasized having power over others to make them do my bidding or somehow affect them merely by chanting a few phrases or burning a few pinches of something or the other in my fireplace. Okay, to be perfectly honest, I used to wish I could do something really nasty to Buford, my evil ex, and get away with it. Maybe make his cheating pecker fall off or at the least cause it to shrivel up like one of Diamond's leaves. But I am a Christian of the Episcopal persuasion. I find it hard enough to believe in miracles, much less magic. Still, there were enough stories out there to make a body wonder.

I flashed Diamond a brilliant smile. "Could you share with us an example of a good spell?"

She cocked her head to think, and the straw hat hid her face. "Miss Emily—she my neighbor—get hit by a car crossing Abercorn Street. Miss Emily fall and break her hip. This happen, oh, three years ago. Miss Emily don't have no kind of insurance, and the doctors say she ain't never going walk again, on account of she up in her nineties. So, I make Miss Emily a potion of—well, just never you mind what I put in it. Anyway, I gets Miss Emily's niece to give her the potion, and before you know it, she up on her feet and walking."

"Well, I'll be!" Mama clapped her hands.

Diamond turned her head and smiled. "Oh, that ain't all. When Miss Emily come home from the hospital, there a man waiting for her in front of her house in a stretch limousine."

"Ed McMahon?" I asked, tuning into one of my own fantasies.

Diamond cackled. "Ain't no Ed McMahon! This some rich black man related to Miss Emily. Stutter

Evans his name. Went up to Motown in the sixties to be a singer but couldn't sing worth a damn. Didn't matter, though. Stutter, he a record producer. A rich as sin record producer. He pay all Miss Emily's bills and give her money to spare. Folks said it was a miracle, but I knew different. I knew it was because of the ju-ju."

Mama couldn't help glancing at Diamond's outfit again. Wisely, she bit her tongue.

"Oh, I know what you be thinking," Diamond said, "but it don't work that way. My good spells only work for other people. And that's why I come to see you."

"Why us?" I croaked.

" 'Cause someone want to kill you," Diamond said just as calmly as could be.

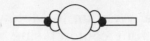

10

"**O**h, Abby," Mama wailed, "what have you done this time?"

"*Me?*" I turned to Diamond. "*Us?*"

The straw hat bobbed. "Miss Amy say you should leave town right away. Go back to where you came from."

"Hey, wait a minute! I thought you said her name was Miss Emily, *not* Miss Amy."

Diamond sighed. "I done told you that last night, but I guess you didn' listen. Miss Amy the white girl up in Bonaventure Cemetery."

"Ah, the dead white girl. So, you're a medium as well."

"Dead folks talk just as much as live folks, ma'am. It just that most folks can't hear them."

"But you do." I didn't mean to be rude, although it came out as a sneer.

"Yes, ma'am. Always have. Ever since I a little girl. The gift my mama called it."

"Nuts," I mouthed to Mama.

Diamond had ears like an elephant. "Don' bother me what you think. I'm supposed to help you anyway. That what Miss Amy say, and that what I fixin' to do."

Mama fingered her pearls as if they were worry

beads. "What exactly did Miss Amy say? Did she mention us by name?"

"Miss Amy don' never mention anybody by name. But she say, 'Diamond, you warn them two itty-bitty white women to go back where they come from. She have me waiting at the gate last evening when you come. And believe me, you don' wanna be anywhere near that place after dark."

"Itty-bitty!" I cried indignantly.

Diamond nodded. "That what Miss Amy say. She say you no bigger than she when it happen."

"What happened?" Mama asked in an itty-bitty voice.

A line of sweat beads had appeared above Diamond's upper lip, and she wiped it off with the back of her hand. "Miss Amy, she drown in the Atlantic Ocean off Tybee Island. It happen on her birthday. She walking along the beach, and this big wave wash her right out to sea. They not find her body for three days. By then the fishes had had themselves a snack. Her eyes, her lips, they gone."

I shuddered. "Gross."

"But now Miss Amy see everything. She tell me everything too. Only she don' use no names."

"How old was she when this happened?" Mama asked.

"She be nine."

I jumped to my feet. "That does it! I will not be compared to a nine-year-old girl."

"Sit down," Mama said in a tone that only God would dare disobey.

I perched on the bench, but swung my legs angrily. "Isthay omanway isay azycray."

Diamond's cackle made an overhead starling take

flight. "I ain't crazy. I just be telling what is. Y'all go back home now like Miss Amy say."

"We will," Mama said, "just as soon as Abby here gets a few loose ends tied up."

Diamond scooped the bits of detritus off her lap and stuffed them back into the felt bag. "Don' you be tying up no strings, hear? Ain't no time for that."

"Don't worry," Mama said, "we'll be careful. And don't let this old body fool you. I'm pretty fast for my age. I can take care of myself. In fact, I'm teaching myself karate."

Diamond's talons all but met in my humerus. "I ain't talking about you, ma'am," she said to Mama. "It this child who in danger."

"*Me?*" I wailed.

Mama's eyes were wide as magnolia blossoms. "Lord have mercy!"

I turned from Mama to look in Diamond's direction, and it was my eyes' turn to widen. Diamond was gone. My arm stung as if she was still pinching me, but the woman was nowhere in sight. I mean *nowhere* in sight. She had simply disappeared.

We left Chippewa Square in a daze, telling ourselves that Diamond had somehow managed to slip into a car or maybe a passing bus. I even went so far as to ask Mama if Diamond could possibly be a product of our imagination. Mama allowed as how I didn't have that much imagination, and if Diamond was a production of *her* imagination, she wouldn't have been wearing white sandals. I couldn't argue with that.

We drove to Gaston Street and found parking a block away from Aunt Lula Mae's row house. This was as charming a street as I'd ever seen. And as colorful.

"Have you ever seen so many azaleas?" I burbled. "Look, the curb is covered with them for as far as you can see. Isn't it just gorgeous?"

"Too many colors, dear. Pink, red, purple, and—"

"White? Mama, azaleas are allowed to bloom before Easter. Dogwood too."

"Yes, but they shouldn't mix them like that. It disturbs the senses."

I thought for a moment. "This wouldn't be sour grapes speaking, would it?"

"Whatever do you mean, dear?"

"Well—and forgive me for saying this if I'm wrong—but doesn't it bother you that Aunt Lula Mae left her house to me and me alone?"

Mama walked faster. "Nonsense."

"Well, it would me, if I were you."

"Don't be silly. You were her niece."

"Yes, but Toy was her nephew." I prudently refrained from adding that Toy seems to be Mama's favorite child. At least, he is the child who in her eyes can do no wrong.

"Your aunt was free to leave her possessions to whomever she wanted. It doesn't bother me in the least if she ignored half her brother's descendants, not to mention the woman who loved and cared for her only brother for most of his adult life. I cooked his meals, ironed his shirts, bore his children. . . ."

"Ah, so that's it! You wanted her to leave the house to *you!*"

Mama stopped so suddenly I couldn't help but rear-end her. Fortunately all those crinolines functioned like an air bag, and I came to a rather comfortable stop. I have heard reports that real air bags can be dangerous to children and small adults. Petticoats, I assure you, are no problem.

I extricated myself from the starched slips. "That's it, Mama, isn't it?"

Mama turned, her face every bit as pink as the azalea next to her. "I never inherited anything, Abby. My parents didn't have anything. And I've never won anything either. The lottery, video poker, bingo—I never win at any of those things. No, I take that back. Once I won a free Pepsi by scratching stuff on a card. But just once before I die, I'd like to get something for nothing."

I squirmed in my size fours. I don't claim to have had an easy life—*au contraire*—but I've been pretty lucky in the freebie department. Two years ago a relative died and left me her antique shop, even though I already had one of my own. Shortly after that an elderly acquaintance bequeathed me a fabulous Kashmir sapphire worth a fortune. And now, of course, there was this Savannah town house. But I've had bad luck, too. My shop has been burgled, the sapphire is now at the bottom of the New River Gorge in West Virginia, and a house I had yet to see had somehow come between me and my mother.

I crossed the fingers of both hands behind my back. "You're mentioned in *my* will."

"Really?"

"Absolutely." Well, why not, after all? Who was to say I wouldn't go before Mama, and why should my children get everything? Surely the woman who endured thirty-six hours of excruciating labor deserved some amount of financial reward.

Mama's face brightened. "Oh, Abby, you were always my favorite child, you know that?"

"You mean it?"

"Of course."

"But all I ever hear is Toy this, Toy that. Tell me one thing you like about me that you can't say the same for Toy."

Mama sighed. "Don't spoil our little fantasy with facts, dear."

"But I really do have a will," I wailed.

Mama smiled. "Of course you do. But I'm not in it, am I?"

"Well—"

"Don't lie to your mama."

"Okay, so you're not. But you could be. Is there anything in particular of mine that you want? You seem to especially like my end tables. They're yours for the asking. Heck, take the sofa, too."

"That's all right, dear. I just wanted to know if . . ." Mama mumbled something that was swallowed by the normal sounds of a street. A not very busy one at that.

"What did you say?"

"You heard me."

"No, I didn't."

"I just wanted to know if you loved me."

"Of course I love you!"

Mama sniffed. "Well, the same thing goes for me. Now let's quit being so maudlin and go see your new house."

We could hear the music loud and clear from where we stood at the foot of the steps. In fact, so could a small crowd of tourists who had gathered there.

"Savannah is home to many famous musicians," the tour guide with the flower-basket hat chirped.

"How did *she* get here?" I whispered to Mama.

"Shh!" a tourist said, and actually shook a fat finger in my face.

The guide blessed the disciplining tourist with a smile. "As I was saying, Savannah has a rich musical heritage. There was Johnny Mercer—he was a world-famous lyricist, and there's Emma Kelly—you can sometimes still catch her over at Hannah's East, a nightclub located just above the Pirate's House Restaurant. Then of course there is the renowned Savannah Symphony Orchestra. Why, I bet that's one of their musicians you're hearing right now. "Moonlight Sonata" has always been one of my favorite pieces."

"Lovely, just lovely." A middle-aged woman in white spandex shorts and a purple tank top was wagging her head like the needle of a metronome.

That's the opening of Tchaikovsky's B-Flat Minor piano concerto," Mama said in a loud voice. "And if you ask me, the bass could be a little stronger."

The guide with the blooming head turned and gave Mama the evil eye.

Mama shrugged. "Well, I happen to know this piece."

The guide tossed her head angrily, almost losing her hat. Amidst a chorus of sympathetic mutters, she led her flock down the block and around the corner.

I turned to Mama. "You're just full of surprises, aren't you?"

"Whatever do you mean?"

"I had no idea you knew so much about music."

Mama patted her pearls. "Well, I *am* in the choir."

I bit my tongue. "But this is classical music. All you listen to on the radio is Mix 106.1. I thought Frank Sinatra hung the moon for you."

Mama sniffed. "This Tchaikovsky concerto was your daddy's favorite piece of music. We listened to it on the hi-fi all the time."

That bit of knowledge alone was worth the trip to Savannah. Surely my daddy had played it on the hi-fi when I was still living at home, but I must have forgotten. The music was familiar, however, and beautiful. Mama was just plain wrong about the dragging bass. Then again, I must have been wrong about the address. After all, dead women seldom play piano with such gusto.

I glanced at the slip of paper on which I'd written the number of Aunt Lula Mae's house. I wasn't about to walk around carrying a complete copy of her will, so I had jotted the number down on the Heritage pad. I've been known to transpose numbers, particularly phone numbers, but this one was easy to remember. It was only one digit away from my ATM PIN code.

"Maybe I've got the wrong number, Mama."

"Well, there's only one way to know, dear." Mama charged up the steps like a platoon sergeant in a World War II movie and rang the doorbell.

The concerto continued unabated, so Mama rang again. The third time I rang. Finally the music stopped, but no one answered the door. Mama tapped her foot while she rang three more times.

Finally the door opened a crack. "I don't push my religion on you," a young female voice said, "so don't push yours on me."

Mama gasped, then giggled. "We're not Jehovah's Witnesses, dear. We're Episcopalians."

The crack widened enough for me to see a gray eye. "I'm an Episcopalian too," the girl said, "and we don't go from door to door."

"We're not here to sell you religion," I said soothingly.

"Well, whatever it is you're selling, I'm not buying any." The door closed.

That did it as far as Mama was concerned. She would have leaned on that bell all day, if need be. The woman has stamina. Mama claims she and Daddy won a dance marathon, that they were on their feet eleven days straight. She told me this after Daddy passed, and although I can find no one to verify this, I am not surprised—*if* the marathon folks had been able to provide Mama with fresh starched crinolines on a daily basis, clean pink frocks with cinched waists, and a dancing hairdresser.

The door opened wide enough for me to see a pair of large gray eyes behind the chain. "Go away or I'm calling the police."

"You do that, missy!" Mama hissed. "You'll see!"

The gray eyes blinked. "Who are you, and what do you want?"

I pushed Mama gently aside. "Is this the residence of the late Lula Mae Wiggins?"

The chain came off, and the door opened to reveal a strikingly beautiful woman. She was tall, and her tight jeans came practically up to her armpits. A full mane of dark hair framed an ivory face of flawless complexion. But it was the enormous grays, now regarding us with the frankness of youth, that made her so stunning.

"Miss Wiggins is dead."

"I know. So, is this—I mean was this—her residence?"

"I asked you before, who wants to know?"

I smiled. I was finding the girl's cheek more amusing than annoying. Had my own daughter, Susan, spoken to me that way—well, that's another story.

"My name is Abigail Timberlake. I'm Miss Wiggins's niece."

That seemed to startle her, but she was quick to recover. "Who's the pushy one?"

Mama's hand flew to her pearls. "Why, I never!"

"The pushy one, as you so aptly describe her, is my mother. Miss Wiggins's sister-in-law. Now do me the courtesy of answering the same question. Who are *you*?"

"I'm Amanda." She moved to one side and motioned us in.

We stepped into a cacophony of pinks. A pearl pink sofa and armchairs on a deep rose carpet clashed horribly with salmon pink walls. A bubble-gum baby grand piano, a painted fuchsia chandelier, and peony pink drapes screamed at each other in the discordance. The plethora of pinks made me want to puke.

Mama shook her head in amazement. "Oh, Abby, you have work to do here."

Amanda leaped in front of Mama like a denim-clad gazelle. "Excuse me?"

"Excuse you what, dear?"

"What did you mean about her having work to do here?"

"Well, this is her house now. You really don't expect—"

"*Her* house?"

"That's what I said, dear. Her aunt left it to my daughter in her will."

"You sure about this?"

"Of course we're sure," I said, moving Mama gently aside like she was a dog who wouldn't sit when commanded. "Now, Amanda, how did you get in here, and what are you doing here?"

"I have a key. I was practicing." She pointed to the piano.

"We heard you," Mama said. "You were a little slow with the bass, don't you think?"

The gray eyes clouded. "Are you some kind of an expert?"

"Well, I know this piece—"

"I wasn't making any mistakes, ma'am," the gazelle said through gritted teeth. "This was my recital piece last term at Juilliard. I got top marks."

Mama rolled her eyes. "You don't say."

"*The* Juilliard?" I asked, pushing the pesky poodle aside yet again.

Amanda nodded. "I'll play it again, if you'll promise not to interrupt."

"I'd love that!"

Amanda bounded over to the piano and plonked herself down on the padded pink bench. But before she could strike the first note, there was the sound of a key turning in the front door.

We turned and stared.

11

The woman standing in the doorway stared back. She was an African-American, of medium complexion, her black hair sculptured and moussed into an elaborate tiara of loops and swirls. She was wearing a bright orange smock over a pair of faded blue jeans. The smock bore a logo of a smiling bumblebee, over which were embroidered the words *Busy Bee Cleaners*. Under the logo was a name: Moriah Johnson. In her right hand the intruder still held the key, in her left hand a plastic bin full of brushes, paper towels, and a variety of spray bottles.

"Can I help you?" I asked calmly.

Miss Johnson, if indeed that was her name, glanced from me to Mama, to Amanda, and back to me. "Who are you?"

"I think the question is, who are *you*?"

The cleaning woman gestured with her chin. "You can see who I am. Moriah Johnson of Busy Bee Cleaners. I don't see any labels on you."

It was time to stop being so paranoid and mind my manners. I extended my hand. Moriah pocketed the key, and we shook.

"I'm Abigail Timberlake, and this is my mother, Mrs. Wiggins, and this young lady, we've just learned, is Amanda—uh, I don't believe I've learned her last name."

"Gabrenas," Amanda said.

Moriah nodded at Mama and Amanda but didn't offer to shake their hands, nor they hers. "I don't suppose you folks would mind telling me what you're doing here."

"Not at all, dear," Mama said, and turned to me proudly. "My Abby inherited this house from her Aunt Lula Mae, and Miss Gabrenas here was just about to butcher my favorite concerto."

Amanda gasped. "Why, you old bag!"

I gave Mama a warning glare and turned back to Moriah. "Turnabout is fair play, right? So what are you doing here?"

"I clean here."

"I can see that, but why? Surely you know that my aunt passed away. In fact, she's been dead for several months."

Moriah nodded. "Dust still settles, doesn't it? And no one told me to stop."

"The agency still has this house scheduled? Who pays them?"

The maid shrugged. "That's not my business, ma'am. I just do what I'm told." She looked me in the eyes. "And I do it well."

"I'm sure you do. How many times have you been here since my aunt passed on?"

"I come every other week—so maybe five times altogether. But like I said, ma'am. There's still always something to do."

There was no point in arguing. "Yes, well, you tell the agency that I'm discontinuing the service. Or should I call them?"

"No, ma'am, I'd be happy to tell them." She

looked around the room again, her eyes resting briefly on Amanda. "Well, I best be going."

"Sorry about the mix-up," I said and saw her out. Moriah was halfway down the stairs before I remembered. "The key!"

"Ma'am?"

"The house key. You forgot to give it back."

"Ma'am, the agency gave me the key. They said to never let it out of my sight."

"That may be," I said patiently. "But my aunt's dead now, and I inherited everything, including that key. I would like it back."

Moriah had the audacity to sigh as she reached into her smock pocket. "Take it, then. I'll just tell the agency to deal with you."

"You do that."

Moriah slapped the key into my open hand. "You better be who you say you are."

"I am indeed."

The maid turned without another word, took the steps two at a time, and strode down the street, the plastic bin banging against her thigh. As I watched her disappear, swallowed up by clumps of tourists, I couldn't help feeling like an ogre.

"Well, fiddle-dee-dee," I said to comfort myself.

I didn't have much time for self-loathing, however, because just as I turned to go back inside, the front door opened and out stormed Amanda. The door slammed behind her.

"Your mother is nuts!" she practically screamed.

"She does tend to get on one's nerves."

"No, I mean really whacked. That women belongs in an institution."

"Well—"

" I did go to Juilliard, you know. And I really do

know how to play that Tchaikovsky concerto."

"I'm sure you do. It sounded beautiful to me."

"It did?"

"Like heaven. So, Amanda, do I take it that you no longer go to Juilliard?"

She let out a long breathy sigh, the likes of which can be only be produced by someone for whom adolescence is a recent memory, and plopped on the concrete steps at my feet. "Yeah, I had to drop out."

"Why, if you don't mind my asking."

Amanda crossed her long legs. "Well, since you're asking, I might as well tell you. Your aunt was my benefactor."

I felt a tightness in my chest, along with a reluctance to pursue that line of questioning any further. "What do you mean by benefactor?"

"She was the one paying for my schooling."

"You're kidding!"

"I kid you not. In fact, it was even her idea that I apply."

"How did you two meet?"

"She was my piano teacher. Ever since the first grade—or was it the second? No, I was six when I started playing."

I shook my head in amazement.

"What's the matter? Don't you believe me?"

"Well, it's not that—I mean, did my aunt even play the piano?"

Amanda laughed. "Now *you're* kidding, right?"

"I'm afraid I didn't know my aunt very well."

"Boy, I'll say! Lula Mae was one of the best classical pianists in all of Georgia. She may not have been professional, but she was really good. She drove up to Atlanta all the time to give concerts. You really didn't know that?"

I hung my head in shame. Fortunately, with my short neck, it didn't have far to go.

"Wow! I thought everyone knew about Lula Mae Wiggins. And you're her niece!"

"We weren't a close family."

The gray eyes locked on mine. "So then why did she leave everything to you?"

"Because I'm her only living relative—blood relative that is. Well, except for my brother, Toy. But he's becoming a priest, albeit an Episcopal priest, and they don't have to take a vow of poverty. Still, it wouldn't hurt him any. That man knows how to waste money like a teenager wastes brains. Uh, no offense intended."

"Bullshit!"

"I beg your pardon!"

"You and your brother were not Lula Mae Wiggins's only blood relatives."

"My daddy is dead," I said coldly.

"Yes, but Moriah Johnson isn't."

"*What?*"

"The maid, the woman you just ran out of her house—I mean, your house."

"What the hell are you talking about?"

"Geez! You don't know very much, do you? Moriah Johnson is no maid. She wore that getup every time she came to see your aunt."

"What are you saying?"

Amanda smiled triumphantly. "Moriah Johnson was your aunt's niece, too. I guess that would make her your cousin, right?"

"Oh, my." I sat down beside Amanda. "Actually, she wouldn't be my cousin, since she was only my aunt's niece by marriage. In fact, she wouldn't be a blood relative at all."

"Hey, you're not prejudiced, are you?"

"I like to think I'm not. Are you?"

"Hell, no. I just don't like to see you taking your stuff out on Moriah. She's okay, you know? Your aunt really liked her."

"Tell me about my aunt."

"Like what do you want to know?"

"Anything and everything."

Amanda lifted both legs and stretched them in front of her. They were easily twice as long as mine.

"Let's see. Well, you knew your aunt was married, right? And that her husband wasn't white?"

"Yes. But I only recently found out, only yesterday, as a matter of fact."

"Hmm. Did you know that your aunt's husband, Kevin Johnson, left her?"

"He did? I guess I just assumed that he'd died."

"Well, he did. A couple of years ago from cancer. But he left your aunt a long time before that."

"Do you know why?"

"No. I was just a little girl then." Amanda stretched her arms and arched her back. Her left hand came so close to hitting my face that the fine hairs on her arm tickled my nose.

I recoiled and then smiled graciously. "You realize, don't you, that I might well sell this house."

"Yeah, that's what my mom says. She says I ought to get used to the idea and start practicing at home. But it's more peaceful here."

"I see. I take it you and your mom don't get along very well."

"We have our *issues*. That's Mom's word. Anyway, if you ask me, she's jealous of my relationship with your aunt—I mean what we *used* to have—well, you know what I mean."

"Yes."

"Lula Mae didn't bug me about things," Amanda volunteered. "Mom's always on my case."

"That's part of the job, dear."

Amanda snorted. "Yeah, but it isn't my fault Lula Mae died. And it's not my fault Mom can't afford to keep me in school."

"There is just your mom?" I asked gently.

"Yeah, my dad died when I was just a baby. Mom works as a waitress over at the Pirate's House Restaurant, but she can't afford a place like Juilliard. And let's face it, I'm not good enough to get a full scholarship. So, Mom wants me to get a job. Does that suck or what?"

"It has got to be a huge letdown. I bet just living in New York was exciting."

"Yeah." Her face lit up like an ember fanned by a gentle breeze. "You know, a lot of people think New Yorkers are rude, but they aren't. No more so than people here or anywhere else I've been. I guess New Yorkers just seem that way because they're almost always in a hurry. But when you get to know them . . ." The ember died.

"You're homesick, aren't you?"

She struggled to a standing position like a colt getting its first legs. This gazelle, when down, was not a graceful creature.

"Well, I gotta be going. I promised Mom I'd look for a job. But no waitressing! There's an opening at Penney's at the mall. What do you think?"

"I hope they let you model. If so, you'll sell a ton of clothes."

"Thanks!" she said. Then, because she was once more a gazelle, she bounded gracefully down the steps and disappeared into the humid lushness of Savannah.

I watched her go with envy. Oh, to be that young and nimble again! I did a clumsy pirouette on the step. The point was to convince myself that I still had it. Instead I stubbed my toe, tripped, and almost tumbled down the stairs. I might well have broken my neck.

Fortunately only my pride was hurt. Directly across the street from my new house was Forysth Park, and sitting on a bench facing the house was the cute guy Mama thought was Tom Hanks. I waved feebly at him, and he waved back. Then much to my relief he got up and walked in the direction Amanda had taken. It was only then that I realized that I had forgotten to get the key back from the girl.

A wise Abigail would have bounded, gracefully or not, back into the house and checked on Mama. The very fact that I had been able to have a halfway decent conversation with Amanda was cause for suspicion. Mama was clearly up to something.

But it was spring, the sun warm on face, and the sound of bees buzzing about the azaleas hypnotizing. Too short to technically sprawl across the steps, I reclined along the width of one and let the cares of the world fall away. How blessed I was to have a loving if meddling mother, two healthy children, good friends like Wynnell and C.J., a hunk like Greg Washburn hankering after me, and money. *Lots* of money.

The green stuff may not buy happiness, but it does buy security. Take it from one who has seen both sides of the financial coin; I'd rather be rich and

lonely than poor and lonely any day. And thanks to
Aunt Lula Mae, whose steps I now graced like a less
than life-sized sculpture, I was rich beyond belief—
and apparently about to become richer.

I was dreaming about an extended cruise on one
of those smaller ships with the la-de-da clientele
when I heard familiar voices and smelled the stench
of a cheap cigar.

"Miss Timberlake?"

I opened one eye.

"Ralph Lizard. We met yesterday afternoon outside Dewayne Kimbro's office."

I sat. "And that's Raynatta with an A and a Y,
right?"

The platinum plaything nodded, pleased at the
recognition. She was wearing spandex leopard-print
slacks and a black halter top. Her breasts billowed
ominously above me, and I prayed that the restraints
would hold. One sneeze, brought on by spring pol-
len, and I could be smothered in an avalanche of
mammary glands.

Ralph puffed on his cigar, although mercifully the
breeze had shifted and the smoke now blew the
other way. His black nylon shirt was unbuttoned almost to the waist and showed through the cheap
fabric of his white slacks. He wore no socks, and his
ankles were every bit as shiny as his pate.

"Miss Timberlake, you given it any thought?"

"You mean about selling this house?"

"Yes, ma'am. I list only high-end properties, and
it would be an honor."

"I'm sure it would, Mr. Lizard. However, I have
barely had a chance to look the place over. I'm not
ready to make that decision just yet."

He squinted, and so did I. A sunbeam glancing off

his shiny bald head would be enough to destroy the sight in these sore eyes. Not to mention the fact that the impossibly large stone in Raynatta's ring was blinding in broad daylight.

"Ma'am, you're not listing it with someone else, are you?"

"No, I am not. Like I said, I haven't made a decision. What do you want? That statement in blood?"

Raynatta giggled, and then realizing her mistake, clamped a pudgy paw over her scarlet maw. I noticed for the first time that she had lime green fingernails with iridescent purple dots centered just above each cuticle.

Ralph cocked his head while he sucked on the stogie. "Ma'am," he said at last, "you aren't thinking of actually living here, are you?"

"And what if I am?"

"Well—uh—ma'am, it's not that folks in Savannah aren't hospitable. We're a very friendly bunch when you get to know us. It's just that we tend to be—well, somewhat *clannish*." He whispered the evil word. "Do you know what I mean?"

I did indeed. Both Atlanta and Charlotte have been overrun by Rust Belt refugees to the point that their natives are imperiled and thus protectively silent. But Charleston, South Carolina, is another story. No amount of money can buy one entrée into Charleston society. That city is sociologically divided between "north of Broad Street" and "south of Broad Street." NOB and SOB, as Mama refers to them. Ironically, NOB residents are *not* the nobility of Charleston. It is a SOB address that is so desirable, but there is a world of difference between just owning a house south of Broad and belonging to the gentry. You may well sit next to your neighbors in church, greet them on the street, and even treat them as patients, but you will never be invited into their homes. Even in little Rock Hill, where I was born and Mama still lives, natives and transplants peacefully coexist but seldom, if ever, break bread together in private. True, I had just that morning sat in the Quarles parlor, but that was a family tainted by Yankee blood.

"I know exactly what you mean, Mr. Lizard. However, I was thinking of maybe keeping this as my second home. You know, a getaway. I'd keep my friends in the Carolinas."

Ralph smiled, supporting the cigar with his thumb and first two fingers. His teeth were tiny and pointed like those of a fish.

"I hear you. But with all due respect, Miss Timberlake, I'm not sure even that would be such a good idea. The taxes alone are going to be a killer, and a house this old—well, it may look all right on the surface, but it's going to take a lot of upkeep. And then, of course, there are criminals to consider."

"Does Savannah have a particularly high crime rate?"

"No, ma'am. But keeping a house empty most of the time just invites trouble."

"I'm sure you're right. And I'll certainly keep that under advisement. In the meantime, however, I have come nowhere near to making a decision."

Raynatta poked Ralph in the side with one of the green and purple claws. "Just make her the offer, why don'tcha?"

"I'm getting to that," Ralph growled.

"Offer away," I said patiently. "But it isn't going

to make a bit of difference right now. I need time to think."

"Ma'am, I'd like to buy your house flat out. Direct from you to me. There won't be any commission to take into account, and I'll pay the closing costs and any other pertinent fees. Fair market value of course."

"Why?"

Ralph blinked, which may or may not have had anything to do with the wad of ash that fell on a bare foot and slid into his loafer. He kicked off the shoe but managed not to look down.

"Well, you see, ma'am, Raynatta and I are getting married. Raynatta, show Miss Timberlake your ring."

Before I could protest or ask to borrow a pair of sunglasses, Raynatta thrust the rock beneath my nose. "It's five carats."

"It's very impressive, dear. Congratulations."

"Anyway, ma'am, we really like this location, and while I have never actually been inside *this* house, I've sold enough like it to have a good idea of the floor plan. Historic houses like this don't come up on the market very often, and I—well, I want to give it to Raynatta here as a wedding present."

Raynatta giggled. I tried to imagine her platinum tresses and leopard spandex in such an important house. Unfortunately, thanks to Aunt Lula Mae's penchant for pink, it was not hard to imagine. The newlyweds wouldn't even have to redecorate. Raynatta's tastelessness would be the icing on Aunt Lula Mae's unpalatable cake.

"I'll think about it," I said. "Now, if you'll excuse me, I really have to get back inside."

Ralph's eyes narrowed. "You don't have another agent inside now, do you?"

"No."

Raynatta poked her intended in the ribs again. "Make her a better offer."

"There is no need for that," I snapped. "Not that it's your business, but my mother's waiting for me inside."

Little did I know how wrong I was.

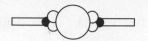

12

"**M**ama?"
She wasn't in the pink living room. Nor was she in the dining room or any of the bedrooms. Of course, I checked the predictably pink powder rooms. I even checked the closets. Once Mama and I took a tour of luxury homes in Charlotte, and while I was gazing at the fourteen-foot ceilings, she wandered off. After a futile and frantic search I was about to call the police when one of the tour directors discovered Mama asleep in a walk-in closet. Aunt Lula Mae's house did not have walk-in closets, but given the fact that Mama can sleep while virtually standing, I even checked the broom closet. I went so far as to check underneath the beds. *Nada.*

"Mama, if you're hiding somewhere, come out now, or I'm never speaking to you again!"

My angry words echoed through the three-story house, but they were followed by sepulchral silence. While I have always been fond of hide-and-seek (especially when my boyfriend Greg is involved), I didn't find my current predicament at all amusing. I'm not saying I believe in ghosts—I mean Apparition-Americans—but neither am I declaring that I don't. All I'm saying is that a disappearing progenitress in an all-pink house in which an unknown aunt has committed suicide is—well—spooky. I needed a breath of fresh air.

I ducked out the back door and into a courtyard that separated house from garage. It might once have been a beautiful little garden centered on a goldfish pool, but three months of neglect was starting to show. Leaves and twigs blown in from a neighbor's oak crunched underfoot, and the pond water was mossy and ripe with the scent of decaying vegetation. Either the fountain had been turned off, or the pump was broken. At any rate, the bronze boy no longer micturated, although he still smiled mischievously.

Mama has an aversion to spiders, so there was little need to check the boxwood bushes, but I poked them with a stout oak limb nonetheless. Hearing no painful squeals, I turned my attention to the garage. As far as I knew, Aunt Lula Mae had not owned a car at the time of her death—at least, there was no mention of it in her will—so I expected to find it empty. Boy, was I wrong! The surprisingly narrow space was stacked to the rafters with paint cans. And not only cans of pink paint either, but just about every hue imaginable. Apparently Aunt Lula Mae had gone through a chartreuse phase, a cobalt blue phase, and much to my surprise, a beige phase.

"Mama, are you in here? 'Cause if you are, you're putting us both in danger. There is paint thinner in here too, and as you know, it can be highly flammable. Just these fumes are enough to make one sick. Mama, you don't want to make us both sick, do you?" To be absolutely honest, I didn't smell anything except for dust and perhaps the odd rat-dropping, but my mother is very sensitive to the power of suggestion.

Mama didn't have the grace to answer.

"The fumes will eat away at your pearls," I shouted. Okay, so it was a lie, but it wasn't far from the truth. Pearls are organic gems and really rather fragile. They should never be subjected to hair spray or come in direct contact with perfume, and if one should accidentally dribble salad dressing on them in a restaurant, the best thing to do is to immediately dunk the necklace in a glass of plain water. This is, of course, easier accomplished if the necklace is first removed. Those folks with very small heads or who find themselves in restaurants with exceptionally large water glasses may use their own discretion.

When Mama didn't respond to the potential threat to her pearls—no matter how bogus—I was forced to conclude she was not hiding in the garage. I trotted back to the house and slammed the kitchen door loud enough to wake the dead over in Bonaventure Cemetery. It was time to drag out the big guns.

"Mama! If you don't answer this minute, I'm going to tell the ladies in your book club that you color your hair."

Nothing. Not even a clock ticked in that old house. It was so quiet you could hear a mouse belch. Clearly Mozella Wiggins had flown the pink coop.

I would have called the Heritage and checked to see if she'd taken a cab and returned to the room, but Aunt Lula Mae's phone service had long since been disconnected. And since Savannah, beautiful as it is, has more one-way streets than hell, it took me a half-hour to get back to the hotel.

The room, alas, was empty.

"Did you check the bar?" Ashley Hawkins, the young receptionist with the strawberry-blond tresses, hadn't recognized me at first. *Me!* How many four-foot-nine-inch strikingly beautiful brunette adults does she run into on a daily basis?

"My mother doesn't drink—well, not before five in the afternoon, and even then it's only half a glass of wine topped off with water."

Ashley rolled her eyes. "Did you try the gift shop?"

"I did. You *sure* there aren't any messages?"

"No, ma'am, there aren't any messages."

"Well, if you see her, tell her I'll be down on River Street, grabbing a bite of lunch."

"Yes, ma'am." Ashley was starting to sound testy.

I turned, took about three steps, and turned again. "Miss Hawkins, have I done something to offend you?"

"Ma'am?"

"Well, yesterday you were so friendly and helpful. You recommended a place where I could board my cat, and you had extra bedding sent up and—"

"Ma'am, it's your friends." She said it so softly I wouldn't have heard her had I not had a good go at my ears with a cotton swab that morning.

"My friends? What about them?"

Ashley glanced around. The manager had his back turned.

"Miss Timberlake, your friends paid a visit to Club One last night."

I shrugged. "What is that? A bar?"

The manager disappeared into an office, and Ashley was able to speak up. "It's a gay nightclub. The one Lady Chablis used to perform at. You know, the female impersonator mentioned in The Book."

That certainly surprised me, but I tried not to

show it. "Well, it is still a free country, isn't it? What they do is their business."

"Yes, ma'am, I'm not saying that. Lots of tourists drop into Club One. It's just that generally they don't jump up on stage during the drag show and critique the performers."

"My friends did *that*?"

"They were drunk, ma'am. Drunker than a marine on a three-day pass. But that's still not an excuse for the things they said. I've never been so embarrassed in my whole life."

"You were there?"

Ashley glanced nervously at the office door. "They were critiquing *me*!"

"You mean—I mean—well, you certainly look convincing."

The red mane shook vigorously. "No! I really am Ashley Hawkins. But this job doesn't pay a whole lot, so I've been pretending to be a guy named Wade Johnson whose stage name is Connie the Barbarian. To make a long story short, last night I got fired."

"Wow! I'm sorry."

"The young one tugged on my hair. She said it was the worst wig she'd ever seen."

"C.J. is just jealous. She has hair like shredded wheat. But tell me something, weren't you afraid that someone from the Heritage would recognize you moonlighting at Club One?"

"Nah. I don't wear much makeup on this job, as you can see, and after my sister works her magic— well, you wouldn't recognize me."

"Your sister is a beautician?"

"Used to be. Still does makeup for some of the movies filmed around here, but her kennel keeps her pretty busy."

"Her kennel?"

"Yeah, the one you took your cat to."

"Lougee Hawkins is your sister?"

Ashley nodded. "Lougee took after Mama in her looks, I took after Daddy. I guess that's why I'm so good at playing a drag queen. Well, I was—until last night."

"Sorry again about that. But thanks for reminding me. I need to check on my cat."

"Well, I can tell you he is doing just fine. I stopped by my sister's this morning, and she had him out in the run. When he saw me, he came right up to me and rubbed against my legs, just begging to be picked up."

"And did you?" I asked incredulously. Dmitri was meant to be born a Japanese chef. He can slice and dice along with best of them, only instead of steak, his specialty is strangers. Especially strangers who foolishly make the first move.

"Oh, yeah. He purred his little heart out. Just hated to be put down. Not that he's lonely or anything. Lougee spends a lot of time with her boarders."

"Well, in that case, I guess I could postpone my visit."

"Absolutely. He's in good hands."

I thanked Ashley for her time and skedaddled just as her manager stuck his head out of the office. Far be it from me to get Ashley fired twice in one twenty-four-hour period.

I took the back elevator down to River Street. The Heritage Hotel is built along the Savannah River bank and straddles a significant change in elevation. The lower entrance opens on a quaint cobbled street, whose stones were brought as ballast on early sailing ships. The bluff side is lined with old warehouses that once served as cotton and naval stores but are now restaurants, gift shops, and art galleries. Along the river is moored a replica of a pirate ship and a veritable flotilla of yachts. The lucky boat-owners who hail from half a dozen states up and down the eastern seaboard sip their cocktails on polished teak decks while studiously avoiding the gaze of tourists. Every now and then a huge cargo ship passes up or down the river, and the anchored boats bobble in its wake. The young at heart wave at Greek and Italian seamen, and if the waving tourists are attractive enough, the seamen wave back.

There is a long tradition of waving along the Savannah River. From 1887 until 1931 a woman by the name of Florence Martus waved a greeting or farewell to every ship that passed through the port of Savannah. Today a bronze statue of Florence and her dog mark the spot where she stood. The monument is appropriately called the Waving Girl.

I was walking along River Street, just yards from the Waving Girl, when I spotted the Tom Hanks look-alike. He was sitting on a bench, of course, but his head was thrown back, and his eyes were closed. How he could be sleeping was beyond me, because just beyond him was a ruckus the likes of which would wake a mummy with earmuffs.

I scurried silently past the ubiquitous bench-sitter to see what was going on. Imagine my surprise when I spotted C.J. and Wynnell. Both women were soaking wet, their hair plastered against their heads, and Wynnell was missing her left shoe. A group of tourists with *Tokyo* emblazoned on their T-shirts stood off to one side, the shutters of their cameras clicking nonstop.

Wynnell saw me first. "Abby! Just look what your friend did."

I pretended the inquisitive tourists were shrubs. "What happened?"

"She pulled me into the river," Wynnell barked, "that's what happened!"

"What do you mean, pulled?" I turned to C.J. "What were you doing? Going for a swim with the dolphins?"

"I was waving at a ship, that's what. I guess I got too close to the edge and fell in. I didn't mean to pull Wynnell in."

I surveyed the scene of the supposed accident. "There's a railing. Y'all weren't sitting on it, were you?"

C.J. snorted—or she may have merely been trying to clear her nose of water.

"Well?"

"We couldn't help it," C.J. whined. "This Italian freighter went by, and the deckhands were so gorgeous."

"I can't believe this! Wynnell, you're married, for crying out loud!"

Wynnell hung her head in shame. "There isn't any harm in looking, is there?"

"Apparently there is. Just look at you. You might have drowned, and who knows, you could very well come down with some horrible bacterial infection. That isn't exactly spring water."

"Oh, no!" C.J. clamped her hands on her midriff. "I could be pregnant!"

"*What?*"

"There were porpoises, Abby."

"So?"

"My cousin Tina back in Shelby fell into a frog pond and—"

"Let me guess. Nine months later she gave birth to a baby boy with webbed feet, right?"

Several of the Tokyo tourists gasped.

"How'd you know?" C.J. demanded.

"Because I read about it in the *National Intruder*, that's how. The same place you read it!"

"Yes, Abby, but that really happened. I used to baby-sit for little Freddy all the time. He always wanted me to take him down to the creek in our backyard. Boy, was he ever a good swimmer!"

I laid a calming hand on C.J.'s glistening arm. "Don't worry, dear. I guarantee you have not been impregnated by a porpoise."

"Pregnant by a porpoise!" the Tokyo guide cried, as shutters clicked furiously.

"You see?" Wynnell hissed. "None of this would have happened if we had good moral leadership. I'm a happily married woman, and I wouldn't have been sitting on that rail waving to gorgeous guys from Genoa if it weren't for President Clinton."

"President Clinton!" Heads swiveled, shutters momentarily silent.

I addressed my friends. "You guys see Mama?"

Wynnell shook her head, and I dodged water droplets.

"Clinton, Clinton," the guide began to chant, and almost immediately the entire group joined in. "We want to see Clinton!"

I had to shout so Wynnell could hear me. "If you see Mama, tell her to go straight to the room and wait for me there." I turned to the tourists and waved my arms like a traffic cop. To my amazement they hushed instantly. "That's better. Now listen up, folks. I'm afraid there has been a misunderstanding. To my knowledge, President Clinton is nowhere near Savannah."

The moans coming from the disappointed tourists were heart-wrenching. They had come twelve thousand miles in search of something truly special to photograph, and who was I to deny them their Kodak moment?

I waved my arms again. "Okay, okay! I wasn't going to spill the beans—"

"Spill the beans?" The guide scratched his head.

"Reveal a secret."

"Ah so!"

"So, anyway, these two women are in disguise. This one"—I pointed to Wynnell—"is really Linda Tripp, and that one is Monica Lewinsky."

"Lewinsky!"

"Abby, you'll pay for this!" Wynnell roared as the group lunged at her and C.J. Cameras were no longer clicking; it was autograph time.

I barely escaped the crush of the throng. But Wynnell was right. I was about to pay dearly.

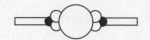

13

Ashley shook her head when I walked into the lobby, so I went straight to the room. Still no Mama.

I dialed Greg at his office.

"Washburn here." I could tell he had a mouthful of food.

"Is it tasty?"

"Abby! Where the hell are you? Why haven't you called?"

"I'm sorry, I really am, but it's been a zoo. I had to board Dmitri, Aunt Lula Mae left me a pink house and a valuable penny, C.J. thinks she's been impregnated by a porpoise, and I've lost Mama!"

Greg swallowed loud enough for me to hear. "Mozella's missing? How long has she been missing?"

I glanced at the bedside clock. "About an hour and a half."

He chuckled. "Sweetheart, that hardly counts with your mother. Now, start at the beginning."

As I described Savannah and some of its daft denizens—who weren't, alas, nearly as daffy as the trio I'd brought with me, mind you—Greg ate his lunch. I could almost smell the roast beef sandwich from Arby's.

"Did you get extra horsey sauce?" I interrupted myself.

"*What?*"

"Never mind. Anyway, as I was saying, she didn't come out the front door—I know that because I was sitting on the steps—and I can't imagine why she'd just sneak out the back. We weren't having a fight or anything."

"Un-huh. Had she expressed a desire earlier to see something in the neighborhood? Maybe take a peek in one of the shops?"

"No. Oh, Greg, I'm worried. You know how Mama is about directions. Whenever we go to the mall, I have to look for her at the food court. Thank heavens she can find that with her nose. Isn't there anything we can do?"

"You mean *me*, don't you? Abby, you know a missing person report can't be filed for forty-eight hours. Just give her time, hon. She'll wander back to the Heritage or maybe take a cab—she does have money on her, doesn't she?"

"I don't know!" I wailed. "I'm not my mother's keeper."

"Then stop acting like it. She's not senile, she has good vision, and despite those damn heels she always wears, she can walk up a storm. I'd say she's perfectly capable of taking care of herself."

"I guess you're right."

Greg slurped loudly.

"Is that the Jamocha shake?"

"Abby, why the sudden interest in my diet?"

"It's been a long time since breakfast," I wailed. "I was on my way to get a bite for lunch when I ran into Monica and Linda. Then, for some reason, I just had to come back to the room. I've got this feeling, Greg, that I just can't shake."

Greg started humming the tune to "I Can't Help This Feeling." Fortunately he has a good voice and knows when to stop.

"Abby, might I suggest you eat a nice big lunch and then book yourself on one of those tours of the city. Who knows, you might spot your mother, but more importantly, you might actually have a good time. Savannah is a city meant to be enjoyed."

"Will do."

I hung up and dialed the Rob-Bobs. Rob Goldburg and Bob Steuben are life partners and co-owners of The Finer Things. Their shop is arguably Charlotte's finest antique store, and they are the most knowledgeable dealers I've ever had the privilege of knowing. They are also two of my closest friends.

"The Finer Things!" Bob boomed in a voice that would make a bullfrog jealous.

"Hey, Bob, this is Abby."

"Abby! Rob and I were just talking about you. Are your ears burning?"

"Not a bit. So it was all good stuff, I take it."

"The best. It was about you and Greg. He came in here yesterday afternoon, asking a lot of questions."

"What kind of questions?"

"Questions like do you prefer white or yellow gold, and which did we think was classier, a marquis or the traditional brilliant cut."

If my heart had possessed feet, my ticker would have done a little soft-shoe. I'm not ready to get married again, but it feels good to be wanted—what's more, to be wanted by a man who is willing to do a little homework first. And there is nothing wrong with a long engagement, is there?

"Tell Greg that bigger is not always better."

"Abby, you're wicked!"

"I'm talking about diamonds! You know that. Clarity, color, and cut are just as important as carat."

"Yeah, the four Cs. Abby, Rob's standing here shooting me daggers. He wants to talk to you while I wait on that rich bitch from South Park with two noses."

"Those aren't two noses, dear. Her plastic surgeon proved in court that he wasn't seeing double when he operated and that the left nose is really a very large wart. But you're right, her manners are definitely from up the road a piece."

"Hey, watch it, Abby! I'm from Toledo, remember?"

I heard some good-natured bantering while the phone changed hands. "Abby?"

"Hey, Rob. What's up?"

"You tell me. You're the one who called. Is everything all right down there?"

I smiled. Rob is like an older brother. He is a Charlotte boy born and bred and has impeccable taste, which means we agree on just about everything. He—okay, I confess, he's even more handsome than my Greg. If Rob were straight, I'd be all over him like white on rice.

"Rob, I'm calling to ask if either of you has ever heard of a numismatist named Albert Quarles."

"Absolutely."

"What can you tell me about him?"

"He's supposed to be one of the best. Bob and I met him at a trade show at Metrolina Expo. Bob," Rob whispered, "thought he was cute. 'Devastatingly cute' I think his words were. Fortunately for me the guy was as straight as Dan Quayle."

"Cute? Well, then, we must not be talking about the same man."

"You sure? Monocle, swarthy complexion, little orange apricot ears?"

"Well, what do you know, it is the same man!"

"Why the background check, Abby?"

"Oh, Rob, you're never going believe what happened."

"Try me."

I gave him the *gontzeh megillah*, as he calls it. You know, the whole enchilada. By the time I finished, Rob was so breathless it was nearly obscene.

"Abby, why do these things always happen to *you*? I pay my taxes, I treat my mother kindly, I give to the poor, I seldom kick dogs—"

I gasped.

"Just kidding," he said. "You know I love animals. But hell, I don't have near the luck you do."

"Maybe it's karma, dear. Maybe in a past life you did kick dogs."

"Or maybe you were perfect."

"Yeah, right. Look, Rob, I need to know if you would trust this guy."

"With Bob, no." He paused so I could chuckle politely. "But all kidding aside, I would say yes. I would trust him."

"It's not just his professional opinion I'm talking about, Rob. Would you trust him to broker the collection?"

"What's wrong with yours truly?" It didn't take second sight to catch the hurt in Rob's voice.

"Nothing, dear," I hastened to assure him. "It's just that—well, you said he was the best and—"

"I said he was *one* of the best."

I slapped my own cheek. "Are you as knowledge-able as he? Regarding coins, I mean."

Rob's sigh cooled my stinging cheek. "No, I guess not."

"Then, if you were me, would you trust Albert Quarles?"

"The man has a reputation to uphold. He isn't going to cheat you. Just make sure you inventory everything and make him sign a receipt. Assuming this mythical collection exists."

"But you think it might?"

"I'd say there's a good chance."

"Thanks, you've been a dear."

"Anytime. Say, Abby, did you hear the one about Al Gore and Pinocchio?"

"Later, okay? I've got to go now. Give my love to Bob."

Rob groaned. "It's his turn to cook tonight. He's making emu burgers a l'orange."

"Yuck!"

"Tell me, Abby, is that a Yankee thing?"

I blew a kiss into the phone and hung up.

If Greg was going to buy me a diamond ring, the least I could do was take his advice. It was time to enjoy Savannah.

At the very least, a proper lunch was definitely in order. The Heritage has its own restaurant, but I was feeling guilty for having tricked the Tokyo tourists. To cleanse my karma I walked over to Yoshi's Downtown, which is located on the corner of West Congress and Martin Luther King. It bills itself as Savannah's best sushi bar, and who am I to argue? But I chickened out on the raw fish and had the deluxe *bentou* box: *negmaki*, *kakfurai*, *tempura*, and *gyoza*.

In other words, rolled beef with scallion, fried oysters, fried shrimp, and fried dumplings.

When I was quite satiated, I collected my car and drove over to the Visitors Center, which is lodged in some old cotton warehouses, and caught one of the Blue Line trolleys. Its boast was that it offered passengers more points at which to embark and disembark at will than any other tour line. I hoisted myself into the last remaining seat just seconds before departure.

"Good morning, y'all," the guide began. "How many of you are Savannah natives?"

No one raised their hand, but several eyebrows, including one of mine, were raised. Frieda Sheinwold had the strangest southern accent I'd ever heard.

"How many Georgia natives do we have?"

Five hands rose and a couple more eyebrows.

"How many do we have from the South altogether?"

About a third of us, including my seatmate, raised their hand.

"I'm from the south, too," Frieda said in her weird hybrid accent. "Can anyone guess where?"

"Louisiana?" I asked. I didn't think it was Cajun, but that was my most intelligent guess.

Frieda chuckled.

"South Jersey?" someone with a northeast accent asked.

"No, I mean the real south. I'm from South America."

Most everyone groaned.

"I'm from Argentina, but I moved to Savannah when I was sixteen."

"Oh, great," my seatmate muttered, "no doubt she's the offspring of itinerant Nazis."

I turned to look at an attractive woman my age, dressed in a lavender pantsuit, with enough gold bangles on her wrist to sink the Spanish Armada. She returned my frank gaze and smiled.

"My name's Sheila Cohen," she whispered. "I was born in Memphis, but my parents spent some time in Argentina. They fled Hitler and settled in Buenos Aires, but then after the war there were more Nazis per square foot there than back in Munich. That's how I ended up in Tennessee."

Fortunately Frieda had a strong voice and the microphone worked well enough so that I had no compunction about carrying on a whispered conversation. And just to prove that I try to mind my manners, I want you to know that I glanced around every now and then for disapproving looks and kept one ear open for silencing "shhs."

"Abigail Timberlake," I said. "Born in Rock Hill, South Carolina, but live and work in Charlotte, North Carolina. You here by yourself?"

Sheila sighed. "My husband, Getzel, would rather play golf than breathe. You can guess where he is right now. How about you? Your husband playing hooky too?"

I showed her my bare left hand. "Divorced, but I'm not here alone. I was coerced into bringing my mother and two friends. Oh, and my cat."

"We brought our cat too!"

"Oh, where are you staying?"

"The Olde Harbour Inn."

"Dang! I tried there, but they were all booked up."

"Nice place. We often leave Boots alone if it's just for a few days—you know, leave out plenty of dry food, lots of water bowls, and several litter boxes. In fact, our veterinarian says it's less stressful for the cat than boarding him or even having someone come by to feed him. After all, Boots sleeps ninety percent of the time. But lately he's been getting into trouble, so we lugged him along."

"What kind of trouble?"

"Well, last time we came back from a long weekend and couldn't find him anywhere. I tell you, my heart just leaped into my throat. We were beginning to believe we might have accidentally locked him outside—and he's a strictly indoor cat, mind you—when we heard a faint meow coming from the fireplace."

"Oh, my gosh!"

Sheila nodded. "There's a ledge inside the fireplace just beneath the flue. Boots used to get up in there and take naps when he was a kitten. We always had to check before we built a fire. But you see, Boots is a Maine coon cat. He weighs twenty-two pounds now." She chuckled. "I can laugh now in retrospect, but it sure wasn't funny then. Poor Boots was stuck, and the only way we could get him out was to squirt oil on him with a turkey baster."

"You're kidding!"

"I kid you not. I was afraid that would drive him further up the chimney, but we managed to get him so slippery he plopped right down into the grate, which was still full of ashes—Getzel loves to start fires, but isn't much on cleaning up. Anyway, you've never seen such a mess. I had to get a special shampoo from the vet to get all that oil and soot out of his fur, and even that wasn't one hundred percent effective. On the bright side, we had no trouble with hair balls after that for at least a month."

"Wow! That's quite a story."

Then I proceeded to tell a few Dmitri tales. We chatted amiably, pausing every now and then to listen to Frieda's spiel, until approximately halfway through the tour.

Sheila stood. "This is where I get off. That's Temple Mikve Israel over there. It's the third oldest synagogue in the country and the only gothic one. It also houses the oldest Torah in America."

"Oh? What is a Torah?"

"Our sacred scroll containing the Five Books of Moses. And I read there is a wonderful little museum—say, would you like to come with me?"

"Uh—well—I—" I was tempted to disembark with Sheila. I could use some diversion.

She who hesitates is lost, however, and before I could make up my mind, an amazon woman with saddlebag thighs clambered aboard, pushed past Sheila, and tried to squeeze past me to the vacated seat. In order to avoid being crushed, I scooted over to the window side.

"Have a good time, Sheila!"

"Thanks, Abby. See you!"

My new seatmate wasted no time. She was still panting from the exertion of boarding, but she extended a hand as large as a loaf of bread.

"My name is Alice Bickendorfer."

I shook hands reluctantly. "Abigail Timber—"

"This is my first time in Savannah. How about you?"

"Actually—"

"I almost didn't make it to the airport in time because Aunt Bernice's bursitis was acting up, and I had to take her to the doctor. Usually Little John does that kind of thing when I'm on one of my trips, but Coco's got a good chance of winning best show in Indianapolis this year, and he needed the time to groom. Do you have dogs?"

"No, I—"

"Well, there's cat people, and then there's dog people, I suppose. Little John is definitely a dog person. He looks just like his bichon frise, if you ask me. Personally, I never cared much for either—cats or dogs, I mean—not Little John and Coco. Now gardening, that's my passion. Do you garden?"

"Not—"

"Because I'd like to see some of these gardens put on tour. Of course, I can't grow stuff like this up in Indiana, but that doesn't mean I don't enjoy seeing it. Still, I shouldn't complain. I've been having such a wonderful time and all. I took The Book tour yesterday and—did you read The Book?"

"I wrote it."

"Of course, it's a shame they can't take you inside Mercer House but—*what* did you say?"

"Nothing."

"Yes, you did. You said you wrote *Midnight in the Garden of Good and Evil.*"

I squirmed. "You must be mistaken."

Alice Bickendorfer stared at me. She had a large doughy face with small dark eyes like glazed raisins.

"Say, I've seen you before!"

"I don't think so, ma'am."

"Of course I have! You were at Seasons restaurant this morning, weren't you?"

"Guilty. My, you've got a good—"

"You were drinking champagne. I never touch the stuff myself—well, I guess that's not strictly true. I did have pink champagne once at a Valentine's party. Now, there's a holiday I've always hated.

Couples, that's what it's all about. That and making money for the retailers. If you don't have anyone special in your life, then you're made to feel inferior. I'm not talking about myself necessarily. I mean, I've got Aunt Bernice and Little John, and where is it written that Valentine's Day is for lovers only? But there are some people who have no one—did you ever see that *Twilight Zone* episode about the astronaut stationed on the moon? Or was it Mars? Anyway, he has this female robot with him to keep him company, only he forgets it's a robot, see, and . . ."

I zoned out, not coming fully back to my senses until the trolley reached Monterey Square and started to turn north, back down Bull Street. "Excuse me, please. This is my stop."

The raisin eyes looked right past me. ". . . so I told Little John that the next time Aunt Bernice's bursitis flares up, it's his turn to take her to the doctor. That's only fair, don't you think? Of course, I wouldn't expect Little John's help if it was some sort of female problem. Aunt Bernice has those too, boy, does she ever! Just last week her—"

I crawled to freedom over the massive thighs. I'm not sure Alice from Indiana noticed. As the trolley pulled away from the stop, I could see that her lips were still moving. I said a silent prayer for Aunt Bernice and Little John.

When I turned to take stock of my surroundings, I noticed first with dread, then with anger, the Tom Hanks look-alike sitting on a bench not ten feet from me. Monterey Square is as inviting as any of Savannah's parks, but seeing this was too much of a coincidence. I marched resolutely up to the gorgeous young man.

"Have you been following me?" I demanded without preamble.

He looked up at me with bedroom eyes. "I beg your pardon, ma'am?"

"You seem to be popping up on park benches everywhere. You're like toadstools after a rain."

"Maybe if you kiss me, I'll turn into a prince." He laughed.

"I said toad*stool*, not toad, and I'm not kidding. Why are you following me?"

He laughed again. "Ma'am, I'm not following you. You just got off the trolley, and I've been sitting here for nigh on to half an hour."

"Well, you have to admit this is a bit strange, me running into you everywhere I turn."

"Ma'am, this is Savannah."

When all else fails, try good manners. "My name is Abigail Timberlake," I said, and extended my hand.

He took it gallantly. "Joe Quarles at your service."

I stared, wide-eyed as a scarecrow on steroids. The studmuffin lounging before me had a perfectly normal neck. There was not a hint of wobble to his handsome head.

"Any relation to Albert Quarles, the numismatist?" I finally asked.

Bench-warming Joe laughed. "He's my daddy."

"Oh. Somehow I got the impression he didn't have any children."

"I'm sure that was intentional. Daddy—Mama, too—would just as soon forget I was born."

"I can't believe that!"

"Believe it. Mama thinks she married into high society, and Daddy acts like I committed a cardinal sin by dropping out of school. He being a teacher and all."

"Your daddy is a teacher as well as a numismatist?"

"*Was* a teacher. Now he just plays around with coins full time."

"At least that's an honorable profession."

"Yeah, well mine's older than his."

I arched my brows. "What do you do?"

"I romance tourists. For money, of course." He treated me to a dazzling white grin. "You in the mood to buy me lunch, Abigail Timberlake?"

"When geese wear shoes," I said pleasantly and went on my merry way.

No encounter with a park bench hustler was going to get me down. The sun was shining, the mockingbirds singing, and all was right with the world. Attitude, I told myself, it's all attitude.

And Greg was right. I'd been overreacting about Mama. A seventy-year-old woman does not need to ask her daughter's permission to come and go as she pleases. Let's face it, I had been acting stupidly, not at all in my own interest. My children were just now becoming adults, freeing me of responsibility, and I should have been gratefully enjoying my status as an empty-nester instead of trying to control the life of someone who was quite capable of taking care of herself.

"Just relax and enjoy the moment," I said aloud to myself as I unlocked my new front door. In the words of my children, 'take a chill pill.' "

Instead, I screamed.

14

Before me lay a scene of utter devastation. The pearl pink sofa and its cushions were in shreds, the goose down scattered about like hoarfrost. I stumbled to the kitchen. The cabinets were open, boxes and cans dumped on the floor. The silver drawers were empty, but the contents spilled, not taken. Even the refrigerator was open, bare as Mother Hubbard's cupboards. In short, the house was almost as messy as my daughter Susan's room her senior year of high school.

I screamed again. This time it was a cry of pure, unadulterated rage at the waste that lay all around me. If someone wanted the damn coin collection that badly, they could have tried more civil means, like holding a gun to my head or a knife to my throat. Of course if that had been the case, I might well have added to the mess with a couple of quarts of blood, given the fact that I had no idea of the collection's whereabouts. Still, there was no need to smash a jar of perfectly good artichoke hearts, was there?

"Are you all right?"

I whirled, my hands up to protect my face. Albert Quarles was standing not six feet behind me. He was wielding a hot-pink lamp vase as if it were club.

"Damn it, Albert, you scared me half to death!"

"Sorry, Abby. I didn't know if you were in here alone or not. I wanted the element of surprise in case you weren't."

I gasped. "Oh, my God, I hadn't thought of that! We may not be alone!"

Albert nodded, somehow managing to keep the monocle in place. "Let's go out front. I have a cell phone. We'll call the police from there."

I beat him to the door, although not by much. I had the feeling that although Albert Quarles was a gentleman, he was first and foremost a self-preservationist. Frankly, I found that quality rather charming.

"So," I gasped, catching my breath on the steps, "how did you happen to come along at just the right moment?"

Albert picked something invisible off one of the lapels of his cream-colored suit. In the sunshine his complexion looked even more jaundiced. The dried-apricot ears were positively orange.

"Well, I—uh—Abby, perhaps I should call the police first. Then we can talk."

"By all means."

When he was through giving directions, he slipped the tiny phone back into an inside breast pocket and straightened the paisley tie.

"Okay, Albert, what's the story?" In a nearby oak a mockingbird was trilling at the top of his or her lungs.

"Well—" He compulsively touched the corners of his clipped black mustache. After four repetitions, I figured it was time to goose the goose.

"Spit it out, Albert. The cops will be here any minute."

"I came to see you."

"Me? But how did you know I'd be here?"

"I didn't. You didn't say where you were staying, and I guess I could have tried tracing you through my brother-in-law, Calvin, but I had some errands to run, so I thought I'd give here a try."

That seemed plausible. "What did you want to see me about?"

"I wanted to warn you." The mockingbird stopped singing.

"*Warn* me?" The hair on my arms stood on end, and because I'd been so busy lately, the hair under my arms followed suit.

"I thought you should know about the girl."

"Amanda?"

The monocle popped out of his eye, and if it hadn't been for the gold chain attached to it, would have fallen on the steps and might well have broken. Perhaps dropping the monocle was not an unusual occurrence, because Albert made no move to catch it.

"You know about her?"

"We met. She was here playing the piano the first time I stopped by. So now *you* tell *me*, what do you know about her?"

"Well, I only met her a couple of times, but I don't think she did all that." He gestured toward the house.

"Ah, but you have met her before—which means you've been here before. Right?"

Albert started to sit and then thought better of it. I don't blame him; the suit was a dandy.

"Yes, ma'am. I have been here before. Your aunt and I were—well, we were friends."

"Were you lovers?"

He gaped at me and then replaced the monocle to get an even better look. "No, ma'am! I would never cheat on Miranda."

"Maybe so, but back at your house you practically denied even knowing her. 'Didn't do the social scene' I think is the way you described her."

He glanced around, no doubt checking the azalea bushes for spies. Given my experiences thus far in Savannah, it seemed like a prudent thing to do.

"Ah," he said suddenly, "there's the squad car now. I'd better be going."

"What do you mean, going?"

"Later, Abby." Albert was already a yellow blur. Before I could react, he was halfway down the block.

"What's with this city?" I wailed. "Folks pop in and pop out like characters in a stage play."

The mockingbird resumed singing.

Sergeant Albergeria may have had Portuguese ancestors, but she was as southern as biscuits and red-eye gravy.

"Ma'am, are you all right?"

I nodded and then shook my head. "No, actually I'm not. My aunt's house—I mean, my house—has been totally vandalized."

Sergeant Albergeria gave her partner, Sergeant Polk, a meaningful look. Sergeant Polk cleared his throat.

"With your permission, ma'am, I'd like to go inside and have a look around."

"Look away," I said, "but be careful. The perpetrator might still be in there."

The officers exchanged glances.

"Well, that's what you call criminals, isn't it? Per-petrators?"

"Right." Sergeant Albergeria put her hand gently on my elbow. "Ma'am, maybe we should talk in the squad car. We'll have more privacy that way."

I was about to resist, if not resent, the suggestion, but I noticed a flock of tourists headed our way. They were being led, wouldn't you know, by the woman with the bouquet for a hat. I could hear her high-pitched voice a block away.

"The car would be fine," I said.

I let Sergeant Albergeria steer me to the car, which was parked under an oak tree directly in front of my house. Overhead the mockingbird sang his heart out.

"Front seat or back?" I asked.

She smiled. Up until then she had been merely a pretty girl with chestnut hair and calm gray eyes. Now she was fascinating. Sergeant Albergeria had two rows of teeth, top and bottom.

"Up front. Unless we both sit in back. But that would look a little kooky, wouldn't it?"

"Yeah." I climbed into the right front of the car. "Fire away."

"I beg your pardon?"

"Well, don't you have a million questions to ask, like 'Did you leave the door unlocked? Did you in-vite strangers in? What special insurance policies do you have?' That kind of thing."

"Hmm. You sound a bit cynical."

"Forgive me, but I date a police detective. No one is beyond suspicion."

Sergeant Albergeria laughed, giving me an even better view of her chompers. Surely she was a den-tist's best friend.

"I just want you to tell me what happened in your own words. I'll let my partner do the interrogating."

"Well, in that case, it's very simple. I inherited this house from my aunt, who drowned in her bathtub New Year's Eve. I know that sounds strange, but that's what happened."

The sergeant nodded. "I remember the case. It was eventually ruled accidental, right?"

"Heart attack. But I'd still like to know what color the champagne was."

"I beg your pardon?"

"You haven't been inside yet, or you'd know. My aunt wouldn't be caught dead in anything but pink. Anyway, I live up in Charlotte, but I came down to settle the estate. I'd never been in the house until this morning. My mother came with me to check it out, and I swear everything was fine. But then I returned just a few minutes ago to find the place looking like I'd rented it out to a college fraternity."

She jotted something down on a clipboard. "How long were you gone?"

"About three hours."

"Where is your mother?"

"I don't know—*What*? You don't understand! Mama and June Cleaver are one and the same. She irons her cotton panties, for crying out loud. She'd rather have a root canal than—" I clamped a small hand over a very big mouth. How insensitive could one get?

Sergeant Albergeria didn't seem to notice my gaffe. "I have an aunt like that. She irons socks. Okay, where were we? Was there any sign of forced entry?"

I shook my head. "I don't really know. The front

door was locked, but it is such a mess in there I didn't even think to check the back door."

"I see. Okay, here's one of the questions I'm sure you've been anticipating. Does someone besides you have a key?"

I shrugged, which is not the same as lying. I didn't want to get young Amanda into trouble. Not for playing the piano. Nor did I want to see Moriah Johnson, my aunt's niece by marriage, suffer. Not only can loose lips sink ships, mine have been known to sink entire armadas.

"Did your mother have a key?"

"No, and I thought we settled that. Besides, any number of people could have had keys—neighbors, friends, you name it."

"You're right about that. Some folks even give keys to—"

A loud burst of static drowned out the sergeant's voice. She got on the car phone, and although all I heard was gibberish, she seemed to understand every word. She babbled back, radioed her partner, then turned to me. "We've got to go. Where can we reach you?"

"The Heritage. Tell me, what's going on? Was there a bad accident somewhere?"

"Burglary."

"Oh, please, can I ride along? I promise to stay in the car, if you let me come."

She glanced at the front door and back at me. "I don't think that'd be such a good idea."

"Pretty please? We have a ride-along program back in Charlotte. I've been on it twice and never gotten into any trouble."

"But you formally applied for that, right?"

"Yes, but I'd give my eyeteeth—" I bit my tongue until it bled. It was still bleeding intermittently when I hobbled back into the Heritage.

"You have a visitor," Ashley said immediately.

"My mother?"

"Over in the bar," she whispered. "It's a man."

"Tall, dark, and handsome with a smile capable of putting your eyes out?" This described Greg perfectly—Superman, too, come to think of it, although only Superman could have flown from Charlotte to Savannah that quickly. Still, it never hurts to dream. And I wouldn't mind changing my name to Lois Lane.

Ashley wrinkled her nose, thereby connecting a hundred or more freckles. "He's kind of old. And ugly. I don't think he's your type."

"Did he leave a name?"

"Yeah." She handed me a slip of paper that must have started its life as spit-wad. A telepathic pharmacist couldn't have read what was scrawled on it.

"Jumbo? Does that say Jumbo?"

"Didn't sound like it."

"Jimbo?"

"Nah, not that either. But you can't miss him. Like I said, he's old, and he's got these real thick glasses."

"Kimbro!"

"Yeah, that's it. Hey, he's not really your boyfriend, is he? I mean, if he is, I take back what I said."

"Relax, dear, he's not my boyfriend. He's my lawyer."

"Your lawyer?" The freckles on the girl's forehead came together in orange stripes.

"Just business."

I thanked Ashley and before she asked any more questions lit out for the bar. To get there I had to cross the lobby, which meant plowing through a mass of milling teenagers. The boys were wearing tuxedos, and the girls were all decked out in identical floor-length black velveteen dresses. It was only four o'clock in the afternoon, for Pete's sake. I tried to imagine the occasion. A choral group? A prom for Moonies? The annual convention of Junior Undertakers of America?

Despite their formal wear, the kids were anything but decorous. The boys pushed and snapped each other's suspenders. The girls hissed like stray toms, or was that hair spray I smelled? There was such a high concentration of hormones that by the time I crossed the room even I had a face full of zits.

I spotted Dewayne Kimbro sitting by the window. He seemed startled to see me, but being a proper southern gentleman, he immediately found his feet.

"Sorry about the pimples, Mr. Kimbro. Who knew they were so contagious?"

"Uh—I just didn't expect you to show up. I mean, you weren't in. I had no idea how long you'd be out."

"Well, I'm here now."

"Please sit," he said, and remained standing until my fanny kissed the chair. "Can I get you something to drink."

"That would be nice. What are you having?"

"A Bloody Mary. Somehow it seems healthier, what with the tomato juice, celery stick and all— especially so early in the day."

I chuckled. "In that case I'll have a Bailey's Irish Creme. Isn't the milk mustache a symbol of good bones?"

He nodded absently, his face turned to the river below. There weren't any passing freighters, and I didn't see any dolphins. And—praise God, hallelujah—I didn't see C.J. or Wynnell thrashing about either.

"So, what's this all about?" I asked brightly.

"Miss Timberlake, I'm afraid I haven't been entirely forthcoming."

"I beg your pardon?"

"There is something important I feel obligated to tell you."

"That you're in love with me?" It was of course a joke, and a stupid one at that. No doubt it had to do with the lingering hormones I'd picked up in the lobby.

He turned in my direction, but I still couldn't see his eyes, thanks to the light that came glancing through the window. I was grateful for that.

"It regards your aunt's will."

I prayed that my gasp had been felt only and not heard. "It's valid, isn't it?"

"Yes, ma'am. It will stand up in any court of law."

"So, what's the problem?"

"It's not a legal problem, ma'am. I guess it's more of a moral dilemma."

"*What* is?" I wanted to grab him by his white lapels and shake him like a James Bond martini.

"You see, ma'am, for years your aunt had another will."

"Of course. She was married."

I think he stared at me. "To my knowledge your aunt never married."

"Yes, she did. She married—" I caught myself just in time. If Aunt Lula Mae's scandalous marriage had been forgotten, then who was I to bring it up? "What

I mean to say is, what does an earlier will have to do with me?"

Dewayne Kimbro folded his massive hands around a half-empty glass. Perhaps he sensed that if the waitress didn't take my order soon, I was going to ask him to share.

"Ma'am, I just want to see that the right thing is done."

"By whom?" My mouth was so dry you could plant cactus in there.

Dewayne Kimbro took his sweet time before answering. "I'm afraid I might have some bad news," he finally said.

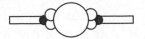

15

"What bad news?"

Tiffany, our cocktail waitress, chose that moment to make her appearance. Although I had no designs on Dewayne Kimbro, it still irritated me to see Tiffany giggle and jiggle far more than was necessary to get a good tip. I couldn't help placing my order with a scowl.

"Spill it, dear," I snapped as Tiffany waggled off. If I didn't watch myself, I was going to end up every bit as tart-tongued as Magdalena Yoder, an innkeeper I once met up in Pennsylvania.

'Well." Dewayne cleared his throat. "I don't know where you are on the integration issue, but . . ."

"I have no problem with integration," I said, and then, dreading what was surely to come, tried to make a joke. "If Yankees don't mind moving in next to me, then I don't mind them."

"I'm not talking about Yankees," he said, not cracking a smile. "I'm talking about coloreds."

"Excuse me?"

"Blacks, then. African-Americans. Your aunt— well, she was involved with one."

"I know."

"Oh?"

"Yes, in fact I think she married him. And just for the record, Mr. Kimbro, it doesn't bother me a bit. I

151

don't know how long your people have lived in the South, but I bet if you shook my family tree, more than a few dark-skinned folks would fall out. I doubt that few or any of the so-called best families are lily white. I know for a fact that my great-great-grandmother was Cherokee."

"You may be right. Please don't misunderstand me. I'm not prejudiced or anything like that. I just didn't know how you'd take the news."

"Perhaps it's time you told me," I said through gritted teeth. "Let's see."

He drained the last of his Bloody Mary. "In her first will, your aunt left everything to—uh—a certain Amanda Gabrenas."

"The budding pianist?"

"You know about her?"

"Yes, I met her this morning. At the house. She's a very talented young woman. Tell me, why did my aunt change her mind? And what does this have to do with race?"

He cleared his throat again. Despite the thickness of his lenses, I could tell he was looking desperately at Tiffany, who incidentally appeared to be flirting with the bartender.

"Miss Gabrenas is—uh—African-American."

"She most certainly is not."

I think he blinked. "Your aunt seemed to think so."

"There must be some mistake. Amanda is as white as you or I. Not that it matters in the least to me, Mr. Kimbro. Amanda could be blue for all I care. However, I would like to know why my aunt changed her will."

"Amanda's mother found out about the will and wouldn't have it. Said if your aunt didn't drop

Amanda from the will, she was pulling her out of Juilliard."

"Wow! That's incredible. Why would she do that?"

Dewayne Kimbro shrugged. "I don't know. But I got to feeling bad about that. I know your aunt was putting her through school. Now that your aunt's dead—well—I guess young Amanda had to drop out of school, didn't she?"

"Yes, she did." I sighed. "Okay, so now I feel guilty too. I tell you what, I'll help her look into scholarships."

He smiled. "That would be right nice of you."

Tiffany sashayed over with our drinks. "Here y'all go. One Bloody Mary—"the woman bobbled her breasts in Dewayne's face—"and one White Russian."

"I asked for a Bailey's," I said calmly.

"Yeah, right. But a White Russian has Kahlúa in it. I like it a lot better."

"Then you drink it. Bring me the Bailey's."

"Geesh!" Tiffany stomped off, her knickers, if indeed she wore any, in a knot.

I smiled at Dewayne. "Please allow me to leave the tip."

He actually chuckled. "I had a waiter serve me fish once. Tried to tell me it was chicken."

"That's funny. Mr. Kimbro—"

"Please call me Dewayne."

"All right," I said, but didn't offer him an "Abby" in return. The man was holding something back, and it irked me. "Dewayne, I'd like to return briefly to the matter of my aunt's will."

"Like I said before, Miss Timberlake, I'm sure it will stand."

"I'm not worried about that. What I want to know is why my aunt then picked me as her beneficiary. Why not some charity? Why not just establish a scholarship at Juilliard if she wanted to help Amanda so badly?"

Dewayne took a long slip through one of those narrow cocktail straws. "She had just celebrated a significant birthday—her seventy-fifth, I think—and was feeling a need to reconnect to her birth family. I suggested she change the beneficiary to you and your brother."

"That was very nice of you, Dewayne. By the way, why *wasn't* my brother Toy included?"

"Your aunt heard through the grapevine that he was a ne'er-do-well. Your aunt couldn't abide fools."

"Amen to that." Of course, I felt guilty, now that Toy was no longer a ne'er-do-well but a wannabe man of the cloth. Although whether or not he actually became a priest remained to be seen. Always a poor student, Toy somehow managed to get admitted to a medical school in the Caribbean but dropped out the first week of classes when he was assigned a cadaver. Since then my brother has dropped in and out of a chef school, clown school, two art academies, and the U.S. army. He's held more minimum wage jobs than a boatload of refugees, and to my knowledge has never stuck with any long enough to get a raise—well, except for his last job, parking cars out in Hollywood at some highfalutin restaurant.

Dewayne sucked the last of his drink with a loud slurp. I, on the other hand, had yet to see my Bailey's.

"Miss Timberlake, I'd like to change the subject altogether, if you don't mind."

"Ah, you want to talk about your fee, right?"

"No, ma'am. Your aunt took care of all that. I was wondering if you'd seen the movie *Titanic*."

"Most of it."

"You didn't like it?"

"I loved it, but I made the mistake of buying a large soft drink along with my popcorn. The last hour or so I did a better job of floating than the ship in question. It was hard to concentrate."

"I hear the musical is playing over at Oglethorpe Mall."

"There's a musical version?"

He nodded. "With dancing. I read somewhere they lost several of the dancers in that final deck scene. At any rate, I was thinking of seeing it tonight and was wondering if I might have the pleasure of your company."

"That's a very nice offer Mr. Kim—I mean, Dewayne, but I'm seeing someone back home."

"Why is it the best ones are always taken?"

Fortunately it was a rhetorical question. Nevertheless I shrugged and chuckled appropriately.

"No, I mean it, Miss Timberlake. A nice, pretty woman like you—of course you'd be taken. But why is it I never meet someone like you *before* they're taken? This someone you're seeing back home—I bet he's really good-looking, isn't he?"

I knew where this conversation was headed and made a snap decision to head it off at the pass. "It's a *she*. And she's gorgeous."

Dewayne Kimbro recoiled in surprise. "Oh?"

Tiffany the barmaid inadvertently came to my rescue by plunking the Bailey's in front of me. Bless her pea-picking little heart.

*   *   *

The mysterious mob of bedecked teenagers had disappeared, perhaps beamed up by their mother ship. At any rate, I was able to cross the lobby without further exacerbating my acne. I had just pushed the elevator button when I heard the now familiar voice of Ashley.

"Oh, Miss Timberlake. One minute, please."

I watched the doors open to reveal an empty car and, alas, close again. I watched Ashley leave her post behind the counter and trot over to me. She was much younger than I, after all.

"Miss Timberlake," the big girl said, slightly out of breath, "you have a message."

"I do?" I glanced at Ashley's empty hands.

"Not a written one. Your mother called while you were in the bar talking to Mr. Kimbo."

"That's Kimbro, dear. What did my mother have to say? And why didn't she just leave it on the answering machine in my room?"

Ashley smiled. "She says she hates machines."

I nodded. That was Mama, all right. The woman doesn't own an answering machine or a VCR or even an electric can opener. She does push a dilapidated old Hoover around—wearing her pearls, of course—but her vacuum was manufactured back in the days when a man by the same name was wearing dresses and running the F.B.I.

"What's the message?"

Ashley could have written it down, but apparently it was more fun to screw one's features into a semblance of deep concentration. It was certainly more dramatic.

"Let's see. She said to tell you she'd met some old friends—one was a Mrs. Williams, I think—and they'd decided to drive down to Saint Simons Island."

"Saint Simons Island? How far is that?"

Ashley shrugged. "I've never been there. But I don't think it's that far. Maybe an hour or two south of here. Anyway, your mother said to tell you not to worry in case they decide to spend the night."

"Spend the night?"

"That's what she said. She said if they really liked it, it might be two nights. Hey, you're not worried, are you? 'Cause your mother seems like a really cool woman."

"She's cool, all right." I paused to let the dripping sarcasm puddle at my feet. "And no, I'm not worried, but I *am* annoyed. If she calls again when I'm not in, tell her I'm going back home day after tomorrow at the latest. If she's not back in time—well, she's just going to have to find a ride home with Mrs. Williams or whomever. I am not a taxi service."

"Yes, ma'am, I'll tell her that."

"And if you see either of my two friends, tell them—"

"Tell us what?"

I whirled. C.J. was standing at my elbow. A careless gesture and I might well have poked her in the knees.

"If you ladies will excuse me . . ." Ashley backed away a few steps and then practically sprinted to the desk.

I pushed the elevator button again. "Where's Wynnell?"

"Ooh, Abby, you're not going to believe what happened to Wynnell."

"Try me."

"She ran off with that group of tourists. You

know, the ones who were taking our picture by the statue of the Waving Girl."

"The tourists from Tokyo?"

C.J. nodded. "I don't want to be too hard on you, Abby, but I think you went overboard that time."

"No, that was you two," I said, and giggled.

"I'm serious, Abby. You told the tourists Wynnell was Linda Tripp and I was Monica Lewinsky."

The elevator arrived, and I ushered C.J. in. "That was only a joke, dear," I said as I pushed our floor. "Nobody took me seriously."

"The tourists did. They all wanted my autograph, and some of the men even wanted—well, you know what. It was humiliating."

"I'm sure they were just joking, dear. They had to have known that I was. You don't look anything like Monica."

"Yeah, but Wynnell does look sort of like Linda Tripp."

"Linda is prettier," I said, and clamped a hand over my mouth.

We reached our floor, and the door opened. "But Abby, it's like Wynnell suddenly started believing she was Linda Tripp. The guide asked her if she wanted to join his tour, and she accepted. You don't think she hit her head on something when she fell in the river, do you?"

"No, I do not! Wynnell said I'd pay for my practical joke, and that's exactly what she's trying to do. She—"

"Oh, my God!" C.J. said.

I screamed as icy talons dug deep into my arm.

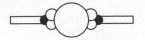

16

"**D**iamond!"

The old woman cackled. "Got you scared real good this time, didn't I, child?"

I staggered to the wall and slumped against it.

"Yes, ma'am, I got you real good."

"You scare me like that again," I panted, "and all the mojo in the world isn't going to protect your scrawny neck."

"Hush, child. It you that be in trouble, not me." Diamond aimed a claw in C.J.'s direction. "Who might you be?"

C.J. thrust a hand forward. "I'm Jane Cox from Shelby, North Carolina, but all my friends call me C.J."

Diamond gave C.J. the once-over. "That ain't enough name for a girl like you. Crystal, that's how I sees you."

C.J. grinned. "Crystal what?"

"Ain't no need for no other name 'sides Crystal." Diamond turned back to me. "Where your mama?"

"She must have heard you were coming," I said naughtily, "because she's skipped town."

"Where to?"

"Saint Simons Island."

Diamond nodded, and the chicken foot and black

leather pouch bobbled between her sagging breasts. "Good. She safe, then."

C.J. sucked in her breath sharply and then exhaled hard enough to blow out a candle at ten paces. "Ooh, but she isn't."

I straightened. "What?"

C.J. looked at Diamond, back at me, and then at the floor. "I had a dream last night, Abby. Your mama started out looking like she always does—you know, short, dark like you only prettier, puffy skirt, pearls—"

"I know what Mama looks like," I wailed.

Diamond put a finger to her lips. "Shh. Let the child be. I have me a feeling this girl have the second sight."

C.J. grinned, needlessly encouraged. "Like I was saying, your mama started out like her regular self and suddenly she turned into this little dog. Only it being a dream and all, that didn't seem to bother me one bit. Anyway, I walk over to scratch her ears, but the next thing I know she's in one of those carrying cases. Well, I stick my finger through the wire mesh to scratch her anyway, but—well, it was just too awful."

"But *what?*" I screamed.

C.J. was no longer grinning; in fact she looked close to tears. "She was dead."

"*Dead?* Are you sure?"

"Well, not exactly."

I would have grabbed C.J. and shaken her like the paint mixer at Home Depot, but Diamond's claws had found my arm again. "Don't," she said, reading my mind. "This child is something special."

"So is a case of the plague! C.J., finish your sentence!"

"That's Crystal," C.J. said, and tossed her dish-water blond hair saucily.

"Crystal, *please*," I begged. "What happened to Mama? What do you mean by 'not exactly'?"

"Well, okay, since you're using the right name, I'll tell you. It wasn't a dog anymore in that carrying cage, it was a bird. A kind of sparrow, I guess. And it was dead."

I turned to Diamond. "Well, that's not so bad, is it? I mean, what does dreaming about a dead bird prove?"

Diamond fingered the chicken foot. Her dark eyes were barely visible under the broad rim of her straw hat, but what I did manage to see in them didn't look good.

"Dead birds is bad omens."

"Ha!" I said bravely. "Then what about Thanksgiving? Turkeys are birds, and roast turkey is not a bad omen."

"It was for the Indians," C.J., aka Crystal, opined. "Look what happened to them."

"Give me a break," I growled. "The Pilgrims didn't even eat turkey that first Thanksgiving."

"They did so. I studied that in school."

"Don' matter," Diamond said. "That don' change what is, and it sure don' change what to come. Only one thing change what to come."

I may have snorted, but I assure you it was in a ladylike manner. "And what would that be? Some low country voodoo spell?"

"Ain't nothing wrong with *good* juju. But first I got to have me another talk with Miss Amy."

"Your little ghost friend?"

C.J.'s eyes widened. "You have a ghost friend? Ooh, cool!"

Diamond nodded. "Miss Amy done crossed over. She know everything—well, most everything. She know all the best juju."

I glanced up and down the hall. Not even a housekeeping cart in sight. Still, it was the hardly the place to be talking about spirits and spells. Not if we objected to wearing white straitjackets before Easter.

"Ladies, do you mind if we take this conversation elsewhere? We can talk just as well inside the room as we can out here."

Of course they ignored me.

"Can I meet Miss Amy?" C.J. begged.

Diamond sank her nails into C.J. for a change. "Don' see why not. You have the gift, child. Don' you be forgetting that. You have the second sight."

"But very little foresight," I quipped.

I could feel both women glare. Diamond waggled a finger, presidential style, in my face.

"This girl something special. Don' you be giving her no grief." Diamond turned back to C.J. "Y'all meet me tomorrow morning in Bonaventure Cemetery. Ten o'clock. Section N. Corner of Wiltberger Way and Bonaventure. They's what looks to be a little Greek temple. That Miss Amy's home."

I couldn't help but smile. "Do we ring the bell?"

C.J. gasped. "Abby! Don't be rude!"

There is no rational explanation for what happened next. The best I can do is postulate that the elevator door opened at just the right time and Diamond somehow managed to slip into it unnoticed. One second she was standing there, just as much flesh and blood as you and I, and the next second— poof! She was gone.

"Ooh, Abby, now see what you've done!"

I whirled to look around. I even grabbed C.J. and looked behind her.

"*Me?* I had nothing to do with it, I swear. Besides, you're the one with the second sight. You should still be seeing her, right?"

"And now you're making fun of *me!*" C.J. stomped off to our room.

But thanks to her dunk in the brink, C.J. had lost her key, and I had to let her in. Let the record show that I refrained from pointing out that a truly clairvoyant person wouldn't have fallen into a river in the first place, and what's more, she wouldn't have picked an insensitive friend like me.

We freshened up. In the time it took C.J. to shower and change clothes, she'd forgiven me. The woman was born with a generous soul.

My son, Charlie, was born with a generous soul. When he was four, I accidentally backed over his Big Wheels tricycle, which he'd left lying in the driveway. My apologies were, of course, profuse. But somehow I felt even worse when Charlie, his big brown eyes streaming with tears, said in a small voice, "Mama, I forgive you."

I was born with an average soul. I am reasonably slow to anger and only slow to forgive when the wounding party is unrepentant. For my own sake I try to forgive my ex-husband Buford on a daily basis for cheating on me with that bimbo, Tweetie. Some days it is harder to forgive than others.

At least I'm not mean-spirited like that innkeeper Magdalena Yoder, up in Pennsylvania. That woman's tongue is so sharp it can slice cheese. If Buford had been married to her, he'd be grated Parmesan by now.

At any rate, in keeping with her generous nature, C.J. agreed to accompany me for the rest of the day without first even hearing my agenda. Of course, all this generosity comes with a price, and I knew I would have to humor her. No doubt Diamond had created a monster.

"Ooh, goody," C.J. said, when I told her our first stop was my new house. "I can't wait to see its aura."

"Houses don't have auras, dear."

"Yes, they do. My Granny Ledbetter's house back in Shelby has a lavender aura."

"I think you mean odor, dear."

"I know what I mean, Abby. The house is encircled by a pale purple haze. Granny and I are the only ones that see it."

I bit my already sore tongue in the interest of friendship. By the time C.J. and I arrived at my inheritance on Gaston Street, I was talking with a sieve.

"Ooh, Abby," C.J. gasped, "this house has a bright pink aura."

We were still outside, standing on the sidewalk, and trust me, I hadn't said a word about my aunt's monochromatic decor. Either the girl was incredibly lucky, or I needed to keep a more open mind.

"You're sure it's pink? I think I see a green mist."

Fortunately C.J. missed the sarcasm dripping from my punctured lingua. "No, it's definitely pink. But something's not right. Something horrible happened in there."

"You can say that again. I meant to tell you, but some time today—early this afternoon, probably—someone tore the place up. It looks like a teenager's room in there."

C.J. shook her head. "Not that. It has to do with your aunt."

I hung my head in shame. "Yes, of course. You know that my aunt died in there. Drowned in a bathtub full of champagne on New Year's Eve."

"Yeah, that's it! She was murdered."

"Sorry, dear, but this time you're wrong. The coroner ruled it natural causes. Her heart just gave out on her, and she drowned."

"Coroners can be wrong, Abby."

"True, but—well, never mind. Let's go inside."

"Ooh, Abby, I can't go in there."

"Yes, you can. You just follow me up these steps, through the front door and—presto, bingo—there you are! Inside!"

"But the aura! Abby, this is a very disturbed house."

"Then you'll feel right at home, dear." I clamped a hand over my mouth.

"You shouldn't go in there either, Abby. It's not safe."

"Nonsense. Besides, I have no choice." I climbed the first four steps. "There's a treasure hidden in there someplace, and I think I know where to look."

C.J. took the first step. "What kind of treasure?"

"Old coins. Maybe an entire collection."

I climbed two more steps, as did C.J. "What type of coins? Foreign or domestic?"

"Early American pennies."

C.J. sighed. "Well, if you're sure you have to go in, and if there's nothing I can do to stop you . . ."

"Not a thing, dear."

The dear woman grabbed my hand—as much for her comfort as for mine—and followed me in. I found it remarkable she seemed neither surprised nor dismayed at the devastation. I, on the hand, found it even more upsetting the second time; it was worse than I'd remembered. Perhaps C.J.'s youth made her oblivious to such disorder.

"Where's the loot?" she practically demanded.

I brushed away a stubborn tear. "Well, I was sitting next to this woman on the trolley who has a cat— Never mind that. I think it might be hidden up the chimney."

"Ooh, Abby, that's awful!"

"It is?"

C.J. nodded vigorously. "Everyone knows that reaching up chimneys is bad luck. If the treasure is up there, we're going to have to just let it be."

"Cut the crap!"

C.J.'s head froze in midnod, like a windup toy with a faulty spring.

"Sorry, dear, but I don't have time for superstition."

"This isn't superstition, Abby. My Granny Ledbetter stuck her arm up a chimney, and now she only has one arm."

"I suppose a gremlin or something bit it off."

"No, the gremlin bit her toe, but that's okay now— although you can still see the little teeth marks."

"Her arm!" I screamed. "What happened to her arm?"

"A spider." C.J. shuddered. "A brown recluse spider. Granny hadn't used that particular fireplace in a long time, and who knows how old that spider was. It was huge, I'll tell you that. As big as a saucer."

I had been about to thrust my right arm up the flue. I clamped it to my side and took a step back.

"It may have been a big spider, dear, but it

couldn't have bitten off her arm." There may have been just a hint of uncertainty to my voice.

"No, silly, of course it didn't bite off her arm. In fact, she didn't even feel the bite. But a couple of hours after she stuck her arm up the chimney, it started to blister, and she ran a real high fever." C.J. paused to pick her nose.

"*And?*"

"And, well, Granny Ledbetter has always been sort of hard-headed, and she wouldn't go to the doctor. Not that the doctor could have done a whole lot. There isn't any specific antidote for brown recluse spider bites. You know of course that the area around the bite rots."

"Come again?"

"The tissue dies, and the surrounding flesh rots. That's what happened to Granny's arm. By the time she went to the doctor, there was this huge hole and—well, they had to amputate."

I sat weakly on the hearth—but on the very edge. Spiders and I have never gotten along. Little Miss Muffet was not a coward in my book, although I personally prefer to confront arachnids. I face off with shoes, brooms, bug spray—whatever it takes. If you ask me, Garfield has the right idea. The only good spider is a dead one.

C.J. sat beside me and laid an arm across my shoulders. "Cheer up, Abby," she said, not at all cheerfully. "Maybe the treasure is hidden some-where else."

"You've got the second sight," I wailed. "Is the treasure hidden somewhere else?"

C.J. sniffed the air, like Mama does when she senses trouble. No doubt that's where she got the idea.

"I don't smell anything."

"Nothing?" I don't have a first, much less second, sense, but I would have been willing to bet money there was a valuable coin collection hidden somewhere in the house and most probably in the fireplace. "Dust to dust, *ashes to ashes*." What other clues did I need? Handwriting on a wall?

"Well, to be perfectly frank, Abby, did you shower today?"

"How rude!"

"Sorry, Abby. You've gone and got me depressed, and when I'm depressed, things just kind of slip out."

"Why are *you* depressed? It isn't your inheritance that's in a shambles."

C.J.'s sigh rustled the pink drapes across the room. "Because you got me remembering Granny and the spider and—well, I blame myself."

"Whatever for?"

"Well, Granny asked me to bring her a glove— you know, one of those long kind that comes clear up to the elbow? Anyway, I was too lazy to get off my rocker and go get it."

"I'm afraid you've lost me, dear."

"Don't you see? If Granny had been wearing a glove, she wouldn't have been bitten. It's all my fault. Now Granny has to do her pushups with just one arm."

"Nonsense," I said firmly. "Your granny could have gotten her own glove. But you know, a glove isn't a bad idea. I wonder if Aunt Lula Mae—Wait a minute! You stay right here!"

I ran to the kitchen and returned a moment later sporting a hot-pink oven mitten. Given my small frame, the thick protective glove came all the way up to my elbow.

C.J. smiled weakly. "You're smart, Abby."

"It was you who gave me the idea, dear. Thanks."

C.J. brightened. "Any time."

"And thanks for being such a good friend, C.J."

"My name is Crystal now, Abby. Did you forget?"

"No, dear."

I know from experience that often the best way to get through an unpleasant experience is to plunge right in. I met Buford at a water park, and that summer I got to be an expert on the merits of jumping into cold water rather than taking it an inch at a time. The fact that after all this jumping I ended up in hot water is irrelevant.

"Here goes nothing!" I cried, and with eyes closed tightly, thrust my arm up the chimney.

It was hard to feel through the thick, quilted fabric. I patted and pawed at the brick surface, and I could hear soot as it hit the grate beside me. I was beginning to think that with an arm as short as mine I was going to have to practically crawl up into the chimney when I felt the ledge.

"Eureka!"

"Did you find treasure?" C.J. must have gotten down on all fours, because I felt her head bump my stomach.

"Not yet. I found—"

I heard the snap of powerful jaws before I felt their pinch. And then I felt nothing.

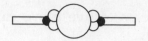

17

"**O**oh, Abby, you're awake!"

I closed my eyes and struggled back into unconsciousness. I didn't want to see the hand that had been bitten by Miss Muffet's mugger. Perhaps Granny Ledbetter could live a happy, productive life with just one arm, but I needed two. I may be small, even tiny by some folks' standards, but I do a great deal of lifting and carrying in my profession. Besides, as soon I got the answers to a few more questions, I was headed straight back to Charlotte and the comforting arms of Greg Washburn. I would need at least two arms to wrap around Greg; given our relative sizes, four would have been even better.

"Ooh, Abby," C.J. wailed, "please wake up again. I left my smelling salts at home, but I could breathe on you. I had a liverwurst and onion sandwich for lunch at—"

"Don't you dare!" I opened one eye. "How bad is it?"

"They're very good. It's better on pumpernickel bread of course, but all they had was white. And beer. You gotta wash it down with beer."

"Not the damn sandwich, you idiot! My hand! How is my *hand*?"

"There is nothing wrong with your hand, Abby.

But your mouth could use a little work. Honestly, you never used to be so rude."

I was lying flat on my back on Aunt Lula Mae's— no, make that *my*—pink shag carpet. Forcing both peepers open, I slowly brought my right hand to where I could see it. It certainly appeared normal.

Not quite convinced, I wiggled my fingers. There were still five of them, and all five moved. They didn't even hurt. I brought the hand so close to my face I could barely focus, but couldn't find a single tooth mark.

"Where's the spider?"

"What spider?"

"The one that chomped down on my hand." To my credit, I said this calmly and swallowed all the epithets that came to mind.

To her credit, C.J. laughed like a single hyena on steroids and not the entire pack. "Ooh, Abby, you're so silly! It wasn't a spider, it was this!" She waved the pink oven mitt above my face. From it dangled a mousetrap.

"What?"

"Nothing bit you, Abby. It was just this silly old mousetrap. But it's a good thing you were wearing this mitt, huh? And it's a good thing I was right there with you to break your fall when you fainted."

"That's it? I was attacked by a mousetrap?"

She nodded. "Just think of the little life you probably saved."

I sat up, the proverbial egg of embarrassment dripping from my face. This happens with such regularity, it's a wonder my cholesterol level isn't though the roof.

"Well," I said, "I guess there's no fool like an old fool. Do me a favor, C.J., and don't tell anyone—

especially Greg—about this little incident. I'll never live it down."

C.J. patted my back with her free hand. "Don't worry, Abby, you can count on me. But the name is Crystal now, remember? You know, I was just thinking, maybe I should get a big crystal ball. Since I have the second sight and all, I could tell fortunes. Every time a customer buys an antique from my shop, they get a free look-see into the ball. What do you think? "

"It is certainly a novel idea, dear."

C.J.—I mean, Crystal—squealed with delight. "Ooh, Abby, I'm so excited. I'm even going to change the name of my shop. Crystal Solutions! What do you think of that?"

"It's definitely unique."

"And because you're such a good friend, Abby, I'll read your fortune anytime you want. You don't even have to buy anything."

"Thank you, dear." I struggled painfully to my feet. I may have landed on my friend, but she's okay. "Well, I guess I should face the truth. There probably isn't any hidden treasure, and even if there is, we're never going to find it."

"Don't you think we should at least do what the note says?"

"What note?" I asked patiently. Lordy, but I couldn't wait to get back home and to the craziness of paying customers.

"The note that was attached to the mousetrap." C.J. shoved her hand into a pocket of her jeans and pulled out a wad of paper. "I was going to show this to you the minute you came to—honest."

I snatched the paper from her. The handwriting was the same as that on the note in the urn.

Good thinking, it read. *Now look in the piano.*

I slapped a petite palm to my forehead. "The piano!"

Suddenly it all made sense. Coin collections are often stored in flat books. They're not kept in bags, like pirate's treasure. Stupid me! I'd been visualizing a cloth sack or maybe a leather pouch with a drawstring!

I flew to the piano. The massive lid was open, and there was of course nothing inside that space but air. Whoever ransacked the place wasn't stupid.

"Damn it! This really ticks me off. I should know better than to get my hopes up."

C.J. peered into the piano. "Maybe it's under the sounding board."

"Say what?"

"Under that." She pointed to a solid metal plate that covered the bottom of the entire space.

"C.J.—Crystal—that's bolted down. We'd need special tools, and even then, I doubt if we could lift that plate."

"Don't be silly, Abby. I can get those nuts off."

"How?"

"With these." C.J. held out her hands. "Granny loves pecan pie, but she's too cheap to buy a nutcracker. I've been shelling pecans with my bare hands since I was six. These"—she nodded at the piano—"are only nuts of a different kind."

Without further ado my loyal friend demonstrated her hands of steel. She twisted off the large metal nuts with as much ease as I unscrew my toothpaste cap.

"Well done, dear, but now what? King Kong couldn't lift that thing."

C.J. leaned well over the edge of the boxing,

spread her gargantuan arms, and with a grunt that would have made King Kong proud, hoisted the incredibly heavy plate above her head. I gaped stupidly, then started praying madly that she'd set the damn thing down before we both were killed.

"You see, Abby? Don't ever say never. Granny always—" C.J. started to teeter under the weight and then, like Goliath hit between the eyes by David's stone, fell backward with a resounding crash.

Actually it was the sounding board that made most of the noise. The entire house shook when it hit the floor, and whatever subflooring lay beneath the pink shag was undoubtedly badly dented. C.J., bless her pecan-crushing neck, managed to land on a hot-pink sofa.

"Sorry, Abby," she panted. "I used to carry Granny's hogs to market, but that thing weighs a sight more than one of those hogs."

I should have been at C.J.'s side, a look of intense concern in my eyes. Instead, and it shames me to say this, I was already staring into the belly of the pink baby grand.

"Don't be sorry," I screamed. "I'm rich!"

We opened the genuine leather portfolios and spread them across the righted dining room table. There were twenty-eight of these books, each holding a dozen coins. All of the books were filled, except for one, which contained eleven coins.

For the better part of an hour we oohed (something at which C.J. was particularly good) and ahed. We even slobbered a little, although we were careful not to get it on the coins. Finally it was time to take some action.

"My kingdom for a cell phone," I moaned.

C.J. giggled. "How much is one really worth to you?"

"You *have* one?" I knew C.J. had phones in both her shop and her house, but you'd never know it by the way the girl acted. She was forever stopping by to use mine.

"Of course, silly. Granny Ledbetter gave me one when I moved to Charlotte."

I held the frown only briefly, since they are known to cause wrinkles. "C.J., dear—"

"Ah, ah, ah! It's Crystal now."

"Crystal," I hissed, "I'd be mighty obliged if you'd quit calling me silly."

"Sorry, Abby."

"So," I hissed again, "can I borrow your damn phone or not?"

C.J. fished around in a fringed leather handbag and finally located an instrument smaller than a bread roll. "You may use it, Abby, but you really ought to get one of your own."

"They cause cancer," I snapped and snatched the phone from her hand.

"Who are you calling?"

"Albert Quarles, a local numismatist."

"Don't, Abby."

"I beg your pardon?"

"Don't call him. C.J. reached for the phone, which I deftly switched to the other hand. She tried again with no luck. Still, it was like playing keep-away with Wilt Chamberlain.

"*Crystal*, dear, a numismatist is—"

"I know what one is, Abby, but you shouldn't call this man."

"Excuse me?"

"I have a bad feeling about this man."

"But you've never met him, have you? Wait a cotton-picking minute! This isn't that so-called second sense of yours, is it?"

She nodded vigorously. "When you said his name, I felt chills run up my spine."

"That's because the heat in here has been turned off for months."

"It's seventy degrees outside, Abby. No, I felt a definite psychic premonition."

"Well, I didn't, and I'm going to call him."

Even a bad driver could have parked a stretch limo on C.J.'s lower lip. "Don't you believe me, Abby?"

"I believe *you* believe, dear, and that's all that really matters, isn't it? I mean, I'm an Episcopalian, and you don't even go to church. Okay, so maybe that's not a good analogy. But you get my drift, don't you?"

C.J. shrugged. "It still hurts my feelings."

"I'm sorry, dear. If that's the way you feel, I'll go find a phone. Better yet, I'll take the collection over to Mr. Quarles's house. It's probably much safer there anyway. You never know when whoever did this"—I waved at a kitchen chair that was still overturned—"will decide to come back and resume searching."

C.J. glanced at the door and sighed. "Okay, but don't say I didn't warn you."

"I won't," I said, already beginning to dial. "I promise."

"And if he tries anything funny, I'll put a hex—"

Albert Quarles must have shared the gift of second sight, because he answered on the second ring. "Good afternoon."

The unexpected greeting threw me only for a second. "I found the mother lode!"

"Lula Mae Wiggins's fabled collection?"

"It's a beaut," I crowed. "Any chance I could persuade you to come over?"

"I'll be right there!" he said, and hung up.

C.J. actually knew more about old coins than did I. The girl is daft, not dumb. She's also more honest than a roomful of nuns, so I had no qualms about leaving her, salivating over the collection, while I made a very personal trip to the upstairs bathroom.

And no, my trip had nothing to do with bodily functions but everything to do with gratitude. Reverently I entered the bathroom where my aunt had breathed her last. The room was even pinker than the rest of the house, if that's imaginable.

I sat atop the hot-pink mohair-covered toilet lid and contemplated the scene of my aunt's demise. Pink bathtub, pink towels, and pink soap. What had my aunt looked like? Was she a smaller version of my father, with pink lipstick and maybe even pink-tinted hair?

"Auntie Lula Mae, you were really something else, you know that? I wish I could have known you. I think we might have been friends. Even good friends. Lord knows I have friends even crazier than you. Heck, I bet you made Mama seem normal.

"Anyway, thanks for all this—the house, the coin collection, but most of all just being you. It's so neat to know that someone in my family stood up for their beliefs to the point of being ostracized. Although frankly, dear, I think you may have carried it too far. I don't mean about your involvement with a black man—I'm sure my grandparents were none too happy about that—but you could have trusted my daddy more, and you certainly could have trusted me.

"Still, I hope you had a happy life, and I guess when one has to go, there are worse ways then dying in a bathtub of pink champagne. The champagne was pink, wasn't it? And did you drink it while you bathed? Of course not, that would be disgusting. But a nice sharp cheese, some Jarlesburg, maybe—"

The doorbell yanked me from my reverie, and I flew downstairs to answer it before C.J. could put a hex on poor Albert. I got there just in time. C.J. must weigh 50 percent more than I, but I gave her a gentle kick behind the left knee, and she stumbled aside.

"Come in," I said to Albert.

He stepped over the threshold and saw what remained of the piano. "My God! What happened?"

"Maybe you should tell us," C.J. quipped.

I gave my friend a look that would turn even wax grapes into raisins. "C.J., this is Albert Quarles."

Albert properly extended his hand.

"And Albert, this is—"

"Crystal," C.J. snapped. Her hand didn't budge.

I smiled helplessly. "Crystal's doctors are still adjusting her medication."

"Very funny, Abby."

I led Albert into the dining room. C.J. tried clumsily to block us but backed off after I collected a sample of her DNA. Who said long nails were passé on mature women?

Albert, of course, could not believe his eyes. He had to steady himself with both hands as he leaned across the table. Finally I made him sit, lest he faint and scratch any of the coins with the wire rim of his monocle.

"Holy cow!" he said more times than I care to remember. Actually, he used a synonym for cow manure, one which no lady would repeat.

"So, Albert, you're really impressed, are you? I thought you'd be. This really blows *my* mind away— although how would I know? I'm not the one who took drugs in the seventies. Still, if I had to guess what a mind-blowing experience would be like, this would be it." I know, I was babbling like an idiot, and of course I couldn't take any credit for assembling such a fabulous collection, but there you have it. Wealth gives me bursts of adrenaline that Gatorade never could.

Albert placed his monocle carefully on the table beside a portfolio. Without the ridiculous eyepiece he looked mildly attractive. If he shaved the mustache and let his hair grow long enough to hide those ears—what *was* I thinking? Albert was married, for crying out loud, and besides, I had Greg— That was it! It had been too long since I'd seen Greg. As soon as I got home, my love muffin was in for a big surprise.

"This collection is," Albert said, drawing out every word, "the finest I have ever seen. I knew your aunt was keeping something back, but I could never have even dreamed it would be this good."

"Would you help me broker it? For a fee, of course."

"I would be honored."

"Unless, of course, you'd like to purchase it yourself."

The orange ears turned red. "I would love to. The truth is, I couldn't raise this kind of money."

"Oh?"

"Yes, I know, on the surface it may appear that I

have money, but most of what you saw at the house was inherited. Which is not to say I don't make a respectable living investing in coins—just not enough to purchase a collection like this."

I realized then that he had removed his monocle so that no man-made object would be between him and the object of his lust. Call me crazy if you will, but I think that at least once in every individual's lifetime he or she should be rewarded with the object of his or her heart's desire. I am not so crazy, however, as to give two million dollars away.

"Albert, it would be my pleasure to offer you the opportunity to buy that portion of the collection you feel you can afford."

"You mean break up the collection?"

I nodded. Generosity is almost as much of an adrenaline rush as money.

C.J. gasped and then gasped again as I took a second DNA sample. Albert seemed too stunned to speak.

Albert's vocal chords sputtered to life, like an old car engine that hadn't been started in a long time. Like that car engine, he misfired a few times.

"I am overwhelmed," he finally said.

"Abby, you can't do this—ouch!"

"I can do whatever I please with what is mine. Take your time, Albert, you don't need to decide right now. Give it an hour or two to sink in—heck give it all night. I would give you more time, but I'm anxious to get back to Charlotte."

Albert cleared his throat and popped the monocle back into place. He was suddenly all business.

"I would like this," he said pointing to a coin in the portfolio directly in front of him. "And these three," he said, picking up another leather-bound book. "Oh, and this."

"Of course you would," C.J. snapped. "Abby, he's up to something!"

Albert bared his teeth at C.J. Against his sallow skin they were startlingly white.

"I am quite prepared to pay Miss Timberlake a fair price for these coins."

"Why those coins?" C.J. demanded. "Why not these?" She pointed to another portfolio, one Albert had glanced at only briefly.

I'd had quite enough. "C.J., shut up!"

"Ladies, please! I do not wish to come between two friends. I picked these coins because they fill gaps in my own private collection. I didn't pick these"—he gestured to the folder C.J. was indicating—"because I already have a complete collection of Capped Bust dimes. You see, collecting coins and investing in them are quite unrelated things."

I gently took the portfolios from Albert. Their leather covers felt like kidskin. The front of each was embossed with gold initials. L.M.W. Lula Mae Wiggins must have been a fascinating mixture of tackiness and class.

"And the fair market value of the coins you just selected?"

Albert squinted through the monocle. "I'd have to do some checking, you understand. Prices are constantly fluctuating. But off the top of my head I'd say close to a hundred thousand dollars."

"Well, what if I give you these coins in exchange for your brokerage services? After I've had the chance to draw up an agreement, of course."

It was Albert's turn to gasp and C.J.'s turn to

shriek. I smiled at one and glared at the other.

"But Abby, you can't do that! Something awful is going to happen because of this man. I can feel it in my bones."

"Get your bones out of my house!" I barked. "I will not have you speaking like that to my guest."

C.J. slunk off like a hyena chased from a lion's kill. Like the hyena, she didn't slink very far. I could hear her banging about in the living room but decided to let her be. Perhaps she'd come to her senses and return to apologize. If I was very lucky, she'd put the piano back together and straighten up the place.

"Albert, I don't know what to say—"

He held up a yellow, well-manicured hand. "Please, there is no need to say anything. I admire loyalty among friends."

"Just the same, I feel bad about the way you've been treated." I smiled warmly. "So, will you consider my offer?"

He held the yellow hand out to me. "Abby, I would be very grateful."

We shook on the deal. It was the first time I'd touched his skin, and I was surprised by how cool and clammy it felt, like a child's forehead when a fever has broken. Or like a snake?

I hate to admit it, but just for a second I too had a premonition. The feeling had nothing to do with Albert cheating me; it was more of an overall sense of dread.

"Is something wrong?" Albert asked quietly.

"No, I just—"

My words were drowned by a deafening crash. The house shook so violently that I ducked under the sturdy kitchen table. I am ashamed to say this, but I left both Albert and the portfolios behind.

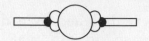

18

"**C**.J.!"

She moaned. The poor girl was sprawled over Aunt Lula Mae's pink marble coffee table. The impossibly heavy sounding board was on the piano. Not in it, but *on* it. It was immediately obvious that all the king's horses and all the king's men were not going to be able to put that baby grand back together again.

"C.J, are you all right?"

The big gal hauled her lanky limbs back to a central location and slowly stood. "Yeah, I'm all right. Just had the breath knocked out of me, that's all. Abby, who moved that coffee table?"

"Nobody moved it, dear. Besides, this is your first time in this house. How would you know it was moved?"

"I know the name of a good chiropractor," Albert said helpfully.

"I bet you do." C.J. growled like a rabid dog. "I bet you know the names of all the vermin in Savannah."

"C.J!" I said sharply. "You apologize to Mr. Quarles."

Albert twiddled one end of his mustache. "That's not necessary. I was just leaving."

"But Abby—" I reached up and clamped a hand

over her mouth. I couldn't quite cover it, but she got my point and hushed.

"For shame," I said, after I'd seen Albert to the door. "Didn't your Granny Ledbetter teach you any manners?"

"I'm just trying to protect you, Abby."

I pointed to the smashed piano. "I think maybe someone needs to protect me from *you*."

C.J. hung her massive head. "Sorry, Abby. I know you told me to get out, but I was trying to do you a favor and straighten up a little first. Go ahead and yell at me. I deserve it."

"You certainly do. However, I have a better idea. Instead of yelling at you, why don't we go find ourselves some dinner?"

"What?" My young friend looked like a sheep who had been asked an algebra question.

"Well, I'm starving, and I prefer not to eat alone. How about it?"

I know, I should have given C.J. the boot and sent her a bill for the piano. Call me sentimental, but I found her loyalty endearing. Besides, maybe I really was in danger—only not from Albert, of course—and could use a five-foot-ten-inch giant with dishwater blond hair.

My young friend might call herself Crystal, but she has a heart of gold. "You buying?"

"I'll buy, but the choice of restaurant is mine."

That was fine with C.J. She really is an easy woman to please, which is one of the reasons I like her so much. She is also exceptionally generous, and she volunteered to hide the coin collection before we left. When I accepted her offer and suggested the chimney, she turned the color of Mama's Easter lilies.

"But Abby, what if that brown recluse spider gets me?"

"Nonsense. I didn't get bit, did I? At least you won't have a mousetrap snapping at your fingertips."

"Yeah, but—"

"We're going to the Pirate's House."

"Ooh, goodie!" C.J. squealed. "I've always wanted to go there."

"And now you shall. Just put these portfolios up in the chimney and off we go. And mind you, handle them gently."

She did as she was told, but not without a good deal of lamenting. The way C.J. carried on, a passerby might well have thought the girl was being tortured. My children seldom made that much fuss when I made them help with housework.

I know, I should have hustled my bustle over to the bank, but it was only ten minutes until closing time. Rather than break my neck trying to get there, only to have the door slammed on me, I did what I honestly considered to be the second-best thing.

The Pirate's House is a favorite of locals and tourists alike. It was first opened as an inn for seafarers in 1753 and fast become a rendezvous for bloodthirsty pirates and sailors from the seven seas. Here seamen drank their heady grog and discoursed, sailor fashion, on their exotic high-seas adventures from Kingston to Bombay, Lisbon to Manila.

The sense of maritime history is almost palpable in this old inn. It is said that in the Captain's Room, with its hand-hewn ceiling beams joined with wooden pegs, shorthanded ships' masters negotiated the abduction of unwary seamen to complete their crews. Many a sailor was supposedly drugged and carried unconscious through a hidden tunnel from the Old Rum Cellar beneath this infamous room.

Robert Louis Stevenson made numerous references to Savannah in *Treasure Island*. Some of the book's action takes place in what is most likely the Pirate's House, and it is commonly believed that old Captain Flint, who originally buried the fabulous treasure on Treasure Island, died here in an upstairs bedroom. Many folks swear the ghost of Captain Flint haunts the place on moonless nights. It was broad daylight when C.J. and I arrived, and the forecast called for clear skies. Still, I would not have been surprised to see the pegleg himself clomping about the ancient inn.

We didn't have reservations, but because it was still early, we managed to be seated right away. Unfortunately we had to settle for a table in the Treasure Room, a small, busy thoroughfare that leads to the bar. The rough plank walls were decorated with framed but yellowed pages of the Stevenson book, and we amused ourselves by reading these until our server arrived. C.J. nursed a tomato juice while we read, and I had a little Mary with my blood.

After a few minutes C.J. stopped reading and cleared her throat. "You know, my great-granddaddy Ledbetter was a pirate."

"You don't say." I kept reading.

"Yup, he sure enough was. Captain Hook Ledbetter was his name."

"Uh-huh."

"Had a black patch, a wooden leg, and everything. Even swallowed a clock."

I took a deep draught of Mary. "C.J., dear, I think

maybe you're a tad mixed up. Captain Hook was in *Peter Pan,* and *he* didn't swallow the clock, the crocodile did."

C.J. scowled. "Don't be silly, Abby. Why would a croc swallow a clock?"

I got acquainted with the bottom of my glass. "Why would your great-granddaddy swallow one?"

"To keep track of the time, silly. Pirates had lots of sword fights and didn't have time to look at clocks, that's why."

"Well, they could wear watches."

"They didn't have them back then. Besides, a watch could get damaged in a sword fight. So, Great-granddaddy found him a little clock and rubbed it all over with butter."

"Why?"

"So it could go down real easy. But then the butter smelled so good Great-granddaddy licked it off. Of course he had to put more on, only he licked that too. Had to butter that clock five times before he got around to swallowing it. That's where they got that saying, you know."

"Which saying?"

" 'Takes a licking but keeps on ticking.' "

I groaned. "That's a Timex ad, and it's about a watch, not a clock."

"You sure?"

"Positive."

"Just the same, I know for a fact Great-granddaddy swallowed *something* that ticked. Even when he was dead, you could hear it ticking from his coffin."

I decided to fight fire with fire. "My great-granny was Tinkerbell."

C.J. nodded. "I always wondered why you were so short."

Fortunately for C.J., our server finally arrived. She was an attractive but tall woman about my age, and she started speaking well before she got near our table. Fortunately I still have a mother's ears.

"My name's Judith and I'm sorry to keep y'all waiting, but Janet got sick and I had a flat tire, even though it was a new one I just bought, so there was a slight backup in the kitchen, but Cassandra just arrived so from here on out it looks like smooth sailing and oh darn I forgot to check the specials, but I can highly recommend the medallions of pork with the black-eyed pea salsa and of course the swordfish steak with Savannah rice and peaches." Believe it or not, she said it all in one breath.

C.J. clapped her hands. "Wow! That was good. Say something else."

"Crystal!" I hissed. C.J.'s new moniker was satisfyingly sibilant.

Judith smiled warmly. "That's okay, I know I talk fast and sort of run on, but I guess I come by it honestly because my mama always talked that way, only now she doesn't anymore on account of her stroke, but if you ask her questions she blinks her eyes real fast, you know, two blinks for yes and one blink for no, except that sometimes it's hard to tell the difference and can be right confusing, like if you were to give her a true or false test or—"

I waved both arms like a referee. "Please, if you don't mind terribly, could we order?"

"Of course, but like I said I didn't check the specials, although I think I overheard the chef telling Cassandra we had fresh tuna on tonight's menu, in which case I'd recommend that as well, because you know most folks have never even tasted fresh tuna, just that stuff that comes out of a can, although I'm not saying that's bad, and it certainly is nice that all those tuna companies have started to care about saving dolphins, which might well be every bit as smart as us, only they can't talk like us, because of course they don't have the same vocal chords, although I guess they could blink their eyes like Mama—"

"Medallions of pork with black-eyed pea salsa," I said firmly.

"Good choice, because—"

I kicked C.J. under the table. Unfortunately in order to do that I had to slide under the table and practically lie on my back.

"Uh—I'll take the swordfish," C.J. said.

Judith nodded her approval. "The swordfish is wonderful, which is not to say that the medallions aren't too, but of course they aren't seafood, although some folks just don't like seafood at all, which really surprises me because I've basically liked everything I've ever tasted, except for liver, but that isn't so much the taste as texture, because I do like pâté de foie gras, which tastes a little bit like liver, because it is liver, only it comes from geese, but that was until I learned they force-feed the geese by stuffing corn down their long necks which is pretty cruel if you ask me, just not as cruel as what they do to calves to produce veal, which I refuse to eat under any—"

"Oh, miss!" a man mercifully called from an adjacent table. "Can we get some service over here?"

Judith gave an embarrassed little gasp, blushed, and excused herself. Try as we might to tune her out, we could hear her regale her new audience with an explanation of the term "medallions" as applied to meat, and the real medal her daughter won at a science fair in junior high.

"Geez," C.J. moaned, far too loud for my comfort. "That woman's a few pickles shy of a barrel."

"I beg your pardon?"

"She's got some loose shingles on her roof."

"I know what you meant, I just can't believe you—"

Judith interrupted me just in time. "Sorry I forgot, but you ladies get a salad with that, although personally I don't eat a whole lot of raw greens because they require dressing, and even if you use a low-fat dressing, it can all add up, like it does with elephants, which most folks don't realize eat nothing but greens, only of course they eat up to three hundred pounds of the stuff a day, which is probably more than most people could eat, although I've seen a few folks over at the Shoney's salad bar—"

C.J. rolled her eyes. I had to order mine not to do the same.

"We'll both have the low-fat ranch dressing."

"But Abby," C.J. whined, "I prefer blue cheese."

"Then blue cheese it is." I handed the menus to Judith. "Say, you wouldn't happen to know if a Mrs. Gabrenas works here."

Judith's gray eyes widened further. "I'm Judith Gabrenas, except of course Gabrenas is only my married name because my maiden name was Tatweiler, which isn't too common in these parts, although come to think of it Gabrenas isn't either, and since we only have a daughter—"

"Named Amanda?" Sometimes one just has to be rude.

"Why, yes! How did you know? Although I guess I shouldn't be so surprised, since most folks think we look so much alike, even though Amanda is adopted—"

"She is?"

"Yes, she is," Judith said, her voice suddenly very defensive, "but I assure you I couldn't love her any more than if I'd given birth to her myself."

I smiled. "I don't mean to sound patronizing, but what you did was very admirable."

"Thank you, but I don't think of it that way. Amanda has brought a lot of joy to our lives."

"I'm sure she has. But adopting a biracial child, that takes a certain amount of guts. Especially here in the South."

Judith Gabrenas's mouth hung open so wide she could have swallowed Jonah *and* the whale. At first she seemed incapable of speech.

"Spit it out," C.J. said, not minding her own business.

"H-h-how d-d-did you know?"

There was no need to lie. "My aunt's attorney told me," I said gently. "Mr. Dewayne Kimbro."

"W-w-what ex-ex—"

"Come on, girl," C.J. said with the callousness of youth. "You can do it."

I flashed C.J. a matching set of daggers. "Mrs. Gabrenas, please don't be upset with Mr. Kimbro. Apparently he didn't think that information was confidential. Personally, I think it's wonderful."

Judith smiled weakly. "I want you to know that we are very proud of Amanda. It doesn't make a bit of difference to us that her birth mama was black, or perhaps I should say African-American."

"Of course not."

"Although actually Amanda's birth mama was only half black, which is just the same as far as most people are concerned, but it ought not to make a lick of difference because people are just people after all."

"Amen to that." I was affirming both her statement and its brevity.

"Of course it does make a difference because Amanda's birth grandpa got into all kinds of trouble trying to raise her on account of she looks so white, so that's why he put her up for adoption, which is the best thing that ever happened to my Marvin and I, except maybe for us finding each other, which is a miracle in itself, because—"

I was going to have to get used to being rude. "What happened to Amanda's mama—I mean birth mama—if you don't mind my asking?"

"Her name was Rose, and that was so tragic what happened to her, not that every death isn't, especially when it involves a young person like that, but to have your car get stuck on a railroad track and your baby right beside you—" She paused on her own, tears welling up in the large gray eyes.

"How awful," I said, quite sincerely. "Now, you said Amanda's birth grandpa was black, but what about her other grandparents? And what about her daddy?"

"Oh, he was white, but what you'd call a ne'er-do-well, and it's a lucky thing he and Rose were never married, and as for his parents, well, they were real bigoted and wouldn't even look at the little tyke, much less take her in, on account of she had "the wrong sort of blood," and as for Rose's mama, well she was just so damned eccentric by then—pardon my French—that letting little Amanda be raised by her was out of the question, but the old lady still got to participate by sending her to Juilliard and—"

"*What?* I mean, how can that be? It was Lula Mae Wiggins who sent your Amanda to Juilliard."

Judith Gabrenas nodded. "Yes, and she was Rose's mama and my Amanda's birth grandma—"

"Wait just one dang second. Are you saying Lula Mae Wiggins had a child?"

"Miss? Oh, miss," the man at the next table called, "do we get to be waited on, or what?"

"Or what!" I screamed.

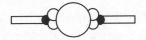

19

"**O**oh, Abby, you've got yourself a black cousin."

I stared at C.J. "So what? Do you have a problem with that?"

My protégée shook her head vigorously. "I always wanted to be African-American. *Ebony* is my favorite magazine, and I think Denzel Washington is the cutest man who ever lived. But"—she sighed deeply—"I'm one hundred percent Scotch-Irish." She giggled. "Granny Ledbetter says that when she drinks she's twenty percent Irish and eighty proof Scotch. That's funny, Abby, isn't?"

I was barely listening. The Wiggins's family secrets were being peeled away layer by layer, just like an onion. And I don't mind sharing that this onion, although only metaphorical, was causing my eyes to tear up in a major way.

What kind of a world was it where skin color kept families apart? And not even just skin color but minute amounts of "the wrong sort of blood?" It was a ridiculous world, that's what. If a tongue of flame appeared above the head of every native southerner who had a drop of African blood in his or her veins or that of some other unsuitable ancestor, the entire region would go up in flames. And from what I hear, folks in the North wouldn't miss out on the conflagration either. We humans are but one species and have been mixing since the beginning of time. Recent anthropological finds even suggest that some of us, Europeans in particular, may even have a little Neanderthal blood in our veins.

"Ooh, Abby, you're crying!" C.J.'s voice was loud enough to cause a spring avalanche all the way up on Mount Mitchell. It certainly turned every head in the Pirate's House.

"I am *not* crying. I'm merely weeping."

"But why?"

"I'm weeping over the inequities of this world."

C.J. nodded. "Yeah, life isn't fair, but Granny Ledbetter always says—"

"Stifle the Ledbetter stuff!" I wailed.

"All right. It's just that Granny says we usually really cry for ourselves, even when we say we're crying for others."

I dabbed at my eyes with a nice soft cloth napkin. The Pirate's House is, after all, a classy joint.

"I beg your pardon?"

"Maybe you're really crying for yourself, Abby."

"What?"

"Well, if Amanda is your Aunt Lula Mae's granddaughter, then shouldn't *she* be the one to inherit the house and that fabulous coin collection?"

I recoiled as if struck by a snake. "But that's ridiculous. She's just a young girl. Someone that age— well, it just wouldn't be right."

"Why not? I bet you Amanda's only a year or two younger than me, and I handle my own financial affairs, don't I?"

"But you're a special case." I meant that in the kindest way possible. C.J. may knit without yarn most of the time, but she's no nitwit when it comes to money. How many other twenty-three-year-olds do you know who own their home and business outright?

"It's only natural to feel this way about it, Abby." C.J. sounded uncannily like the counselor I hauled the family to when Buford announced his intention to get a divorce. "I mean, you've already gotten used to the idea of owning a house in Savannah, and that coin collection is enough to knock the socks off a goat."

"Goats don't wear socks," I said archly.

"Yes, ma'am, Granny Ledbetter's goats wear—"

"Can it, Crystal. You're forgetting that Aunt Lula Mae wanted *me* to inherit her estate. She didn't even mention my brother in her will."

C.J. regarded me placidly. She may as well have been a cow and I the moon.

"Maybe she thought you would do the right thing by the money and Toy wouldn't. I mean, wasn't he always kind of a selfish guy? And a touch on the vain side?"

"He's studying to be a goddam priest," I snapped. Although C.J. had never met Toy, she was right about his character. Tall and blond, the man inherited all the looks in this family and has never met a mirror he didn't love—he is always looking for a mirror—and may have, in fact, made love to a few of those mirrors. Such intense vanity is, of course, just one of the many forms of selfishness. One Easter my Aunt Marilyn, bless her clueless spinster heart, gave us a basket of candy to share. Because he is younger than I, Mama decided Toy should be the one to do the divvying.

Well, Toy divvied all right. He gave me one broken chocolate bunny—hollow, no less—while he took the rest. And lest you think I'm being hard on my kid brother, allow me to inform you that we were both in high school at the time. All I can say is, thank heavens for karma and caramel. Aunt Marilyn's gift ripped the braces right off Toy's teeth, and he got to spend several more hours in the orthodontist's chair than would have been necessary otherwise. What's more—as long as I'm telling tales out of school—he got a horrible bellyache and enough pimples to scare a flock of geese silly.

Of course, I somehow managed to get blamed for Toy's metal mishap and had to turn over my babysitting money for an interminable period of time to help pay the additional expense. This should prove once and for all that you may be able to take the boy out of the mama but not the mama out of the boy. Or is it the other way around? At any rate, C.J.'s bland expression never altered while I pondered her hypothesis.

"Well," she said at last, "if I were to leave my money to anyone other than Granny Ledbetter—and Cousin Horace and Cousin Melba Lou and Aunt Pickney's stepsons by her eighth marriage, although I guess they aren't exactly related to me because Aunt Pickney isn't either—I'd leave it to you."

"You would?"

She nodded vigorously. "Yeah, because even though you've already got plenty of money, you would know how to do some good with the money I left you."

"Thanks for the vote of confidence, kid, but I don't think Aunt Lula Mae was thinking that far. She didn't even know me. In fact, I'm surprised she'd even heard of me."

"So, you going to do the right thing and leave it all to her granddaughter?"

I recoiled again. Clearly the striking serpent was greed.

"I don't know. Let's drop the subject, okay? My food's getting cold."

C.J. sighed. "Yeah, there's nothing worse than cold swordfish, unless it's cold shark. I read somewhere that in Iceland they bury shark meat in sand for three weeks to ripen it. It's considered a delicacy."

"Shut up and eat," I said gently.

The meal was delicious despite C.J.'s gross comment, and we chatted pleasantly about girl stuff. You know, is bigger really better, is it safe to do it in the tub, and is every day too much. In the end we agreed that the new pocket-size hairdryers out on the market were adequate, but you'd have to be a fool to use them while in the bathtub, and the only people who should wash their hair on a daily basis were teenagers with exceptionally oily skin and auto mechanics.

I suppose the only reason I was able to carry on such a mundane conversation was because I was still in shock. It isn't every day one has one's house ransacked, finds a multimillion-dollar coin collection, and acquires a cousin of a different color—well, in a manner of speaking.

It wasn't until Judith returned to our table bearing a dessert menu that reality set in. "Y'all care for some dessert?" she asked quietly.

We waited for the litany of interesting descriptions to begin, but alas, there were none. Judith Gabrenas just stood there, pen poised over pad, like any other good waitress.

"That's *it?*" C.J. finally asked. "You aren't going to babble on and on about our choices?"

"C.J!"

"Well, it's the truth, Abby. Even I—"

"Enough!" I said sharply.

I believe Judith winced. Either that or she winked at me.

"That's all right. I know I tend to carry on about things. Sorry about that."

"Still, that's no excuse for my friend's rudeness. I'm afraid she left her manners back in Charlotte."

Judith shrugged, not altogether an appropriate gesture under the circumstances, if you ask me. Perhaps her medication, if indeed she was taking any, had kicked in.

" Excuse me for asking, ma'am, but may I know your name?"

"Abigail Timberlake, and my ruffian companion is—"

"Crystal!"

I held out a hand. Judith either didn't see it or refused to shake. That really was fine with me. Handshaking is an obsolete custom that ought to be abandoned. It began centuries ago as way of showing that one was truly unarmed—no palmed daggers, etc.—but it is now the number-one conveyor of colds and influenza. Much better, in my humble opinion, to bow to one another like the Japanese. Bad backs are generally not contagious.

Judith glanced around the small room. Her other customers were busy chowing down.

"Miss Timberlake, you going to do right by my girl?"

"Excuse me?" It took moxie to ask a stranger for moolah, I'd grant her that.

"You aren't going to say anything to my Amanda about—well, you know, her being Miss Wiggins's biological granddaughter and all."

"She doesn't know?"

"No, ma'am. Everyone kind of figured it would be easier that way. Then we wouldn't have to explain the other part."

"What other part?"

Judith glanced around the room again. She was like a monkey on a barbwire fence.

"About her being black," she whispered. "I mean, part black."

"You mean she doesn't know?" I'm sure my voice woke more than a few of the dead over at Bonaventure Cemetery, no doubt giving some lucky late-afternoon tourists the thrill of their lives.

Judith shook her head. She looked as miserable as a cat in a cold rain.

"But that's impossible," I cried. "You blurted it out to us, and we're perfect strangers."

"I can't believe I did that. It's just that the subject has been in my mind a lot lately, on account of Amanda has started asking more questions about her past."

"Well, you should tell her. Because you're likely to just blurt it out to her too."

"Seems to me life is complicated enough," she said still in a whisper. Frankly, I was surprised she hadn't fled the room.

"Life's a bitch," I agreed, "and then you die. But you have no right to deprive someone of her heritage. Amanda deserves to celebrate all of her history, and trust me, someday she's going to find out, whether you tell her or not."

"The time just hasn't been right," Judith whined. "I can't pick just any moment."

"There will never be a right time, not if you've kept the secret this long. But I can tell you this. If she hears it on the street, it's going to be worse."

I realize that my children's situation and Amanda's was not at all the same—or was it? There is no shame in having African heritage. Likewise, there should be no shame in having a cheating father, but Susan and Charlie felt it just the same. Because Buford is Charlotte's most successful divorce lawyer, we were a high-profile couple. The children heard about Buford's bimbo at school, and they were mortified on my behalf. *Twin Peaks* had been on television by then, and that's what the kids called Buford's mistress. The guys in Charlie's class wanted to know if he was getting "a piece of the action." After all, Tweetie—Buford's silicon slut of a secretary—was only a few years older than our son.

I'm not saying I could have prevented my children's pain by preempting the rumors, but I could have helped prepare them for their friends' reactions. Maybe. Perhaps Charlie wouldn't have been hurt so much when he opened his locker and found the anatomically correct inflatable doll labeled *Your new mom*. And maybe Susan wouldn't have felt the need to defend me against allegations that I had forced my husband into an affair by being frigid. But I said nothing to the kids. For months I knew that, thanks to his political clout, Buford was going to kick me out on the street. That kind of thing ought not to happen, especially in a society that has traditionally bent over backward to honor the rights of motherhood, but let me tell you, it does.

What I'm about to say is an explanation, not an

excuse. I honestly thought I was shielding my children by not telling them what the rest of the world so obviously knew.

Of course, Amanda Gabrenas was not my daughter—my cousin, yes—and it was up to Judith to fill her in, not me. All I could do was encourage the woman.

"Please think about it," I said gently. "Not that I could do any good—for her I mean—but I'd be glad to be there if it will help you. I've been through a similar situation myself."

Judith's eye twitched. Surely she wasn't winking this time.

"Thank you, ma'am. You've given me a lot to think about. If there's anything I can do for you—"

"Extra desserts would be nice," C.J. said. "On the house, of course."

I grabbed my fork and gave C.J.'s funny bone a quick workout. The girl didn't even have the decency to yelp.

"Mrs. Gabrenas," I said just as calmly as could be, "you can tell me why you refused to have your daughter named in my aunt's will."

Judith rubbed her eyes on a large freckled forearm. Even in the dim light of the restaurant I could see the mascara streaks on her cheeks.

"I guess I was really in denial then."

"I thought it was de Savannah River," C.J. said with a lopsided grin.

"That was you in the river, dear. Now, if you don't mind, please shut up." I turned back to Judith Gabrenas. "Please explain."

"Like I said, I thought it was better for Amanda if everyone just assumed she was white. But your aunt thought otherwise. She was always talking about 'claiming' Amanda, as if she was a pair of sun glasses or a wallet at the lost and found. "

"So you threatened to pull Amanda out of Juilliard if her own grandmother named the girl in her will?"

Much to my consternation, Judith began to sob. "It was for her own good."

"There, there," C.J. said as she got up and put her arms around the weeping waitress. "My friend doesn't realize that although she may be little, she can be a big bully."

"I am not a bully!" I got up, intending to hug Judith Gabrenas as well, but given the disparity in our sizes, ended up pawing her back like a puppy at the kitchen door. But it was the thought that counted, right?

Judith Gabrenas seemed to think so. In a few minutes she stopped blubbering and returned to being our waitress. C.J. and I returned to our seats, and Judith whipped out her order pad. Free or not, it was time for some dessert.

I made up my mind first. "I'll have—"

"Oh, my God!" C.J.'s gasp deprived the tiny room of half its oxygen.

"What is it?" I demanded, when I could breathe again. Judith was still gulping for air.

"Look over there, Abby. You're not going to believe your eyes."

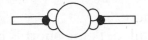

20

"**I** can believe my eyes, all right," I growled. "That woman with the flower garden on her head has been following me all day."

"That's Wilma Pridgen," Judith said, her voice gaining strength with every word. "She brings tour groups in here all the time, but she leaves the lousiest tips, which is worse than leaving none at all if you ask me, because then at least I can pretend the customer forgot, which can happen I suppose if you're paying cash, but isn't so likely to happen if you're paying with a credit card, because it asks you right there what gratuity you want to leave, although I suppose I should count my blessings because in some countries they don't live tips at all, whereas here in America folks are expected to give at least a fifteen percent tip during the day and twenty percent at night—"

"Ooh, good, you're back on a roll," C.J. said not unkindly, "but I'm not talking about the lady with the daisies on her hat. Abby, I'm talking about Wynnell."

I stood on tiptoe to get a better view of those patrons waiting to be seated. "*Our* Wynnell?"

"Ooh, Abby, she's wearing a kimono. No fair, I always wanted to wear one."

"*What?*" I still couldn't see Wynnell.

"Look over there."

"Where?" I wailed. Being short is both a curse and a blessing. I have to look at the world from a child's-eye level, but at least I don't see the bald spots on men—or women—and I avoid a lot of halitosis by speaking to folks face to navel.

Finally the hostess led the irritating tour guide and her flock of victims to an adjoining dining room. Sure enough, the Tokyo tourists were standing in a bunch by the hostess's stand, waiting to be seated. Several of the women who had been wearing jeans earlier in the day were now wearing brightly colored kimonos. Among them was Wynnell.

C.J. was right after all. I couldn't believe my eyes. I opened and closed them several times before my brain finally accepted the absurdity. My friend was indeed wearing a kimono. It appeared to be silk and was predominately red with embroidered images of black and white cranes. There was also a lot of gold thread here and there to represent trees. It was definitely *not* something a middle-aged woman of Scotch-Irish descent would wear to dinner in the Deep South.

"In my next life remind me to get some normal friends," I said, and then immediately clamped a tiny hand over not such a tiny mouth.

Fortunately C.J. didn't appear to hear me. Wynnell and her entourage of Tokyo tourists were causing quite a stir. The hostess who was about to seat them had dropped a menu, and when she bent to pick it up, the entire party bowed, even Wynnell. This unnerved the hostess so much that she dropped another menu, and everyone bowed again. The hostess—and I shall call her Madeline to preserve her anonymity—must have relished her new-found power, because she bowed again, this time without dropping anything. Unless a third party intervened, Wynnell and the tourists were going to snap off at the waist from all that repetitive movement.

"Wynnell," I practically shouted. "Over here."

Wynnell straightened and looked around. Who did she think she was fooling? Even a male Kabuki dancer with a stylized mask didn't have eyebrows that big. If Wynnell wanted to pass for someone foreign, her best bet was a Persian carpet salesman. One who wore his wares on his face.

I stood and waved my napkin. "Over here. Third table to your right. With C.J." Alas, due to my size, it sometimes pays to give folks coordinates.

Wynnell left her groupies and tottered over. She was wearing wooden platform sandals over white silk stockings.

"I should be mad at you, Abby."

"You're not?"

She shook her head. Her face had been painted and then powdered white, like a floured biscuit. Her graying black hair was done up geisha style. She even had what looked like a pair of lacquered chopsticks stuck in the elaborate coiffure.

"To tell you the truth, I've never had so much fun in my life. In fact, I want to thank you, Abby."

"You do?"

"Yes. If it hadn't been for your mean little joke, I wouldn't have made all these wonderful friends. My *new* best friends I call them."

That stung like a hornet behind the ear. "Wynnell, dear. You barely know these people."

"Oh, but I do. Maybe they don't all speak very good English, but we communicate. Yoko-san has a brand new grandbaby that's just the cutest thing you've ever seen—she showed me pictures—and Hatoyama-san and his wife Yoshi are celebrating their fiftieth wedding anniversary, and Ikeda-san—that's our leader—just got a major promotion. This is his last tour. I think he's going to be a vice president of the August Moon Travel Agency."

I attempted a friendly smile. "That's nice. But tell me, don't you feel at least a little bit—well—odd in that getup."

"Oh, no. Folks just think I'm part of the group."

C.J. wrinkled her nose. "Are you sure? 'Cause you're a foot taller than any of the others, and you walk kind of funny, sort of like my cousin Alvin when he tried to saddle-break Granny's prize breeding bull."

"It's the—hell, I forget what you call them. You know, the shoes. But I'm getting better. I only twisted my ankle twice."

"That's nice, dear." I turned back to Judith, who'd been waiting patiently. "I'll have the pecan praline pie."

"I'll have the double chocolate cake," C.J., said without a second's hesitation. The girl would use chocolate toothpaste if it were available.

Judith left to get our orders, but Wynnell seemed reluctant to budge, even though her party had by now been seated. It was an awkward situation. I wanted to tell Wynnell about my discovery, but I was too miffed at the moment.

Finally Wynnell spoke. "So, Abby, do you mind if I sit down for a minute? There's something I need to talk to you about."

"What about me?" C.J. whined.

Wynnell smiled, the white paint on her face cracking slightly. "You too."

I scooted over to the far side of the booth. "Sit. Assuming you can in that outfit."

Wynnell managed it quite well. "Look, I know you think I look ridiculous, but it was Yoko-san's idea. I really am enjoying myself. In fact, that's what I wanted to talk to you about."

"Oh? You mean you want us to dress up in costumes too? Would that make you like us better?"

Wynnell sighed deeply. "I know I hurt your feelings with that comment about my new best friends."

"Hurt them? Why, you stomped on them first and then ran them through a blender. When you were done, you threw them on the floor again and did the jitterbug."

C.J. nodded in somber agreement, a fact that really surprised me. The girl is usually so quick to forgive.

"I didn't really mean it," Wynnell said, her voice breaking. "I was just trying to pay Abby back, and I guess I went too far. I'm really sorry."

C.J. and I exchanged meaningful glances, but I spoke first. "Forget it. And I'm sorry about playing that joke on you. I sometimes go too far as well."

Wynnell slapped a silk kimono sleeve around my shoulders and gave me a tight squeeze. "You'll always be my best friend." She looked at C.J. and scrambled for words. "And you're very special too. I really do love y'all. I want you to understand that. But"—she released me from her grip—"I need something more in my life right now."

"Oh, no," C.J. wailed, "you're becoming a Moonie."

"What?"

"You're joining a religious cult. I saw it on *20/80*."

"That's *20/20*," I said kindly.

"Not on Granny Ledbetter's television. The picture tube blew out, and now all you get is the sound."

Wynnell laughed nervously. "I'm going to miss you, C.J."

"Don't be silly. You and Ned can come over to my house anytime. You know I love having company. Hey, how about coming over for Easter brunch. You too, Abby."

"My husband's name is Ed," Wynnell said with remarkable patience, "and I'm afraid that won't be possible."

"Why not?"

"Well, it would be awfully expensive, for one thing."

My scalp prickled, and my hair began to rise like that of a good watchdog when he hears an unfamiliar footstep. "Wynnell, dear heart, this sounds ominously like you're going away."

Wynnell nodded. "I leave tonight."

"Ooh, cool," C.J. cooed. "You're going back to Charlotte dressed like that?"

Wynnell shook her head so vigorously one of the chopsticks in her hairdo broke its lacquer hold and sailed across the narrow room, just barely missing the thigh of a dedicated diner. Fortunately neither Wynnell nor the other woman noticed.

"No, I'm going to Tokyo."

"*You what?*"

"My friends—I mean, my *new* friends—tell me there are lots of antique shops in Tokyo for sale. Of course, prices are very high there, and I won't be able to afford much in the beginning, but I'm not too old to start over again. Am I?"

I ignored her question. She wouldn't have liked my answer anyway.

"What about Ned?" I wailed.

"That's *Ed*," Wynnell growled. "And what about him?"

I swallowed my irritation. "Will he be going with you?"

The hedgerow eyebrows fused then parted. "Ed doesn't like to travel. Abby, you know that."

"How long will you be gone?"

Wynnell shrugged, and the remaining chopstick wobbled dangerously above my head. "Who knows? Maybe years. Maybe forever."

"You can't be serious!"

"I am."

"But Ed—"

"He and I have needed a break from each other."

"Maybe so, but years is not a break. Years sounds more like a divorce."

"Maybe it is."

"Oh, God, I didn't know."

"Yeah, well, now you do."

"Who gets custody of your children?" C.J. asked.

"Her children are in their thirties," I hissed. Tears filled my eyes, imperiling my mascara. "Wynnell, are you sure?"

C.J. giggled. "Of course she's sure. A good mama knows her children's ages. Well, most of them at any rate. My Aunt Nellie Ledbetter had the darndest time keeping track of her kids' ages until she had them tattooed on their little foreheads."

"C.J., shut up," I said, not unkindly. I turned back to Wynnell. "Is Ed having an affair?"

Wynnell's hedgerows almost hit her hairline. A good geisha would get them plucked.

"*What?* Abby, that's a hoot. Ed's no longer interested in sex. Hasn't been for years."

"Please," I begged, "don't tell us more than we want to know."

"Ooh," C.J. said, her eyes as big as the pork medallions I'd just consumed. "When a man's no longer interested, that only means one thing."

"C.J!"

"That's okay, Abby. Let her be. Ed's having an affair all right—with Mrs. Green. Mrs. Putting Green, if you know what I mean. That's all he's done since he retired. I don't think he'll even notice I'm gone."

"Of course he will. What am I saying? You're not going! You can't!"

"Sorry, Abby, but you can't stop me."

"But your passport!" I cried gleefully. "You don't have your passport with you."

Wynnell smiled, a hint of sadness already on her face. She stood and smoothed the front of her kimono.

"That's why we're leaving tonight. They've changed their flight to leave from Charlotte rather than Atlanta. We'll be stopping by the house to pick it up on the way to the airport."

There was nothing I could do to stop her. Even if there was, it wouldn't have been my place to do so. We are all entitled to our mistakes, even when we get to be Wynnell's age. Who knows, just maybe it wasn't a mistake. Maybe Ed would wake up some morning and *not* smell the coffee. Maybe this was just the nudge he needed.

I sighed and hugged my best friend good-bye.

C.J. and I returned to the Heritage. I had just handed my car keys over to the parking attendant when I smelled the cigar. I allowed my sniffer—

which is vastly inferior to Mama's—to point my eyes in the right direction, and that's when I spotted Ralph Lizard's shiny dome exiting a cab. It was followed seconds later by the faux blond locks of Raynatta with an A and a Y.

"Inside, quick!" I ordered C.J.

"But Abby, it's so nice out here. Why don't we stroll down to the river and see what's happening there? Maybe we can find a nice jazz club."

"Just get inside," I hissed. I grabbed C.J.'s arm and tried pulling her toward the front door. The girl doesn't appear to be overweight, but let me tell you, she weighs a ton. I'm surprised she hadn't sunk straight to the bottom of the Savannah River.

"But Abby, I wanted to go upstairs at the Pirate's House Restaurant to that nightclub. What was it called again?"

"Hannah's," I huffed. "C.J., come on!"

"That's it! Hannah's. I wanted to hear Emma Kelly sing. The woman of a thousand faces."

"You mean *songs*, dear, not faces."

"You're right. Cousin Alma Ledbetter is the one with a thousand faces. Anyway, Abby. After we said good-bye to Wynnell, you stopped being fun. All you've wanted to do is come right back here to the room. You're a spoilsport, Abby, you know that?"

"I am not! I'm just not in the mood for—"

"Oh, Miss Timberlake!"

Alas, the lizard had spotted me and was scuttling in our direction. Raynatta with an A and a Y struggled to keep pace.

"Miss Timberlake, I'm so glad I finally caught up with you again. I've been thinking—"

"*We've* been thinking," Raynatta with an A and a Y rasped. She was out of breath, even though she'd covered just a short distance. Perhaps if she lost the Y...

"Yeah, we've been thinking that maybe we didn't make ourselves too clear."

"Oh, but I think you did."

Ralph rubbed the back of his cue-ball cranium with the heel of his cigar hand. The wad of ash on the tip of his stogie made this seem like a dangerous habit.

"No, ma'am, or else we wouldn't be having this conversation right now."

"That sounds vaguely like a threat, Mr. Lizard."

A narrow grayish tongue flicked about the corners of an almost lipless mouth. "Ma'am, that ain't a threat at all. I just wanted to show you something." He turned to his girlfriend. "Give it to her.

Raynatta with an A and a Y fumbled about in a back velvet bag. "It's in here somewhere."

"Damn! I told you to put it in a safe place."

"I did."

Ralph looked prepared to personally delve into that forbidden territory from which few men emerge unscarred, the female purse. You can't imagine the look of relief on his face when a fistful of lime green fingernails with iridescent purple spots emerged holding a scrap of yellowed paper.

"Here it is!" Raynatta with an A and a Y thrust the newspaper clipping at me.

"Really, y'all, I don't have time for this."

"Please read it, ma'am." The woman was practically begging.

I sighed and carefully extracted the fragile piece from the tangle of claws. The print was small, and the overhead lights not intended to facilitate read-

ing. But I did my best just to send the pesky pair on
their way. At last I handed it back.

"I don't understand," I said. "That article has to
do with General Sherman"—I spat discreetly on the
walk at my feet—"may his name *not* rest in peace."

"Yeah, but it says he stayed in that house of yours
on Gaston Street."

That wasn't the case at all. Near as I could make
out, it was about a wealthy merchant named Charles
Green who offered his house on Madison Square to
the invading general. It was from this house, now
referred to as the Green-Meldrim House, that Sherman sent his infamous telegram to President Abra-
ham Lincoln. Please bear with me while I quote that
audacious message:

To His Excellency
Dear Sir: President Lincoln

I beg to present you as a Christmas gift, the City of
Savannah with 150 heavy guns and plenty of am-
munition and also about 25,000 bales of cotton.

W. T. Sherman, Maj.Gen

I spat again. "This garbage says nothing about my
house on Gaston Street."

Ralph Lizard snatched the ancient article from my
hand. For a nanosecond our skin touched, and I can
tell you for a fact that his was cool, like that of the
pet snake my son Charlie tricked me into touching
when he was in the seventh grade.

"What the hell!" He turned on Raynatta with an
A and a Y. "I told you to bring the other article. The

one that mentioned Sherman visiting my great-great-granddaddy Uriah P. Lizard."

I struggled not to spit a third time. The Daughters of Impeccable Lineage, an organization to which Mama proudly belongs, carry men's handkerchiefs in their purses in which to expectorate every time they hear the S word. I didn't have as much as a tissue in my purse and didn't wish to foul the Heritage's drive any further.

"I brought *both* articles." Raynatta with an A and a Y was pawing in the velvet bag, like a dog trying to uncover a bone. "I know the other one is in here someplace."

Ralph Lizard used the other S word, which I'm too much of a lady to repeat. He dropped the cigar on the walk and snatched the bag from his lady.

"Look," I said sternly, "I don't know what y'all's scheme is, but it isn't going to work. If what you say is true, your great-great-granddaddy was a traitor, and I wouldn't sell you my house if I was flat broke and you were the last buyer on earth."

"But ma'am," Raynatta with an A and a Y wailed—she seemed desperate enough to drop the Y if I asked her—"we got it all figured out. If we charge tourists five dollars a head to visit the house and set up a little gift shop—"

"Shut up!" Ralph had a hand raised as if to strike his pleading platinum sidekick.

"Just try and make me," the woman snarled. She raised a hand of her own.

Ralph must have thought better of tangling with the green talons, because he lowered his hand first. "Now she'll never sell it!"

"You're darn tooting," I said, and finally managed to budge C.J. by poking her in the side with the handle of a rattail comb. The girl can step lively under the right circumstances, and I managed to get her into the hotel while the lovebirds glared at each other.

Little did I know that I was taking C.J. straight from the frying pan into the fire.

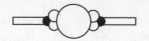

21

Ashley Hawkins descended on us like—well, like a hawk. She practically flew out from behind the check-in counter, her long strawberry-blond hair rising and falling like silent wings.

"You got a message," she said.

I took the small sealed envelope. My name had been printed on the plain white front with black ink. The letters had not been executed with a ballpoint, because the strokes were wide in the middle and tapered at the ends, reminiscent of Far Eastern calligraphy.

"Who from?" I asked.

Ashley shrugged; the wings flapped one last time before coming to rest on freckled shoulders. "I don't know. I was checking in this couple from Ottawa—they couldn't speak a word of English—and the next thing I know, there it is lying on the counter."

"Well, thanks," I said, and slipped the envelope into my pocketbook.

"Aren't you going to read it?"

"Later," I said, and gave C.J. another nudge with the rattail comb. Ashley Hawkins had a lot to learn about manners.

"It could be really important."

"That's my business, isn't it?" I asked, not unkindly.

"Ooh, read it!" C.J. squealed. "Maybe it's from Wynnell."

After a good deal of fumbling I retrieved the envelope from the morass of extraneous items I lug around with me all day, every day. Buford used to accuse me of carrying an entire department store around in my purse, yet whenever he needed something—nail clippers, facial tissue, breath fresheners—they were always available.

"You're supposed to have the second sight, dear. Why don't you tell me what's in it."

C.J. snatched the envelope and pressed it to her broad forehead. "It says: 'Dear Abby, please make sure C.J. gets first pick of my inventory.' "

I snatched it back and laughed pleasantly. Who knew the girl had a sense of humor?

"Wrong! Besides, you have better taste than Wynnell. You wouldn't want her stuff in your shop."

"Ooh, Abby, do you really think so? That I have good taste, you mean."

"The best," I said. Ironically, it was true. Well, almost true. The Rob-Bobs have better taste, but C.J.'s is surprisingly good, despite the fact that her reality piston misfires from time to time.

The auburn hawk was still hovering about. "Open it," she urged. "I'm dying to see what it really says."

I slid the rattail comb handle into a slight gap at the seal, and the envelope opened just as easily as if I'd used the ivory Victorian letter opener I keep on my desk. The missive, however, had been folded in thirds and then folded again, and it took some effort to extract it, rather like prying a walnut from its shell.

Finally I got it loose and spread it flat against my raised thigh. Still balancing on one leg, I read aloud: *Put money in palmetto leaf at base of Oglethorpe statue.* "That doesn't make a lick of sense," I wailed.

C.J. giggled. "Ooh, Abby, I think you got someone else's message. That note's meant for a drug dealer."

"Which I am *not!*" I said for Ashley's benefit.

The auburn tresses lifted and fell several times, but the nosy girl remained earthbound. "Sounds more like a ransom note to me," she said.

"*What?*"

Ashley cleared her throat. "Well, suppose somebody you knew was kidnapped, and the kidnappers wrote several notes, only somebody made a mistake and left the wrong note at the wrong time."

I smiled pleasantly. "You have a lot of imagination. Have you ever considered writing? There is a frizzy-haired blond woman at my church who's published a few mysteries. Maybe I could get her to look at your manuscript."

"I know you think I'm being ridiculous, Ms. Timberlake, but somebody you know *is* missing."

"Who?"

"Your mother."

"She isn't missing! She went to Saint Simons Island with some friends. You said so yourself."

"Yes, ma'am, that's what she told me on the phone. But what if she was being forced to say that?"

My knees felt suddenly weak. A feather brushing against their backs would have sent me collapsing like an old deck chair with loosened screws.

"How did she sound?" I asked, my own voice barely a squeak. "Did she sound stressed?"

Ashley wrinkled her nose in thought. "Well," she

said at last, "I didn't really know her of course, but come to think of it, there was something really odd about the conversation."

"Odd? How do you mean?"

"Well, she said things at odd times. It was kind of like—"

"Like it had been taped?" C.J. wore a look of genuine concern.

"Well—"

C.J. nodded vigorously. "My granny Ledbetter used to do that all the time, only she used to pretend she was God. She had tape recorders hidden all over her house that were motion-activated. If you dropped your socks next to the hamper instead of putting them in, you heard a deep voice coming out of nowhere telling you to pick them up. Or if you were sneaking something from the refrigerator, she'd tell you to put it back. Then one day—"

"C.J., *please*," I begged.

"I'm almost finished, Abby. Then one day she got the tapes mixed up, and after Cousin Alvin got done milking the cow, he heard a voice telling him to put it back. Well, Cousin Alvin Ledbetter O'Leary was a very religious boy and not the brightest bulb in the family chandelier, so he tried to put the milk back. Only Clarabell didn't take kindly to that. She kicked Alvin—which is why he has two foreheads—and then she kicked over the lamp, and soon the entire city of Shelby was in flames."

Ashley Hawkins's eyes were spinning like bingo numbers in a tumbler. "My, what an interesting story," she said, the sarcasm puddling at her feet, "but my conversation with Ms. Timberlake's mother was not taped. At least, not prerecorded. What was odd was that she kept adding things."

I dropped the envelope and message to grab a freckled arm. "What kind of things?" I demanded.

"Well, things like 'I kid you not' and 'Naps are for little children.' That kind of thing. But you see, they didn't fit into the conversation."

I staggered over to a leather armchair in the faux shade of a silk ficus tree. Ashley and C.J. followed close on my heels.

"Abby, are you all right?" C.J. may have a pewter personality, but her heart is pure gold.

"No, I'm not!" I wailed. "Mama's been kidnapped!"

Sergeant Albergeria didn't seem to think so. Or least she was lying through both sets of teeth to keep me calm. We were alone in my room—something about which C.J. was not happy—and could speak without interruption.

"Your mother drinks, right?"

"No, she doesn't."

"Not at all?"

"Well, of course she drinks a *little*, she is an Episcopalian, after all. But besides communion, she might have only a glass or two of wine a month. I don't call that drinking."

"I see, but it isn't against her principles."

"What is your point?" I may have sounded a tad terser than I'd intended.

"Ms. Timberlake, a lot of people change their behavior when they go out of town, and your mother said she met up with some old friends, right?"

"That's what Ashley said."

"Believe me, I've seen it before. Old friends get together, tie one on, and the next thing you know, they've hopped on a plane to Rio."

"Rio?"

Sergeant Albergeria grinned. "It was my ten-year college reunion in Atlanta. We drank a little too much, and I do speak a few words of Portuguese. Everyone says I had a wonderful time, but frankly, I can barely remember the plane ride back." She must have been paying attention to my expression because she added, "Of course I was off duty the entire time."

"Okay," I conceded. "Mama is unpredictable and doesn't always make a whole lot of sense, but how do you explain the coincidence of her phone message and this note?"

The sergeant, who had been casually examining the paper evidence, handed it back to me. "Coincidences are a dime a dozen," she said. "You see them all the time in my line of work. But I tell you what, I'll call Saint Simons Island and have Jim—he's a buddy of mine on the force down there—do a little asking around. See if he's seen a woman matching her description. I'll ask around here too. Ms. Timberlake, I really don't think you have anything to worry about."

I absentmindedly picked at a fine yellowish hair that was stuck to the glue of the envelope. Sergeant Albergeria's words were ones I wanted to hear. And no doubt she was right. If Mama called from Nepal to tell me she'd had an audience with the Dalai Lama, I would be surprised but not shocked. And I would be surprised only because I know she doesn't have a valid passport.

"Thanks for the reassurance. It's been a really stressful day—well, you know that. And speaking of which, any leads as to who might have trashed my aunt's house?"

"We're still working on that, ma'am. There are no signs of forced entry. Whoever did it had a key." Her voice rose just enough to imply a question.

"What? Surely you don't mean me."

The sergeant shook her pretty head. She had thick chestnut locks, the kind that never look mussed. What a blessing it must be to have every day be a good hair day.

"No, ma'am. But can you think of anyone to whom your aunt might have given keys? Do you know any of her friends, for instance?"

"I never even met my aunt. In fact, I never even knew she existed until two days ago."

She scribbled something on a pad and then looked up me. I waited for her to say something, but she just stared at me with all the expression of a dead fish. One with two full sets of teeth, of course. That went on for several minutes until finally I could no longer stand it.

"What do you want?" I wailed miserably.

"Ms. Timberlake, I've been an officer of the law for a long time. I can tell when someone is holding back."

"She's just a young girl," I cried. "Her name is Amanda Gabrenas. She's my aunt's granddaughter—a fact which I just found out tonight."

The sergeant scribbled some more. Again she locked her grouper gaze on me until I sang like a canary.

"Okay, there's woman named Moriah Johnson who had a key, but I made her give it back to me. She's my aunt's niece by marriage—at least, I think she is. After everything I've learned today, I wouldn't be surprised to find out Moriah is my sister!

"But Sergeant, both of those women have had keys for a long time. If they wanted that coin collection—assuming they even knew about it—they had ample opportunity to look for it in a way that would not have brought such attention."

"What coin collection?"

I brought the sergeant up to speed. To her credit she was a much faster study than some other law enforcement officers I've had to deal with. And please understand, I'm not referring to Greg.

"Well, Ms. Timberlake. This certainly sheds a whole new light on the case. I'll speak to my partner at once. I just wish you had shared this information with me this morning."

"I would have told you this morning, but you had to rush off to some kind of emergency, remember?"

"Yes, that. Well, we finally arrested the Phantom Producer."

"Excuse me?"

"Just some tourist who liked it so much down here, he decided to stay, even though he didn't have the funds. He's been going around town telling folks their homes would make great movie locations. Has them take him on tours of the house, gets the owners real comfortable, and then steals something. Always something very small that the owners don't notice missing until he's gone, so up until now it's been impossible to prove anything. This time, however, he was caught in the act of stealing a Fabergé egg."

"Icky Bob Crane!" I said. "You arrested Icky Bob Crane."

"You know the man?"

"We met him this morning when we were coming out of Albert Quarles's house. He obviously thought we lived there."

Sergeant Albergeria nodded. "Just between you and me, that's one weirdo off our streets. A dozen or so more and we'll be a normal city like any other."

"And boring."

"Savannah will never be boring, Ms. Timberlake. Not as long as we still have folks like your late aunt living here. Which reminds me—and I was going to call the hotel anyway to leave a message—I checked with the coroner's office."

"And?"

"The champagne he found in your aunt's lungs was the ordinary kind. You know, that pale yellowish-brown stuff. It was a real popular color on cars a few years back."

I gasped. "Then she *was* murdered."

"Perhaps that's jumping to conclusions."

"Not if you knew my aunt."

"Which you didn't," she reminded me gently.

"Yes, but *everything* in that house is pink. Carpets, drapes, furniture, you name it. I was in that bathroom. The tile floor is pink, the scale is pink, the toilet brush caddie is pink—even the light bulbs are pink, for Pete's sake. And since there is such a thing as pink champagne—well, I just know she wouldn't have poured any other color into that pink marble tub."

The sergeant sighed. "Okay, you're doing a good job of convincing me. Tell you what, first thing in the morning I'll swing by the coroner's office and take a peek at your aunt's autopsy report."

"You can do that?"

"Bill's an old friend. And it doesn't hurt that his wife's cousin is married to my brother."

"Thanks!"

We'd been sitting on my bed—that is to say, the sofa. She stood.

"But don't get your hopes up, Ms. Timberlake. This is a very cold trail, and even if I do find something that seems amiss, I have to run it by my captain. Then he has to contact Homicide. What I'm trying to say is, I can't promise you results."

"That's all right. Just try. And please, don't forget to ask around about my mother."

"I'll do my best on both counts," she said and smiled encouragingly.

But should one trust a woman with sixty-four teeth?

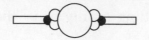

22

C.J. was mad enough to chew nails and spit rivets. I don't know what she thought was going on between the sergeant and me, because she refused to speak to me that night. I know, that might sound like a blessing to some, but with Mama and Wynnell both absent, it was darn lonely in that room.

Under normal circumstances C.J. would have been delighted had I chosen to share the king-size bed, but I took the couch again just to spite her. I thought I might at least force a protest, but no such luck. Her lips were sealed tighter than a clam at low tide, and I had to settle for an angry grunt when I said good night.

The next morning when I awoke, she was gone. I must confess my first emotion was elation, which was immediately followed by guilt. There's no denying the woman is a pain in the rear, but she's as loyal as a steak-fed dog. Jane Cox would stand in the hedge and fill up the gap, if need be. Realizing that made me feel even worse.

Then I saw that her suitcase was open on the luggage rack. She'd packed a few things—or had she just not removed them in the first place? At any rate, it was by no means full. I darted to the bathroom, but it was as empty as Buford's heart the day he announced his intention to divorce. I returned to the bedroom and dressed hastily in a yellow cotton T and pale blue skirt, and anticipating the day ahead, slipped on sturdy leather loafers.

I was just starting to unpack the few things that were in her suitcase when the door opened and in walked C.J. bearing a cardboard tray. She was all smiles.

"Good morning, sleepyhead. I hope you like pancakes and sausage."

I smiled back. "You know I do."

"And coffee with lots of sugar and cream, right?"

"Sounds wonderful."

She set the tray on the kitchenette table and opened the Styrofoam containers. "Sorry I took so long. I was going to get you something from downstairs, but I didn't want to pay their prices, so I walked to McDonald's."

"All the way to McDonald's?"

"I ate the Egg McMuffin on the way back. I hope you don't mind."

"Not at all. This is wonderful."

"Ooh, Abby, I'm so glad you're not still mad at me."

"Me? Mad at you? C.J., dear, it was the other way around."

"It was?"

"Never mind. I didn't mean to sleep so late. As soon as I'm done eating, we've got to hustle our bustles out to Bonaventure Cemetery. Destiny—I mean Diamond—awaits us."

"Ooh, Abby, you're not really planning to meet her there, are you?"

"You're darn tooting."

"But I thought you thought it was all a bunch of hogwash."

"I did. But a lot has come down the pike the last couple of days, and I have a lot of questions to which I'm desperate for answers. If talking to a ghost will get me answers, I'm game."

C.J. shook her head somberly. "Talk to a ghost and you become one yourself within thirty days. That's what Granny Ledbetter always says."

"Nonsense. And what's with this change of attitude? Yesterday you couldn't wait to talk to Miss Amy. You begged to come along."

"That was then, and this is now," C.J. said, like an overgrown teenager.

I took a bite of pancake. "Buck," I said, my mouth disgustingly full.

"No, Abby, those aren't buckwheat. McDonald's only has plain."

"Buck, buck."

"Huh?"

I laid the plastic fork down and flapped my arms like a chicken. "Buck, buck, buck brat!"

C.J.'s lower lip trembled, and her eyes filled with tears. Needless to say, I felt like a total jerk. If I'd been a faster thinker, I would have spilled some of the coffee on my lap, thereby providing a diversion *and* a possible lucrative lawsuit. Dolt that I am, I merely pushed my breakfast aside and gave my friend a big hug.

"It's okay, dear. You can stay here if you want."

C.J. was openly sobbing now, her copious tears as warm as a freshly drawn bath. I got completely soaked to the skin and we went through half a box of the hotel's tissues before I got her calm enough to talk coherently. Even then her conversation was interrupted by the occasional torso twitch.

"Ooh, Abby," she finally managed to say, "I was lying to you."

"No kidding? What about?"

"I don't have the second sight!"

I feigned surprise. "You don't?"

She shook her head vigorously and I got wet all over again. "I just said that because—because I wanted you to respect me."

I wiped my face with a damp sleeve. "I've always respected you, dear."

"You have?"

"Absolutely. You're one of the smartest business people I know."

"That's true," she said. "Did you know I have a genius I.Q.?"

"Get out of town!"

"But," she began to whisper, "when it comes to other things, Granny always said my roof wasn't nailed down right."

"I beg your pardon?"

"I'm half a bubble out of plumb line."

I scratched my head. "Your granny was a builder?"

"Nah, unless you count that two-story outhouse. But she only designed it; Cousin Alvin did the actual building. Frankly, Abby, it was a terrible design. You could never use the bottom floor without an umbrella. But anyway, what I'm trying to say is, I'm three pickles shy of a barrel. Always have been, to hear Granny tell it."

"Ah, that! We're none of us perfect, are we?"

"That's for sure. Take you for instance—"

I grabbed my purse and fled the room. C.J. followed me like a hound to the chase.

*   *   *

She was still listing my negative qualities when we pulled through the wrought-iron gates of Bonaventure Cemetery. I parked the car in the shade of a moss-draped oak and opened the door.

"I need to check the office for a map," I said calmly, "or we'll be cruising around this place all day, looking for Diamond's coordinates."

C.J. paused in her litany. "She said the marker looked like a Greek temple."

"That she did. But look around you; this place looks like Athens. I'll only be a minute."

"Okay." C.J. flashed both hands twice and then held up six fingers. "But don't let me forget where I was."

"You had just listed 'critical,' which I believe you gave as my twenty-sixth fault. Although frankly that doesn't make a whole lot of sense, because you listed 'judgmental' as my eighteenth fault, and not only do you have some overlap there, but you are out of alphabetical order. "

"Abby, you see!"

I slid out of the car and made my getaway to the records office. When I returned with the necessary information, C.J. was still holding up six fingers.

"Now where was I?" she demanded.

"On your way to meet Diamond," I said blithely. "And that delightful little Miss Amy we've heard so much about."

C.J. put her hands in her lap. Bright as she was, that train had just been derailed.

We drove in silence to the corner of Wiltberger Way and Bonaventure. I never would have found it had I not stopped to look at a plot map. There are undoubtedly few pizza deliveries to Bonaventure

Cemetery, and I venture to say any pizza delivered probably arrives cold. Although I'm sure it is greatly appreciated nonetheless.

I parked in what little shade was offered by a Carolina cherry laurel. I had no sooner turned off the engine than Diamond's face appeared at my window. Fortunately I was still belted in, or I would have banged my head on the car ceiling.

"Y'all late," Diamond growled.

I glanced at my watch. It was five minutes past ten.

"Sorry. I overslept."

"Miss Amy don' like folks being late. She say it bad manners."

"Please tell her I apologize."

"Tell her yo'self."

C.J.'s head spun like a top on a stick. "Is she here?"

Diamond cackled. "You see anybody?"

"No, ma'am."

Diamond cackled again and led us a like mother hen to Miss Amy's grave. The monument was truly extravagant. Unlike many of the other ersatz temples, this one was constructed of marble, not concrete. It had twelve instead of the normal eight columns and was circular rather than oblong. The fancy Corinthian capitals supported a marble cupola with a small opening at the top, which was covered only by a bronze star.

I won't repeat the family name, but it was one I'd never heard before anyway. It was cast in bronze and embedded in the center of the floor. Individual family plots radiated from the small temple like the spokes of a wheel, and Miss Amy's actual marker was a simple white stone barely larger than a bread loaf.

Diamond bade us sit under the cupola, facing the little girl's grave. When we were seated, Diamond opened the bag she wore around her neck and removed a piece of candy. A Hershey's miniature! She placed this reverently in front of the little stone and joined us.

"What was that for?" I asked.

"Present for Miss Amy. She mighty fond of chocolate."

"But why such a small piece? Why not a regular-size bar?"

Diamond rolled her eyes in exasperation. "Don' want Miss Amy to be rotting no teeth."

"Isn't it a little late for that?"

"Shh!" Diamond held a crooked finger to her lips.

We sat quietly for a few minutes. The only sounds I could hear were the pulse in my ears and the drone of insects. That and the occasional voices of tourists at the far end of the cemetery who had come to pay their respects to composer Johnny Mercer. It was pleasant enough just sitting there, albeit a bit boring. I must admit I disagree with those folk who say it is better to be buried in Bonaventure Cemetery than be alive anywhere else. Not unless the cemetery adds cable TV.

I am pleased to say C.J. cracked first. "Now what?" she had the nerve to ask.

Diamond glowered at the girl. "Now we sits and bees quiet. Miss Amy ain't gonna show herself if they's a ruckus."

We sat as still as mice in a cattery. Several more buses of tourists came and went, the insects droned louder, and I thought my pulse points were going to burst through my ears. Finally, just when I was seconds away from screwing up enough courage to bolt, Diamond sat bolt upright.

"She here!"

"Where?" C.J.'s eyes were as big as fried eggs.

"Oooooooooooh," I moaned softly.

I thought it was generous of me to lend atmosphere to the occasion, but Diamond was not amused. "Stop that! You want Miss Amy go away?"

"No, ma'am," I said sheepishly. "Sorry."

Diamond accepted my apology with a sniff and turned her attention back to our spectral visitor. "Miss Amy, these womens come to pay you their respect." She chuckled softly. "And to ax you some favors."

"I just want to know where my mama is," I wailed.

Diamond cocked her head. "What's that? You ain't be feeling like no company this morning? That too bad, Miss Amy. How long you been feeling poorly?"

Miss Amy took her own sweet time answering. Perhaps they didn't teach manners down there in grave school. Finally Diamond turned to us.

"Sorry, ladies, but Miss Amy have her a killer headache today. She din' even hang 'round long enough to say good-bye."

"Why, that's absurd!" I cried. "Ghosts don't have headaches! Look Diamond—or whomever you are— this whole thing is the stupidest bunch of nonsense I've ever heard. And with C.J. sitting beside me, that's saying a lot!"

C.J. stomped a foot the size of a small continent. "Thanks, Abby!"

"Whoever," Diamond said.

I'd lost all patience with the woman. *"What?"*

"It should be 'whoever', not 'whomever'. In this case the word in question refers to me, Diamond, who is the subject of your sentence. 'Whomever' is an objective relative pronoun. Although I must say that sentence is particularly confusing, and you would do well to rephrase it." It sounded like the words were coming from Diamond's mouth, but they clearly weren't hers.

"What did you say?"

Diamond's grin was as wide as her face. "I was an English teacher for forty years."

Not only did the cat get my tongue, she batted it around a bit, had a litter of kittens, and played some more before I was able to speak. Meanwhile C.J.'s mouth hung open like a nightjar catching mosquitoes.

"B-b-but," I finally stammered, "y-you—well, you didn't sound like an English teacher. Not until just now."

"Don't worry. I'm not about to accuse you of being a racist. Your conclusion was perfectly valid, given the information I supplied you with."

"With which I supplied you," I said angrily.

Diamond cackled. At least that much of her was real.

"Lord, but this is fun!" she crowed.

"Maybe for you. But C.J. and I don't like being made fools of."

C.J. nodded vigorously. "That's right!"

Diamond shrugged. "Ladies, please forgive me. Perhaps in your case I carried the charade too far. You see, now that I'm retired from teaching, I make a living entertaining tourists."

"How?" I told you C.J. was a pragmatic business woman, despite her handicap.

"Tourists like a good show. Ever since The Book there's been a good market for voodoo spells. A good curse can go for a thousand dollars."

"Aha!" I cried. "You said you didn't do curses. You called it devil stuff."

"So, I lied. I was trying to sound you out. To get a feel for what sort of people you are."

"Why? So you could fleece us?"

The older woman patted her mojo pouch with its disgusting chicken foot. It was like watching Mama pat her pearls.

"I don't want your money, Miss Timberlake. I want you to do right by my great-granddaughter."

"Come again?"

"Amanda," she said proudly. "Amanda Gabrenas."

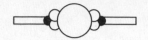

23

"You're kidding!"

"Watch it, Abby," C.J. warned. "This may be part of her scam."

Diamond shook her head like a goat with its head stuck in a pail. "Amanda Gabrenas is my great-granddaughter. Her mama, Rose, was my grand-daughter. Rose's daddy was my firstborn, John. Rose's mama was—uh—well, she was your aunt."

"So that's the connection," I said. "How interesting!"

Diamond gave her head a final shake. "You don't seem surprised."

"I'm not—well, not *too* surprised. I knew Amanda was my Aunt Lula Mae's granddaughter. I just didn't know how you fit in the picture. So your son John was my uncle?"

"John was *not* your uncle," Diamond said, her voice tinged with bitterness.

"Amanda said he was."

"Well, he wasn't. Not legally. Such a thing wasn't possible then."

"Hey, it wasn't my fault."

She sighed. "No, I guess it wasn't. But I have a right to blame that crazy aunt of yours. I told my John that hanging around with white trash would ruin his life, and that's exactly what happened."

"Wait just one cotton-picking minute! My aunt was not trash! She was bohemian, a free spirit."

Diamond's cackle would have made a laying hen jealous. "Bohemian! Free spirit! Sure, she could afford to be a free spirit, because she was *free*. It wasn't the same for a black man back then. Still isn't, if you ask me."

"Which we didn't," C.J. said loyally.

"C.J., hush." I turned back to Diamond. "Look, I'm sorry if you think my aunt ruined your son's life. But like I already said, it isn't *my* fault."

Diamond's eyes glittered like the jewel for which she was named. "Maybe, maybe not. It depends on what you're doing to change the status quo, because if you're not part of the solution—"

"You're part of the problem. That's a cliché, and I resent your implication that I might be racist—well, any more of a racist than you are. Because face it, we all have tribal baggage we need to dump if we're going to get along in this world. And for the record, I think it's neat that Amanda is my cousin."

"Yeah, she's almost as white as you."

"That's unfair, and you know it. I'd feel the same way if Moriah Johnson was my cousin." I gasped. "*Is* she my cousin as well?"

Diamond stared at me.

"*Is* she?"

"No," she said at last. "Moriah is my John's daughter by his wife. His legal wife. She died the year he met your aunt. John loved his wife so much. It was grief over losing her that caused him to act crazy and take up with—"

"Don't even go there!"

She nodded. "Amanda is my concern now. Like I said, all I want is that you do right by her."

"What exactly do you mean by that?"

Diamond took a step forward. It wasn't a threatening move, nonetheless both C.J. and I, who were still sitting on the base of the temple, leaned back away from the woman. As a general rule, I like to keep a certain distance between myself and folks flaunting fowl feet.

"I want my great-granddaughter to inherit that woman's estate." Diamond spoke slowly, as if trying to recall rehearsed words. "Not everything, of course, but her fair share. After all, she is a direct descendant."

"She can have it all."

Diamond stepped back. "What did you say?"

"I said—"

"She didn't say anything!" C.J. practically broke my eardrums.

"Stay out of it, C.J.!"

'But Abby—"

"Shut up, dear." I smiled at Diamond. "I mean it. I want Amanda to inherit my aunt's estate. Her entire estate. It's only fair."

"You're serious?" Amanda's great-grandmother sounded just like Mama when she pretends to open the door to Ed McMahon. Diamond, thank heavens, was not wearing a pink chiffon bathrobe.

"Absolutely. But there is a condition."

I could feel Diamond's sigh on my bare legs. "I knew it."

I swallowed my irritation. Fortunately it was time for a midmorning snack.

"Don't jump to conclusions. It could be dangerous at your age. You might fall and twist your ankle or something."

"Very funny."

"Thank you. Sarcasm has always been my forte. Anyhow, I just want to know something."

Diamond scowled. "If you think I want that money for myself, you're wrong!"

"You're jumping again," I said with commendable patience. "I merely want to know how it is you knew I was coming to town. I mean, it wasn't a coincidence that we met, was it?"

"That's all you want? That's your condition?"

I glanced at my watch. "As of this moment."

Diamond's face softened. "Now that I can help you with. But you have to promise to keep this to yourself."

"Sorry, ma'am, but I'm not going to buy a pig in a poke."

"Well, I can't say that I blame you. Okay. But I'll deny it if he asks me."

"Deny what?" C.J. demanded. "Ooh, Abby, don't believe a word this woman says."

I patted C.J.'s arm in an attempt to calm her. "She said you had the second sight, dear."

C.J. jerked her arm away. "But I don't have the second sight! If I did, I would have known she was a fraud."

"C.J., *please!*"

"But Abby, she's not even a real voodoo priestess, she already admitted that, and—"

"C.J., take a hike!"

Much to my astonishment, C.J. hauled her lanky frame off the temple base and lit out for a group of tourists that had wandered into our section. Why was I not surprised to see Wilma Pridgen, the lady with the spring festival of flowers for a hat, in charge? At any rate, C.J. blended right in with the group, and when a few minutes later they were picked up by a chartered bus, she clambered aboard as well.

Diamond and I watched in astonishment. Finally she turned to me.

"You're really hard on your daughter, you know that?"

"She is not my daughter!" I wailed.

"Uh-huh." She didn't sound at all convinced.

"Do we look alike?"

Diamond's smile was slow and deliberate. "All you white folks look alike to me."

"Be careful what you say. Your great-granddaughter Amanda passes for white."

"Touché."

"So, Diamond, if indeed that is your real name, who put you on to me? Who told you I was here?"

"Dewayne Kimbro."

"So much for lawyer-client confidentiality!"

"Dewayne is a good man, Miss Timberlake. He went to school with my daughter Rose back when they were first desegregated. He sat next to her on the bus. Wouldn't let any of the troublemakers mess with her."

I nodded. "But that still doesn't explain how you caught up with us at the cemetery."

"Ah, that. Well, I may not be a voodoo priestess, but I am not without, uh—shall we say, special gifts?"

"Right." To better let the sarcasm drip from my lips, I bent over to scratch a mosquito bite on my left ankle. "I suppose you're going to tell me you have this homing instinct that allows you to zero in on people if they're within a certain range and that you can just pop in on folks and then disappear at will. Kind of like what's her name?—yeah, Barbara

Eden on that TV show *I Dream of Jeannie*."

Diamond didn't answer. When I looked up, she was nowhere in sight.

I sat there on the base of the Grecian temple and thought. I pondered for about as long as it took for Greek civilization to rise and fall. The dome offered shade for my head and torso, whereas the sun felt good on my legs, especially my mosquito bite. The birds—one mockingbird in particular—provided background music for my little melodrama.

For that's exactly how I was feeling: melodramatic. Here I was sitting alone in a cemetery, for crying out loud! I was forty-eight years old, divorced, and unable to commit to a kind, gorgeous man whose only fault—that I could remember at the time—was wandering eyes. I seemed to be alienating all my friends, and even my mama, bless her padded little bosom, had deserted me. Well, at least I had a cat!

Of course, given my luck, Dmitri would hiss at me next time I saw him. But who could blame him? Being locked up in a cage in a strange house like that. Well, at least he was safe. Lord only knows what might have happened if I'd schlepped him around town with me.

It's a wonder I was still functionally sane, what with all the weird people I'd encountered in the last couple of days. Men with names like Lizard and Bleeks. Women with single Ts in their names, and As and Ys that had no business being there. Not to mention folks of both sexes who popped up hither, thither, and yon, as wanted as pimples on your prom night. Bald heads, platinum tresses, wobbly necks, garden hats, white out of season—folks up in

Charlotte seemed positively normal by comparison. And then there was that bizarre note of the cat hair—a *yellow* cat hair!

I sat bolt upright. No, it couldn't be! *Could* it? Why on earth would Lougee Hawkins, owner of Velvet Paws, kidnap my ten-pound baby? Unless she thought I was loaded. But where would she get that idea? From Mama! My petite, pearl-patting progenitress had blabbed to Ashley, the desk clerk, that I was in town to inherit a fortune. And Ashley was Lougee Hawkins's sister.

I gasped. That was it! After Ashley gave me the note, she stuck as close as white on rice until I read it. There hadn't been any mention of a sum, but hadn't the strawberry-blond clerk herself suggested that it may have been a ransom note out of order? She'd even gone so far as to make me fear for Mama's safety. Why would she do that? Unless— oh, no, now I was being silly. Sergeant Albergeria was sure Mama was just where she said she would be, down on Saint Simons Island partying with friends.

It was absolutely ridiculous, and harmful, for me to entertain, even for a second, the idea of Mama locked in a cat cage while two incompetent sisters got their messages sorted out. But Mama, who is only three inches taller than I, would certainly fit in a cage the size of the ones I'd seen at Velvet Paws. What if she had been in one of these cages since the day before? What if the wicked sisters were feeding her nothing but cat chow and water? What if they made her use a litter box?

Obviously I needed a reality check. I slapped my cheek with my right hand and touched it gingerly with my left. Perhaps I was crazy as a loon—maybe even as crazy as C.J.—but I definitely felt the pain. And the dread.

There was only one way to find out. I left my car parked in the cemetery under the spindly cherry laurel and set out on foot to Velvet Paws. Lacking cat feet I can't quite creep as silently as fog. But mine are tiny feet, and I did a pretty good job. Or so I thought.

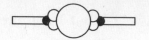

24

My tiny feet took me on a detour to the cemetery office to use a telephone. Sergeant Albergeria was out on a call, and I got Dewayne Kimbro's answering machine. Thank heavens Albert Quarles picked up on the second ring as usual.

"Albert. Abby."

"Abby! I was just thinking about you. In fact, my son was saying—"

"Look, Albert, I don't have much time. I'm calling from the phone in the cemetery office at Bonaventure. It isn't a public phone, and besides, folks come drifting in and out of here like flies on baking day."

"I understand. What can I do for you, Abby?"

I took a deep breath. "Albert, at the risk of sounding paranoid, I just want you to keep track of my whereabouts. You know, in case something happens to me."

He wasted a precious moment in silence. "Abby, please explain."

"Well, you see—uh—I know this is going to sound crazy, but I have a feeling the owner of Velvet Paws is holding my mother for ransom."

Another precious moment dragged by. "What is Velvet Paws?"

"It's a boarding kennel," I said irritably. "For cats.

It's about a quarter of a mile from here toward town. I think that's where they've got Mama."

"Who is *they*, if you don't mind my asking? And why would they be holding your mother for ransom?"

"They is Lougee Hawkins and her sister, Ashley. Lougee is the owner of Velvet Paws, but Ashley is a desk clerk at the Heritage. When we checked in, Mama bragged to Ashley about me being related to Lula Mae. She must have gotten the impression we were rich. Anyway, I think the sisters might be in cahoots."

"Have you called the police?"

"I don't have any proof, Albert. I was going to run my theory by Sergeant Albergeria, because she was there when I got the ransom note—"

"There's a ransom note?" He was finally shifting into gear.

"Well, not exactly. Look, like I said, I can't really talk now. I just wanted to let someone know where I am while I do a little investigating on my own. Will you be home for, say, another hour?" It would take a good fifteen minutes just to walk to Velvet Paws, more like twenty if I was to mimic a feline.

"I'll make a point of it, Abby. I'll be right here."

"Thanks. And I'll call you as soon as I learn something. If I don't call you . . ." My voice trailed off as I thought of the possibilities. Given more time, I would have asked in the cemetery office about the price of plots. Perhaps there was a vacancy near Johnny Mercer. The steady stream of tourists would certainly alleviate boredom.

"You be careful, Abby."

"I will."

"I mean it. Watch your back at all times. Damn, I wish you had a cell phone."

It was sweet of Albert to be so concerned. "Yeah, I'll have to get a cell phone. Okay, Albert, I have to go."

I hung up. A family of tourists had waddled in. And although it may sound unkind, I meant that literally. There were four of them, mother, father, and two teenage kids, but they shared enough excess poundage to create a third child. They were all sweating profusely, their corn-belt faces beet-red from the sun. Upon spotting me, the mother lit up like the dome light on Sergeant Albergeria's cruiser.

"Where's the statue?" she demanded, lumbering at me.

I tensed. If the woman didn't stop in time, I was going to find myself suddenly taller, albeit a good deal thinner.

"What statue, ma'am?"

Mrs. Iowa came to a shuddering stop just in the nick of time. "You know, the one on the cover of The Book. The one of that little girl holding two bowls."

"Ah, that. Those aren't bowls," I said, thinking creatively. "Those are offering plates. They keep the statue in one of the downtown churches, but I forget which one." Actually, I had no idea of the statue's whereabouts, neither did I care.

Fleshy as it was, her brow managed to furrow. "Are you sure?"

"Yes, ma'am." I ducked the ponderous bosoms and scurried out the door, swearing softly to myself the entire time. Heaven forfend Mama should be held captive in a cat cage a second longer just because some tourist family was too cheap to buy a guide.

It took me longer to get to Velvet Paws than I'd anticipated. The shoulder of the road was sandy, and the sand kept getting in my loafers. I preferred to walk on the pavement, but the volume of traffic made this impractical, if not downright dangerous. It was like step aerobics class. Finally, after nearly being creamed by a tour bus traveling at twice the speed limit, I made peace with sand-filled shoes.

Just before I reached the corner of the Hawkins property, I stopped and surveyed the front of the long, narrow lot. Like many older homes on the coastal plain, Lougee Hawkins's house did not have a garage. Unlike most, it didn't even have a carport, just a sandy driveway that ended in a small circle in front of the main entrance. To my relief the drive was devoid of cars.

On the chance that Lougee might still be home or return at any minute, I elected to trespass rather than make myself vulnerable. Fortunately the adjacent yard was bordered by a hedge of red-tip photinias. The shrubs were probably waist high to their owner, but they were head high to me, so I was able to progress unseen until I was even with Velvet Paws. If Lougee's neighbor noticed my presence, he or she was too polite to object.

Once even with the house, I climbed through the hedge and made a quick dash to the cover of one of the enormous camellia bushes that all but obscured the front door. I hadn't realized it before, but the treelike plants had been planted in front of windows. Camellias are evergreen, and no doubt because they do such an effective job of screening, the windows were without curtains or blinds. I peered cautiously into the Hawkins house. The living room was just as messy as I remembered, if not more so. A bra had joined the panties on the living room floor, and the stacks of dirty dishes now rose precariously high wherever there was a flat place. There was, however, no sign of Lougee Hawkins or Mama.

I crept around the house, keeping to camellias and azalea for cover. The back bedroom was so cluttered it took me several precious minutes to determine that it too was unoccupied. With my heart pounding loud enough to wake the nearby dead, I inched around the corner of the house and stole a peek at the back porch.

No humans, just cats. Although I couldn't be positive, the occupants of the first three cages appeared to be the same cats I'd seen when I'd dropped off Dmitri. I can't tell you what a relief it was to see their miserable faces; at least the evil Lougee didn't eat cats.

There were no bushes planted around the back of the porch, and to avoid being seen from inside I had to literally crawl along the foundation. Circumventing the back steps was the biggest problem, but once I got safely around them, I felt like I was home free. Just a quick peek at Dmitri, and I'd hustle my bustle back to the cemetery office to call Albert. No need to call the cops, at least not yet.

I plastered a reassuring smile on my face before raising my head to peering level. Dmitri is not the most sensitive male I've known, but he can read body language almost as well as Greg. At any rate, the occupant of Dmitri's cage peered balefully back at me. Strange, but he'd grown quite a bit since I'd last seen him and—

"Mama!" It was too late to stifle my scream.

"Abby!" Mama screamed back.

As soon as my shocked brain could give directions, I scrambled up the steps and practically ripped off the screen door. The dang thing wasn't even hooked. Nor was Mama's cage even locked. A simple metal bolt jammed through a hasp was certainly no match for my adrenaline.

The door to the cage flew open, and Mama tumbled out. Close on her heels was my ten-pound bundle of joy. Of course, I hugged my mother first. I held her long and hard before scooping Dmitri up into my arms. But just between you and me, Mama smelled riper than my cat. I tried not to gag.

"He wouldn't let me use his litter box," she wailed.

"That's okay," I soothed. "It's no big deal." I put Dmitri carefully down and gave Mama another but more careful hug. "A good hot shower and a change of clothes will fix that. Did she hurt you?"

"Oh, Abby, she was horrid. She didn't hit me or anything, but she said the nastiest things. Made the most awful threats. Said if you didn't deliver the money to some stupid statue in town, she wasn't going to need to buy cat food for weeks."

I released my embrace. "Speaking of which, did she feed you? Did she give you water?"

Mama nodded. "I had to share Dmitri's water, but at least she gave me a bagel."

"How generous."

"She's a greedy woman, Abby. You should have seen how her eyes lit up when I told her you wouldn't have any trouble at all paying her silly ransom. Then I told her about the coin inside the urn—"

"Mama, you didn't!"

"Of course I did, dear. I couldn't let her think we Wiggins girls can't pay our debts."

There would be time to chastise my mother later. "Well, the main thing is that she didn't hurt you."

"She took my pearls!" Mama wailed even louder.

I stared in horror and fascination at my mother's neck. She looked positively naked.

Mama put her hands over her throat. "Abby, don't look! It's indecent."

I tore my eyes away from the ribbon of flesh that had been covered by mollusk secretions for almost two decades. "Can you walk, Mama?"

She took a few stiff steps. "I think so."

"Good, because we need to get out of here. No telling when that witch is coming back."

"Not without my pearls! She doesn't wear them, so I know they're still in this house—" Mama gasped a split second before I heard the screen door slam behind me.

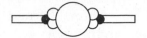

25

I'm sure you'll think I'm exaggerating when I tell you I jumped so high my head hit the ceiling. Please at least believe I jumped out of one of my sand-filled shoes.

"Mr. Quarles!" Mama cried.

I whirled. I was never so glad to see a man in all my born days. Albert Quarles was even more welcome than the anesthesiologist the day I delivered my firstborn, Susan. Dr. Lamaze, you see, had never anticipated a head that large.

"Albert! Thank God you're here!"

"I just couldn't sit home and wait, Abby." He turned to Mama. "You all right, ma'am?"

"Of course she's not. They had her locked in a cage!"

Mama stepped in front of me. "Let me tell it, Abby."

"Be my guest. But hurry, Mama. Lougee could come back any second."

Mama shuddered. "Well, it was just awful. She forced me into her car with a knife and brought me here. She wanted my daughter's money, you see. Now that she's an heiress, I mean. Anyway, she got really mad when Abby here didn't follow the instructions on the ransom note—"

"It wasn't my fault the notes were mixed up."

"So that was it!" Mama turned back to Albert. "Well, like I was saying, she got really mad, so I tried to calm her down by telling her about the fabulous coin collection you said Lula Mae had."

"You told her about the coin collection?" Albert sounded like he'd been sucking on a helium balloon.

Mama nodded. "Of course I couldn't give her any details, except for that penny your brother-in-law found in the urn. But I took the liberty of telling her there were hundreds of those and that if she let me go, she could have them all. But like I told Abby, the woman is greedy—"

"*Please*, Mama, finish your story later. She could return any second."

"Your daughter's right," Albert said to Mama and reached into the inside left breast pocket of his cream-colored jacket. "We better go. But first I'm getting backup."

But then instead of pulling a cell phone out of his pocket, Albert withdrew a gun. A Beretta Model 92 series 9mm automatic pistol, to be exact. I know virtually nothing about guns, but I recognized this one. Greg is issued one just like it.

After several labored breaths, during which the gun was pointed at my face, I managed enough extra oxygen to speak. I had never taken a speech class, however, so my delivery was a bit ragged.

"Albert, dear, is this some kind of a joke?"

"No joke."

"But this doesn't make sense."

"It would make sense for you to shut up."

"But—"

"I said shut up!" The gun wavered but steadied when it was even with my forehead.

I clamped my lips shut, just as tight as a clam

valve at low tide. Alas, Mama did not follow suit.

"How terribly rude of you to speak that way to Abby."

"You shut up too!"

That hiked my hackles, despite my fear and bewilderment. "Don't you speak to my mama that way."

Albert adjusted his monocle with his left hand. "It appears that I hold the power here. I'll speak any way I damn well please."

Mama sniffed. "I smell Yankee in your woodpile."

What a brave woman! Mama was trying to get him to point the gun at her! Well, no way, José. Mama's biological recall date might be sooner than mine, but I wasn't about to allow Albert to accelerate things.

"That's right," I said, feeling my knees grow weaker with each word. "Your brother-in-law is twice the rebel you are. Yes, sir, it's my guess that your granny put out for Sherman or one of his troops—no, make that *all* of his troops."

Albert's eyes widened until the monocle slipped. He practically jammed it back into place.

"I don't have time for this, Abby. Just tell me where the coin is."

"Coin? What coin?"

He turned the gun on Mama. "I'll shoot her if I have to."

My heart pounded. I hadn't the foggiest what he was talking about. There were lots of coins in my aunt's collection. Which *one* coin could he mean?

"I honestly don't know what you mean, Albert."

"The silver dollar," he growled.

I shrugged. "I still don't know what you're talking about."

Albert removed the monocle and tucked it behind the cream silk handkerchief in his lapel pocket. His dark eyes glazed over.

"The 1804 silver dollar. In April 1997, one of these sold at auction in New York for $1,650,000. It's the highest price ever paid for a single U.S. coin."

"So?"

He absentmindedly twiddled the end of his black mustache with his free hand. "For years it's been rumored that Lula Mae had one of these in her collection. Hell, it's been more than rumored. She came right out and told me."

It was time for my eyes to glaze, which they did. I'm sure they resembled a pair of Krispy Kremes.

"She did?"

"More than once. She even talked about it in her sleep."

My eyes cleared. "That's ridiculous!"

Hitler's twin smiled slowly. "Your aunt and I were lovers. We met when I was a teacher and she was going back to school to get her G.E.D. I was a young man then, not seriously into collecting, and she's the one who really got me started. But she never would tell me where that damn coin was hidden. Wouldn't even show it to me. Not a peek. When I broke up with her to marry Miranda, she swore she'd never tell me."

"Boohoo for you," I said.

"Yes, but he who laughs last laughs best, right?"

"You're not laughing."

"Neither did your aunt the night she *drowned* in a tub of champagne."

"You did it! You killed Aunt Lula Mae!" Dmitri rubbed against my ankles and meowed piteously.

"I was a science teacher. How hard do you think

it was for me to make my own cyanide? Stuff that couldn't be traced. You can make it from cherry laurel, you know. And I have one right in front of my house."

"No, the hardest part was getting your aunt to invite me over for New Year's Eve. I had to tell her that I'd left Miranda, that I'd finally seen the light. She'd had a string of beaus, as I'm sure you know, but none for years, and—well, lonely women forgive the easiest. But she still wouldn't budge after all that time. Still wouldn't even let me see that damn coin, so—"

"So," I said, snorting with anger, "you somehow tricked my aunt into ingesting cyanide, and then you made it look like she drowned in her champagne bath. Probably thought you were real clever too, because with all that champagne, no one would smell the characteristic almond smell of cyanide." Dmitri, bless his heart, was rubbing against my ankles for all he was worth. The poor dear knew I was upset, even if he couldn't understand my words.

Albert smirked. "You're a smart lady, Abby."

I wanted to smack that smirk off his face. "Apparently smarter than you. You were her lover once, for Pete's sake. You'd no doubt been in her apartment many times. But yet you were too stupid to stage her death in *pink* champagne."

The smirk disappeared on its own. "Who told you this?"

"The coroner."

"You're lying!"

Mama stomped her foot. "My Abby never lies!"

Albert glanced at Mama, then looked back at me. He hastily put on his monocle, the better with which to think, I guess. Meanwhile the gun wavered ominously. Finally he cleared his throat.

"Well, it looks like I'm going to have to cut my losses."

I cleared my throat as well. With my heart up in my esophagus, it was hard to breathe.

"What do you mean?"

"I mean I'm going to have to kill you."

Mama and I gasped. "You'll never get away with it," she said.

"I beg to differ. I have a fishing boat out on Tybee Island. Y'all would make good fish bait."

"Maybe I would," Mama wailed, "but not Abby. She's too small. You'd only catch a minnow with her."

"I could use her for crab bait." He was shockingly serious.

Mama stomped her foot again. "You're an evil, ugly man. I knew that from the minute I laid eyes on you. You look just like Adolf Hitler."

Albert turned the gun on Mama. "Shut up, or I'll shoot you now."

"Don't listen to her, Albert. She's just a crazy old lady. She suffers from dementia. She probably thinks you *are* Adolf. By tomorrow she'll have totally forgotten your name. So just let her go. She won't remember a thing. It will be much less suspicious if only I go missing. I have lots of enemies."

He clicked off the safety and moved away from the door. The gun remained pointed at Mama.

"Start moving slowly to the door, Abby," he said. "Any funny stuff, and I'll blow your mother's head from here to kingdom come."

I took a wobbly step in the direction indicated. Unfortunately Dmitri, who was practically wrapped around my legs, was most uncooperative. I did not intend to step on his tail, I assure you. The ensuing screech was far out of proportion to any injury he may have suffered.

But the noise startled Albert, who froze in a moment of indecision. That's all it took. Mama's self-tutored karate chop brought Albert's arm down parallel with his body. It was Albert's own finger that slipped, squeezing the trigger.

Apparently Berettas are very sensitive to the touch. Albert dispatched three bullets into his foot before dropping the gun. While the son of Satan writhed in agony, Mama, Dmitri, and I made our getaway.

Fish bait, indeed!

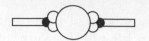

26

"So, Abby," Wynnell said, picking up the last pea with her chopsticks, "did you ever find that million-dollar coin?"

It was amazing that after just a week in Tokyo, my friend had mastered the art of dining with a pair of wooden wands. It was even more amazing that Wynnell had come to her senses in such a short period of time and had safely returned to the bosom of a forgiving husband and a handful of forgiving friends.

I was one of her friends who was still on the fence, so Wynnell had taken me out to lunch at Bubba's China Gourmet on Pineville-Matthews Road. I had suggested the Sushi Barn, but my bristle-browed buddy said she'd had enough fish to last her a lifetime. In fact, she was throwing out her aquarium.

"No, I never found it. At this point, I'm not sure it even exists."

"And you just gave the house, the coin collection, *everything* to this Amanda girl?"

"She's my aunt's rightful heir. In a more perfect world she would have gotten it all anyway."

Wynnell nodded and managed a bite of Jell-O with her chopsticks. Bubba's China Gourmet prides itself on the quality of its fruit-filled gelatin squares served up on a wedge of iceberg lettuce.

"Well," she said, "I'm surprised Albert Quarles's wife wasn't in on his crimes. You did say she had Yankee blood, didn't you?"

I smiled patiently. "Not everyone Yankee is a criminal, dear. Lougee Hawkins and her sister Ashley both belong to Daughters of the Confederacy—well, they did, at any rate—and they've been preying on tourists for years."

Wynnell speared a slice of banana. "How so?"

"Ashley worked at the Heritage, as you know, and she had a good eye for who had big bucks and who didn't. Her usual shenanigans involved credit cards, but she wasn't above stealing directly from the guests' rooms. Lougee, on the other hand, had this totally different persona as a tour guide. Called herself Wilma Pridgen. She used to be a beautician, worked on a couple of movies shot down there. Anyway, when she got herself all dolled up and wore that hideous hat and those pearl-rimmed glasses, even her neighbors didn't recognize her."

"What were her crimes? I mean, besides what she did to your mama? And speaking of whom, how did she get her pearls back?"

"Lougee was wearing the pearls when she was arrested. And as for her crimes—well, she picked tourists' pockets. With her getup she looked so wholesome no one ever suspected her."

A chunk of Jell-O wobbled on the compressed tips of Wynnell's chopsticks and then fell, hitting the Formica tabletop with a splat. It was her first mishap.

"Drat!" She set the utensils down. "Abby, these women sound like petty thieves, not kidnappers. I'm surprised they had the nerve to do what they did."

I shrugged. "They got greedy—thanks to Mama blabbing about the fortune I'd inherited—and they got in way over their heads. Sergeant Albergeria said she doubts Mama would have come to serious harm. Both sisters sang like canaries, and both said they were on the verge of letting Mama go and fleeing for the hills of North Georgia.

"Albert Quarles, however, is another story. He probably would have fed us to the fishes. And all because of his obsession with some stupid coin."

"Which may not even exist," Wynnell said, and waggled her eyebrows at our waitress to get her attention. Perhaps the waitress thought Wynnell was coming on to her, because she studiously avoided us.

I raised my hand and waved.

"Oh, my God!" Wynnell started gasping like a fish out of water.

"What is it, dear? Are you choking?"

"Y-your ring! I just now noticed it."

I fanned my fingers. "Isn't it a beaut? Greg and I made it official the night I got back."

"Congratulations, Abby!"

"Thanks. It's not the biggest stone in the world, but he did mind his Cs, and maybe someday I'll trade up."

"Platinum?"

"Nah, just white gold."

"What matters is that you've got yourself one heck of a man."

"I know. And so do you. That promise of Ed's was really something. For every time he played golf, you two would—well, you know what I mean." I blushed.

Wynnell waggled her brows again. "Indeed I do."

"Even C.J. seems to have prospects. Calvin Bleeks—the mortician who cremated my aunt—

called her last night. Wants to come up and see her this weekend."

"How did they meet?"

"Who else? Mama!"

Wynnell smiled knowingly. "This morning C.J. asked me to call her Crystal."

"Oh, no! She's not on that second-sight kick again, is she?"

"Come to think of it, she did say something about that. Said to remind you she dreamed your mama was in a pet carrying-case, which to her is not that much different than a kennel. Said she was right about Albert Quarles, too."

I sighed. "The girl is going to be insufferable from now on."

"Maybe this Calvin Bleeks will keep her too busy."

"Maybe."

The waitress scurried by, and although Wynnell waggled and I waved, the young woman ignored us again. Wynnell glared at her retreating back.

"I guess I'll just have to pay up front."

We stood simultaneously. Lunch was Wynnell's treat, of course, but I knew that when it came time to settle the bill, some protestation was expected. I dutifully played my part.

"Wynnell, dear, at least let me get the tip."

"Sure, Abby, that would be fine. In fact," she thumbed through a sparsely populated wallet, "why don't you just take care of the whole thing this time?"

"I beg your pardon?"

The hedgerows fused. "Do you know how expensive a last-minute ticket to Tokyo is? And since I wasn't expecting to come back so soon, I didn't have a round-trip ticket."

I sighed and began rummaging through my purse for my wallet. Mama claims Jimmy Hoffa is in there somewhere, and she might be right. I found a can of hair spray, a stack of programs from Ovens Auditorium, a paperback book with dog-eared pages, an empty tube of hand lotion, a fistful of stale Savannah pralines, but no wallet. After a while I got just plain irritated and starting dumping the contents of my bag willy-nilly on the table.

Let me tell you, it was a frightening experience. Things materialized that I had long since given up on. Some items, I swear, I'd never seen before. But I was more annoyed than surprised when the ugly pink bust of a dead composer bounced off the table, landed on the floor, and cracked wide open.

I'll let you imagine how I felt when I saw the glint of a silver coin.

WELCOME TO THE WORLD OF TAMAR MYERS

and her suspenseful
Den of Antiquity Mysteries

Read on for a brief glimpse into the thrilling adventures of antiques dealer Abigail Timberlake, a crime-solving Southern belle with an eye for masterpieces and a nose for murder. . . .

Gilt by Association

Petite, indomitable North Carolinian Abigail Timber-lake rose gloriously from the ashes of divorce to create a thriving antiques enterprise: the Den of Antiquity. But a superb, gilt-edged eighteenth-century French armoire she purchased for a song has just arrived along with something she didn't pay for: a dead body. Suddenly, her shop is a crime scene and amateur sleuthing is leading the feisty antiques expert into a murderous mess of dysfunctional family secrets. And the next cadaver found stuffed into fine old furniture could wind up being Abigail's own.

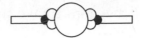

The invoice from the estate auction read as follows:

one Louis XV armoire
one Louis XV desk
one small Louis XV table
one carved and gilded mirror

It said nothing about a body. I read the invoice one more time just to be sure. *No body.*

I sat down rather heavily on a sturdy Victorian side chair. Finding a corpse in a closet is not a daily occurrence at the Den of Antiquity. One should excuse me then for stopping to catch my breath before I called the Charlotte police. I'm sure you will understand as well when I tell you that it took me several minutes to catch that breath.

"Well, well, what have we here?"

I jumped several inches off the chair. There are eight sleigh bells attached to my front door, but I was so distraught I had not heard anyone enter. In my frame of mind, it could well have been the corpse conversing. I whirled and faced the speaker, a middle-aged police officer in a blue uniform.

"He isn't on my invoice," I said stupidly.

"Ma'am?" Charlotte police are invariably polite.

"He wasn't part of the lot. I only bid on the desk, the table, the mirror, and that!" I pointed to the armoire, in which the body sat, slumped in a heap.

"Name?"

"I don't know his name!" I wailed.

"No ma'am, your name."

"I have a right to remain silent, and refuse to answer questions," I began. "I have a right to call an attorney. If I—"

This time I heard the bells and was not surprised when a pair of men stepped in. I mean that literally. Rob Goldburg and Bob Steuben are life-partners who own the shop next door.

"Everything all right?" Bob asked in that wonderful voice. "We saw the car outside. There hasn't been a robbery, has there?"

I pointed to the armoire.

"Holy moly!" It was Bob's turn to sit on the Victorian side chair. He's not as tough as Rob, and his face had turned to white porcelain.

The bells jangled again and I could see that his backup had arrived. He intercepted his reinforcement at the door and the two officers conferred with each other. They nodded in my direction. I could feel them talking about me. Handcuff size, leg irons, that sort of thing.

"I didn't do it," I said to nobody in particular. I think I repeated it several times. No doubt I was beginning to sound like a broken record, or was that a chipped CD?

The Rob-Bobs nodded.

"You always did look good in stripes," one of them said kindly.

Larceny and Old Lace

As owner of the Den of Antiquity, recently divorced (but never bitter!) Abigail Timberlake never thought she'd be putting her expertise in mayhem and detection to other use—until crotchety "junque" dealer, Abby's aunt Eulonia Wiggins, is found murdered by an exquisite antique bell pull! And now Auntie's priceless lace collection is missing and somebody's threatened Abby's most priceless possession: her son, Charlie. It's up to Abby to put the murderer "on the block."

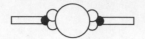

I am better behaved than most things the cat drags home, and closed the door. It was strange to be alone in my own house again—well, you know what I mean. Tweetie either had no interest in decorating or else was forbidden to do so by Buford (the man must have a little taste: he married me, didn't he?), because the only change I could see was the velvet Elvis painting above the grand piano. Even it was of better quality than most.

I gave Scruffles a big hug and let him lick my face a few times. "Next time trying chewing that white suede," I whispered.

Charlie was indeed in the kitchen, chowing down on the remains of an extra-large pizza. Tweetie undoubtedly cooked like she decorated. And what else did she expect a seventeen-year-old boy to do besides eat? Besides *that*, for pete's sake?

"Mama!"

I hugged Charlie and tousled his hair. Thank God the gene for baldness doesn't pass through the father. Even a cue ball has more fuzz clinging to it than Buford.

"What's up, Mama? You want some pizza? The bitch wouldn't let me order extra cheese. Says she's trying to watch her weight."

I accepted dinner from my son. After supper I tousled his hair again. Charlie doesn't mind pizza grease in his hair.

"Honey, Aunt Eulonia died last night. Did you hear?"

He shook his head, tears welling up immediately.

"I was at school all day, then football practice. I just got home."

"Look Charlie, I'll tell it to you straight. Anyway, you're going to read about it in the paper. She was murdered."

He sat bolt upright. "No way!"

"Yes, dear, last night. I would have called you then, but I wanted to tell you in person."

He nodded, a far-off look in his eye. Undoubtedly he was remembering some of the good times he had known with his great-aunt. When he was little he used to spend the night at her house, and the two of them would stay up until dawn, playing canasta and making peanut brittle.

"She was one of a kind," I said. "Why would anyone want to kill an old lady like that?"

He looked me in the eyes.

"I know why she was killed, Mama. I know why they killed Aunt Eulonia."

The Ming and I

Abigail is quick to dismiss the seller of a hideous old vase—until the poor lady comes hurtling back through the shop window minutes later, the victim of a fatal hit-and-run. It turns out the victim had a lineage that would make a Daughter of the Confederacy green with envy. And digging into the long-festering secrets of a proud family of the Old South turns out to be a breach of good manners that could land Abby six feet under in the family plot.

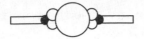

"**H**ello," I said breathlessly, having just returned from the window display. "Den of Iniquity here—I mean, Antiquity!"

"It's me."

It was a familiar voice, but I couldn't place it. "Me who?" I asked politely.

"You don't need to know who I am. But I know who you are."

"Ah, you're the Lock, Stock, and Barrel person," I said. "I recognize your voice."

There was a long silence, but no sound of pearls clicking, so I knew it wasn't Mama. "I want my Ming," the caller said at last.

"Excuse me?" I felt my heart drop down into my stomach. If it wasn't for my small pelvis, it might have hit the floor.

"You heard me. I said, 'I want my Ming.' Do you want me to spell it for you?"

I took a couple of deep, cleansing breaths, courtesy of Lamaze. "Describe it."

"The same vase Ms. Troyan carried into your shop the day before yesterday."

It is times like this I could kick myself for not subscribing to the caller ID service my phone company offers. I should, at the very least, keep a cassette recorder by the phone, and record these kinds of calls. By replaying them when I am not so stressed, I might be better able to pick up on clues. Not that I get many mysteriously ominous phone calls, mind you.

"I don't have your stupid vase," I said loudly, my dander rising. Fear and anger are the flip sides of the

273

same coin, and in my case the coin was spinning like a whirling dervish.

There was a muffled gasp. "What did you do with it?"

"I didn't do a damn thing with it, because I don't know what the hell you're talking about."

"Listen," the voice growled, "if I don't get my vase back, the same thing that happened to Ms. Troyan might happen to you."

So Faux, So Good

Abigail is about to marry the man of her dreams and *has just outbid all other Charlotte, North Carolina, antique dealers for an exquisite English tea service. Then Mama (who is running off to be a nun) stops by to deliver an early wedding present, and it turns out that the one-of-a-kind tea service Abby paid big bucks for has a twin. Then a local auctioneer from a small town in Pennsylvania Dutch country myste-riously collapses outside her shop and has a press clipping of her engagement announcement in his wal-let. Abby heads for the Mason-Dixon Line, where she confronts a menagerie of dubious characters. But Abby realizes that she might just be digging her own grave in—horrors!—Yankeeland.*

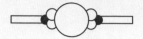

Greg pulled up just as I slammed shut the trunk of my car.

"Where's Mama?" I demanded.

"Uh—well, the truth is, I never made it to the airport."

"*What?*"

"I got an important call from headquarters, Abby."

"And my mama—your future mother-in-law—isn't important?"

"I had to take care of department business."

"Gregory Washburn, I am your business! And now, thanks to you, my mama is getting fitted for her wimple. Well, you're just going to have to hop on the next plane to Dayton and talk her out of it. Who knows, maybe some of the other nuns will defect when they get a look at you."

The Wedgwood-blue eyes failed to dance with amusement. "This department business involved you, Abby."

"I paid those speeding tickets," I wailed. "All five of them."

My betrothed bent his long, lean body and retrieved a crumpled sheet of paper from the front seat of his car. His big hands took their time smoothing it flat against the windshield. Finally he handed it to me.

"This just came in from Elkin, up in Surrey County. You recognize it?"

I stared at the paper. It was a facsimile of my engagement announcement in the *Charlotte Observer*, complete with a picture of me. I had originally planned to have one of Greg and I together, our hands crossed, one over the other, like a four-layer lasagna, but since my intended is a detective, I was told that would be unwise.

"Oh, gross! Look at those bags under my eyes. A family of twelve could pack for a three-week vacation in those."

"This was found in the wallet of a crash victim along I-77. It was folded around an ad for some silver. You just bid on some silver, didn't you?"

My knees felt weak. "Not Mama! She was going to fly, not drive."

Greg briefly put his arms around me. Public displays of affection embarrass him. Apparently giving comfort falls into the same category.

"It's not your mother, Abby. As far as I know, Mozella is fine. The crash victim was a male, age thirty-five, from Bedford County, Pennsylvania. His name was Billy Ray Teschel. Did you know him?"

"No."

"You sure?"

"Pretty sure. A lot of my customers are tourists from Pennsylvania, but they usually don't introduce themselves. Do you have a picture?"

Greg reached into his car again and extracted a second sheet of crumpled paper. He thrust it at me like a hot potato.

I glanced briefly at a photocopy of a Pennsylvania driver's license. I have a friend in Pittsburgh who claims her state's DMV trains their photographers at the Saddam Hussein School of Sadists and Torturers. Billy Ray Teschel's driver's license seemed to confirm that. But even allowing for the chicanery of a disgruntled government employee, the face on the license was not one I'd likely forget. Billy Ray Teschel was my vision of Satan on a bad hair day.

"I never saw him before in my life."

"You positive? Maybe you need a few more facts to jog your memory. Let's see now, the man was five feet eight and weighed one hundred and seventy-five pounds."

I stared at Greg. "What are you driving at?"

"What are you hiding?"

"*Excuse* me? Is there something going on here that I don't know?"

"You tell me, Abby. Why would a good-looking guy like that be driving around with your picture in his wallet?"

I glanced around for something to fling in his face. Perhaps he could compare the two for me. Alas, I had only my key ring, and there was an open storm drain too close for me to take the chance.

"Are you implying that I and this accident victim were having some sort of tryst?" I hissed.

"If the shoe fits."

Baroque and Desperate

Unflappable and resourceful, Abigail Timberlake's expertise makes her invaluable to exceptionally handsome Tradd Maxwell Burton, wealthy scion of the renowned Latham family. Along with her best girlfriend, C.J., he sends Abby on a treasure hunt in his antique-filled manor to find the most priceless item and then split the proceeds with her. But other members of the Latham clan are none too happy to have her poking around the family treasures, and when a maid is found stabbed to death with an ancient kris—with C.J.'s fingerprints all over it—it's up to Abby to use her knack for detecting forgeries to expose the fake alibi of the genuine killer.

"A bby!"

"I'm fine. Just tell me that you didn't confess to a murder."

"She did," Edith said triumphantly. Between you and me I wanted to take Edith's diamonds and shove them down her wrinkled brown throat.

"I'm not talking to you." I turned to my friend. "C.J., is that true?"

"Just a minute," Sheriff Thompson said. "Are you aware that anything you say can be held against you in a court of law?"

C.J. nodded dismally. Tears streamed down her face. It was a crying shame she hadn't taken the time to wash her hair since yesterday's ride in Tradd's convertible. Stringy hair is no way to start a prison stay— or so I've been told.

"Sheriff, are you arresting Miss Cox?"

He smiled. "I'm not in the habit of arresting anyone for murder without first seeing a body."

"Ah, the body." The grande dame made a distasteful face. "I saw her myself, Neely. It's a gruesome sight." She turned to her middle grandson. "Tradd, dear, will you be so kind as to show Sheriff Thompson to Flora's room? You seem to know the way quite well."

Tradd had the decency to blush. "Yes, ma'am."

"I'm coming, too," I said, "and so is C.J."

Edith gasped. "You most certainly are not!"

"Habeas corpus!" I screamed. I wasn't sure what it meant, except that it had something to do with a body. Either that, or it was a town in Texas.

"*What?*"

"No one is arresting C.J. for a corpse she hasn't even seen, and—"

"She just confessed, you idiot. Of course, she saw the body."

"Well, I haven't, and I'm her best friend. Besides, C.J. didn't know what she was doing when she confessed. She didn't really mean it."

"Yes, I did, Abby."

"Shut up, C.J.!"

"Then, let's go."

The two of us followed Tradd to a small, windowless room off the kitchen.

Only a teenager is capable of creating the mess that was Flora's room. Since the maid was well into her twenties at the time of her death, I can only surmise that she was emotionally stunted. That would have explained her involvement with Tradd. The tiny room looked as if a garbage truck had crashed into a section of Victoria's Secret. Bras, panties, and other assorted lingerie items were scattered everywhere, as were food wrappers and containers. An empty Snackwell box adorned one bedpost, a red lace brassiere another. A black, lace-trimmed garter belt hung from the single-bulb light fixture, red-and-white-striped candy canes dangling from its clips. So distracting was the mess that it took my eyes several seconds to spot the body, which was lying in the open, right in the middle of the bed.

"Oh, my god," I said and clamped a hand over my mouth.

Tradd has hands the size of a catcher's glove, and he clamped one over my eyes. "Grandmother tried to warn you, Abby."

I yanked Tradd's hand away. "Just look at that kris! The handle is exquisite—the intricate working of the silver and the superb quality of those apple-green jade insets."

"Abby!" Tradd was genuinely shocked.

"Oh, my," I said quietly. Although, as previously stated, I've seen my share of dead bodies, it's not something I've gotten used to.

Estate of Mind

North Carolina antique dealer Abigail Timberlake makes a bid of $150.99 on a truly awful copy of van Gogh's The Starry Night, *trying to win Mama's approval by supporting the church auction. When her ex-boyfriend shows up and offers ten bucks for the ugly* Starry Night, *Abby pops the frame and is stunned to discover hidden behind the faux van Gogh canvas a multi-million dollar lost art treasure. Suddenly, she's a popular lady in her old hometown, but it's quickly revealed that the mysterious masterpiece conceals a dark and deadly past. Someone thinks the art is worth killing for, and Abby knows she better get to the bottom of the secret scandal before she ends up buried six feet under a starry night.*

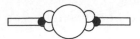

S ergeant Bowater seemed to thrive on delivering bad news. "Look here, the window's been forced. The door is unlocked. You in the habit of keeping your car unlocked, ma'am?"

"I'm not a child," I said calmly. "I'm just short."

"Yup, no doubt about it. Somebody wanted this baby. Can't say as I blame them, though. But they weren't professionals, I can tell you that. A pro wouldn't have left all these scratches."

Sergeant Bowater was dusting for fingerprints. He cleared his throat. "Ma'am, you keep anything valuable in your car?"

"Like the crown jewels?"

"Ma'am, you'd be surprised what people keep in their cars. Pulled over a lady once who had a diamond necklace in her glove box. Thought it was safer than the bank vault. 'Nobody robs glove boxes,' she said."

"What about the trunk, ma'am?"

"Just a jack and the spare tire. Oh, and as of tonight, a painting."

"How valuable is the painting, ma'am?"

"It's not. It's just a piece of junk I picked up at a church auction."

Greg smiled. He has the whitest teeth I've ever seen, although he drinks coffee by the gallon.

"Mind if I see it?"

I obligingly popped the trunk. The faux Gogh was lying there, face up, just where I'd left it. Somehow it had managed to grow even uglier in the interim.

"Oh, man," Greg said, reaching for the painting, "I

love this one. *The Starry Night*. It's always been my favorite."

"The original, yes, but this is a horrible copy."

Greg winked at me. "Tell you what, I'll give you ten bucks for the painting, and you can keep the frame. It's too fancy for me anyway."

"Sold!"

I went inside and got a screwdriver from the kitchen all-purpose drawer. Greg and I popped the painting loose from the frame. It took only a minute to separate canvas from gesso.

"Well, I'll be," Greg said. "This is a two-for-one."

I stared. The horrible copy of *The Starry Night* was just a loose piece of canvas. It flopped to the breezeway the moment it was freed. Still firmly attached to the wooden stretcher, however, was another painting altogether.

With trembling hands, I turned the new painting around 180 degrees. "This one is mine," I said in a small, strangled voice.